What's Your Price, Mr Shivaswamy?

ADVANCE PRAISE FOR THE BOOK

'A fresh, thought-provoking novel about a man stuck in the capitalistic sinkhole that passes for our cities, where a refuge into the spiritual is not just distant but simply unaffordable'—**Arunava Sinha, literary translator**

'M.R. Dattathri distinguishes himself as a gifted novelist within the Kannada literary landscape, celebrated for his receptiveness to innovative ideas. His narratives offer a profound exploration, not merely depicting the external aspects of characters' lives but also delving into their deepest thoughts and emotions. This approach imparts a distinctiveness to each of his novels, enabling his characters to transcend conventional archetypes. The vivid realism in his stories reflects his balanced perspectives, steering clear of bias towards any single ideology. This neutrality empowers him to create narratives that are both authentic and deeply resonant. This novel juxtaposes the modern world with traditional life, highlighting their inherent conflicts through the use of subtle metaphorical language. In this work, he intricately combines thought-provoking concepts with a nuanced narrative, engaging readers with its philosophical depth.

'Dattathri's life experiences are vast, enriched by the years he spent living in various countries and engaging with diverse cultures. Delving into his writings resembles inhaling an intense fragrance. The writings linger in our memory, haunting us for days long after we finish reading them'—**Vasudhendra, author of *Tejo Tungabhadra***

PRAISE FOR THE ORIGINAL KANNADA NOVEL

'Dattathri is one of the fine novelists of contemporary Kannada literature. His prose is poetic, characters are well etched and the plot is well thought out. He studies the human mind with compassion and reasoning, explores where he can fit in these characters in his fiction and does this with finesse.

His use of the Kannada language is very clinical. He never gets enamoured by the prowess of his words and uses them as effective conduits of his ideas. He always has found a fine balance between the plot and characterization.

'In the current novel, Dattathri deals with an ordinary man put in an extraordinary situation to deal with an unusual issue in the most unconventional way. He manages to juxtapose loyalty and ruthlessness, modernity and tradition, and new versus old ideas throughout the novel. He does not take sides at any point. He examines every situation and character with utmost compassion. The characters are fluid and grow with the circumstances rather than the author's predetermined and unbridled enthusiasm.

'One of the best Kannada novels that I have read in the recent years!'—**Guruprasad Kaginele, author of the acclaimed novel *Hijab***

'M.R. Dattathri's *Ondondu Talegu Ondondu Bele* is a remarkable novel that sees the protagonist oscillate between *samsara*—the lure of worldly desires—and *sanyasa*—the path of renunciation. It captivates readers from start to finish with its seamless blend of intellectual contemplation and emotional resonance. While I have admired Dattathri's previous works, especially the prestigious Masti Award-winning *Taarabaayiya Patra*, this novel surpasses his earlier efforts in its profound engagement.

'Through the character of Shivaswamy, a retired HR officer, Dattathri introduces us to a new realm. Here, the clash between life's true values and commercial interests is stark. Predatory builders exploit the naive, including Shivaswamy, who is tempted into buying a house with his retirement provident fund, only to find himself without a home and defrauded. Amidst the comedic hiring of an HR manager for the company, we find a father and son, who control their family business, battling for supremacy, and a daughter-in-law who aspires to dethrone her father-in-law as managing director. The power struggles within an entrepreneurial family are vividly depicted, allowing readers to fully appreciate the discord. Shivaswamy, observing these conflicts, symbolizes integrity. Yet, he is relentlessly challenged by Maya, the illusion, testing his resolve to either succumb to temptations or resist them.

'Dattathri's extensive corporate experience has enriched this novel with profound insights and life reflections. His narrative strength is noteworthy. Consequently, M.R. Dattathri commands a unique position among contemporary Kannada writers'—**Krishnamurthy Hanur, author of *Agnyatha: The Memoir of Tipu's Unknown Commander.***

'I had a pleasant suspicion that Dattathri might have been working on a new book with a unique theme when he frequently engaged in discussions about the meanings of Allama Prabhu's *Vachanas* with me. His insights, as demonstrated in the novel *Ondondu Talegu Ondondu Bele*, confirm this. Discussing his deep engagement with *Vachana* literature, his eagerness to learn more and the breadth of his reading was always a delight.

'Over the ten years since his debut novel *Dweepava Bayasi*, Dattathri has evolved into a proficient novelist. He has acquired the experience and techniques necessary to explore the inner lives of his characters and articulate their emotions vividly. He brings a philosophical dimension to his writing that transcends his corporate experiences while still anchoring the narrative within its context.

'This is why I regard Dattathri as a leading novelist among our new generation of writers'—**H.S. Venkateshamurthy, celebrated Kannada writer**

What's Your Price, Mr Shivaswamy?

a novel

Written and Translated from the Kannada by

M.R. Dattathri

PENGUIN
VIKING
An imprint of Penguin Random House

VIKING

Viking is an imprint of the Penguin Random House group of companies whose addresses can be found at global.penguinrandomhouse.com

Published by Penguin Random House India Pvt. Ltd
4th Floor, Capital Tower 1, MG Road,
Gurugram 122 002, Haryana, India

Penguin
Random House
India

First published in Viking by Penguin Random House India 2025

10 9 8 7 6 5 4 3 2 1

ISBN 9780143471646

Typeset in Adobe Caslon Pro by MAP Systems, Bengaluru, India
Printed at Thomson Press India Ltd, New Delhi

www.penguin.co.in

FSC www.fsc.org MIX Paper | Supporting responsible forestry FSC® C010615

'Only when the fruit ripens within does the skin wrinkle'

— Akka Mahadevi, twelfth century

1

Shivaswamy shouldn't have gone to that interview. A man of sixty-two should have at least a tiny semblance of reality. It was an act of self-flagellation, really. He had known what might happen, but he had never imagined it would hurt him this much. He cursed himself a thousand times for going there.

It was not just the interview; nothing went his way that day. Bad luck stalked him throughout the day—the kind of day astrologers call a *Shani Dosha*, filled with unheard-of difficulties.

For the first time in the history of the Bengaluru Metro, all the trains on the Green Line were stopped for nearly forty-five minutes because of a technical glitch. When the trains resumed service, the station was overwhelmed by a crowd large enough to fill ten trains. The unbearable heat outside was intensified by the delayed monsoon. The black coat, soaked in sweat, clung to his body after years of disuse. The crowd was noisy, and the child beside him cried incessantly.

He decided to call the company to let them know he was running late. He dialled the number of the person who had arranged the interview. She didn't answer. Frantically, he looked up the company's details on his mobile and called their front desk. The call was redirected to the company's head office in Sadashivanagar, not the Dickenson Road office where he was headed. Explaining his situation to the receptionist proved futile; she barely spoke above a whisper. With his free hand pressed against his other ear, he struggled to hear her over the child's piercing cry one metre away.

Then, as the trains resumed their journeys, the rush prevented him from boarding the first two trains. Finally aboard, he found himself trapped in a space so tight he could only wiggle his toes. His neatly ironed clothes now bore the wrinkles of his ordeal.

If someone were to tell this story to Bengalurians, they would certainly not believe it. They would say that such a thing could never happen in *their* metro. In the Shani Mahatmya story, no matter how many times King Vikramaditya claims that the swan from the painting jumped out and swallowed the necklace of the merchant's daughter Alolika, no one believes him. Shivaswamy's situation was no different.

If you alight at the MG Road metro station, one exit leads you to Brigade Road, while another takes you in the opposite direction, towards Kamaraj Road. Shivaswamy was confused about which exit to take to reach DT Software Solutions. He took the wrong one, which added another fifteen minutes to the delay. If everything had gone according to his plan before he left home, he should have been thirty minutes early for his appointment. But instead, he was an hour late. The question of what this meant for him—to be so late for an interview, with thirty-five years of HR management experience—tortured him endlessly.

That day was different for him in other ways too. Until that point, he had always been the one conducting interviews from the safety of the panel, never the one under scrutiny. As an HR representative, he had mastered the art of questioning others, not of answering as an applicant. After a lengthy technical interview, when it was his turn, he would ask a few HR questions and jot down the words: 'The candidate possesses adequate communication skills. Her attitude is satisfactory.' Thus considering his role complete. This was only the second time in his life that he was giving a job interview. A daunting thirty-five-year hiatus separated the first and the second. Would he have written 'His attitude is satisfactory' about an applicant who was an hour late? His brain ached.

By the time he reached, he felt utterly drained. The pain in his knee had flared up after he raced up and down the metro station stairs hurriedly. The heat and humidity were unbearable. Sweat streamed down his face, soaking his south Indian salt-and-pepper moustache. A musty odour assaulted his senses when he tried to wipe it away with his handkerchief.

To add to his troubles, he felt an urgent need to visit the restroom. But the woman at the front desk, who was in charge of escorting him to the interview room, was brusque. 'You're an hour late. Senior executives are awaiting your arrival!' However, Shivaswamy just had to go. His diabetes, presumably, rendered him unable to delay this any longer. With impatience, she pointed him towards the restroom and then busied herself with her mobile.

But the restroom unnerved him further. It was a luxurious lavatory, dazzling white. One wall was lined with flawless mirrors, and the countertops were adorned with flowerpots, all under a soft white light, like beams of the moon. Shivaswamy felt apprehensive, as though his very presence would taint its sanctity. The pungent smell of bleach powder from the toilets of the Ghaziabad office, where he had worked for thirty-five years, was so ingrained in his memory that he firmly believed toilets were defined by that very odour. How could he adapt to the chemical fragrance of this software company's restroom? The thought of skipping the interview and returning home crossed his mind. But it was too late now.

As he entered the interview room, the unexpected sight of someone his age caused the three interviewers to look up in surprise. They hastily skimmed the printed profile of the candidate before them, eager to confirm his age. 'This is just an HR manager's position. You've retired from a senior role at Bharat Electronics Limited. You've come fully informed, haven't you?' asked the woman on the panel.

It is better if what happened at the interview is never discussed. None of the questions pleased Shivaswamy, nor did his answers satisfy the interviewers. The details and examples he offered appeared disconnected from the company's requirements. It was evident to everyone, including Shivaswamy, that his application wouldn't progress further. Despite that realization, he was exasperated by the interviewers' relentless provocation. Had it not been cut short, he would have stood up and left the room. Sensing the situation, it was they who finally brought the torturous experience to an end. By the time he stepped out of the room, he was consumed by both despair and frustration.

Would the day get better now? In his anxious state, he set off for the metro station but lost his way again. On a strangely deserted road, there wasn't a soul he could ask for directions. The blistering sun pierced his neck like sharp needles. A watchman sat slumped on a chair in front of a lifeless bungalow. When woken up, he showed him the correct route, finally.

Going back the same way he had come, after switching two trains, he reached Talaghattapura on the city's outskirts. He was utterly exhausted by the time he walked home from the station.

Whenever Shivaswamy thought about what happened in the interview that day, he was reminded of a scene from a wildlife show he'd once watched on TV: three tiger cubs, newly taught how to hunt, relentlessly pursued an old deer, struggling to make a kill. The deer, for its part, did not give in easily.

2

There was no time to rest even after he returned from the world's worst job interview. Shivaswamy got ready to help his wife, Revathi, prepare for her upcoming trip to the US. She was extremely anxious about the journey because it would be her first time travelling abroad, and, to make matters more daunting, she was going alone.

Although they were originally from Karnataka, life had taken them over two thousand kilometres away to Ghaziabad, near Delhi. As a result, long journeys had become familiar to her. She had travelled alone on occasion, but more often than not, she was accompanied by Shivaswamy or their children. When the children were young, family vacations to Honnali and Masti, their hometowns in Karnataka, were frequent, usually by train. Now, with their children having grown up and living far away, and Shivaswamy having retired, they resolved to journey together wherever they went. It would be a new chapter in their life together. The journey Revathi was taking was an exception.

They had both intended to go to the US to help their daughter during her pregnancy. Even when they applied for a visa at the US consulate in Chennai, they went for it hand in hand, filled with hope and excitement. However, fate had an unexpected twist in store for them in the form of a sudden dispute over an apartment they had bought. Even though all the payments had been made, the builder demanded more. Shivaswamy was forced to stay back and sort it all out.

After retirement, Shivaswamy and Revathi stayed in Ghaziabad for two years, even though they had already decided to return to Karnataka for good. In their middle age, they believed that as long as their children were at home, they would be happy, no matter where they lived. However, this changed in the closing years of Shivaswamy's service.

Shivaswamy was happy to settle down in Ghaziabad for the rest of their lives. He was indifferent to such matters; it was his nature. However, Revathi felt a sudden urge to return to Karnataka, possibly influenced by their children leaving home.

Shivaswamy had paid the first instalment of the down payment for the apartment in Bengaluru when only two more years were left until his retirement. It all started because of his friend, Harikrishna Bhat, who worked in the engineering department of the same company as Shivaswamy.

Harikrishna was well-known for his active involvement in social and cultural activities, especially among the Kannadigas in the Ghaziabad area. One day, he emailed a group of friends announcing that he was going to buy a flat in Bengaluru—near Talaghattapura. The builder was A.P. Lakhani, and the project's name was Anoop Gardenia. A.P. Lakhani was a renowned realtor who had constructed houses in many major cities of the country. Harikrishna warmly welcomed anyone interested in joining him; together they could negotiate for a better price. He also shared a colourful pamphlet of the building under construction and other details of the project in the email. Shivaswamy was tempted; he decided to join him, and soon, many of their friends joined in too.

Years ago, Shivaswamy generously gave away his ancestral home in Masti to his widowed sister. Ever since he left his hometown, he hadn't lived in a house that he owned. He didn't know much about all that went into buying a house. Teaming up with the wise and intelligent Harikrishna Bhat to purchase a flat seemed sensible. His hand quivered slightly as he wrote the first cheque.

Shivaswamy booked a three-bedroom apartment on the fifth floor. Of course, it was still on paper; the construction had just begun. According to the agreement, he had to pay a 20 per cent advance at the beginning, with an additional 70 per cent due after completion. The final step involved registering the sales deed by paying the remaining 10 per cent.

The sales agent had called Shivaswamy and assured him that the construction work had already commenced and was progressing smoothly. He had also assured him that the flats would be ready for handover within a year. That wasn't all. He also sent a brochure printed on fine paper that presented a sprawling six-acre project named Anoop Gardenia. It promised a luxurious lifestyle with amenities such as a swimming pool, a gym, a clubhouse, a tennis court, a children's play area and a serene jogging track. At the heart of the project, a spacious area had been thoughtfully reserved for a magnificent garden.

It was all too good to be true, after all. After Shivaswamy had sent the initial cheque for 20 per cent of the total amount, the builder demanded the second payment of 70 per cent within a year and a half. When Shivaswamy called the builder's office, a man with a coarse voice told him that all the work had been completed, with only two weeks of work pending. If Shivaswamy wanted his dream home prioritized, he needed to make immediate arrangements for the second instalment, he said.

Feeling thoroughly confused, Shivaswamy met Harikrishna in his department. As it turned out, Harikrishna had also received a similar notice, as had several others.

Harikrishna called his brother-in-law in Bengaluru to ask him to check the progress of Anoop Gardenia's construction. His brother-in-law wasn't keen on the task, but after many requests, he reluctantly sent a brief message saying, 'Everything seems to be completed.' Dissatisfied with the lack of details, Harikrishna asked for more information, but his brother-in-law stopped responding, leaving everyone clueless about the apartment project's actual status.

When the notice period expired, another notice arrived from the builder. Shivaswamy and Harikrishna sat down and called the project office on speakerphone. The person who answered was polite but had a commanding tone. He said, 'To secure your home, you must make the payment immediately. It is already overdue. If arranging the money is a problem, please let us know. Many others are waiting to buy completed homes. The demand for our Bangalore constructions is high. We are prepared to refund your payment, along with interest. Please decide.' He offered the solution humbly. Helpless and worried, everyone scrambled to make the payment.

Now, only 10 per cent of the amount was pending.

Six months after the second payment and six months before Shivaswamy's retirement, Shivaswamy's son Tejas, who had moved to Bengaluru for work, took a day off to visit Anoop Gardenia. He called his dad and said, 'Appa, I can say with certainty that there's at least six months of work left at this stage.' Anxious, Shivaswamy called Anoop Gardenia's office repeatedly. Initially, they were cautious, but then they became stern and raised their voices. Eventually, they stopped answering his calls.

Even after one and a half years, the house remained incomplete. While Phase I, where Shivaswamy's flat was supposed to be, remained unfinished, the realtor had started construction on Phase II in the adjacent area. It made no sense to him.

In the middle of this entire saga, other aspects of Shivaswamy's life picked up pace. Their daughter, Sanjana, got married and moved to the US with her husband. Tejas, who was working in Bengaluru, quit his job and went to the US too to pursue his MS degree. Sanjana settled down in California, while Tejas stayed in Texas.

Shivaswamy and his wife continued to live in their rented house in Ghaziabad. In Bengaluru, the new apartment seemed perpetually under construction.

More than sorrow, their housing troubles evoked a sense of revulsion in Shivaswamy. It all went back to his formative years. His austere lifestyle, shaped by a childhood spent at an ashram and a continued commitment to minimalism, never craved excess. It wasn't stinginess but a natural disinclination for desires beyond his needs. The uniform from BEL sufficed, and he had no interest in other clothes. A morning newspaper was enough; he felt no yearning for a television. A book was all he needed to pass his time. Since others at home couldn't adopt such a lifestyle, it was Revathi who looked after the family's needs. Once the salary was handed over to her, Shivaswamy felt his responsibilities had been fulfilled. So, when the house he strived to acquire became a source of torment, Shivaswamy felt more disdain than anger.

One pleasant Sunday evening, Harikrishna and his wife visited their home for coffee. Harikrishna surprised Shivaswamy and Revathi when he said that some families were already moving into the building, even though the construction work was ongoing. Moreover, those who had personally pressured the builder were getting their apartments completed on a priority basis, he added.

'Considering you are already retired and staying in a rented house here, why not move to Bengaluru and stay close to the Anoop Gardenia project? You, too, can personally push the builder to complete your flat,' he suggested. 'Otherwise, it seems their preferences lie elsewhere. Despite the fact that Phase I is not complete, they have already initiated construction on Phase II. That will, most likely, further delay Phase I. Besides, it seems they are starting another major project on Airport Road, one that seems to be twice the size of our Anoop Gardenia.'

Shivaswamy found himself bewildered, unsure of the right course of action. Finally, his daughter, sitting in California, came to his rescue and decided to help him search for a rented house in Bengaluru. Diligently, she scoured websites such as 99acres.com, magicbricks.com and commonfloor.com, registering their need for a house on rent and eventually securing one. The property had two bedrooms and stood right next to Anoop Gardenia in Talaghattapura. At the back of the house, an imposing nine-foot-high compound wall separated them from the vast six-acre estate of Anoop Gardenia. Over a call, Teju couldn't help but humorously remark, 'Once our flat is ready, we can move our belongings without any transport truck!' The proximity to Anoop Gardenia was indeed remarkable.

The only drawback was the steep rent, nearly double what they were paying for their three-bedroom house in Ghaziabad. Adding to this burden, they had to pay a security deposit equal to eleven months' rent in advance to secure the place.

The owner wasn't wicked. His circumstances were such that he couldn't offer any discounts, either on the rent or on the security deposit. He had built this house for himself and was living in it happily with his wife. However, when his office relocated to Whitefield, the area known for a proliferation of software companies in Bengaluru, the daily commute and the distance he had to cover to reach the office finally compelled him to make the tough decision of renting out his house and finding a rented home near his office. The house he had found was nearly half the size of his home in Talaghattapura, yet the rent was double.

Shivaswamy couldn't see any other alternative. Reluctantly, the retired couple had to leave the town they had called home for thirty-five years and move to Bengaluru. Ghaziabad was where their children had spent their childhood in the company quarters. A few years later, even after moving to rented accommodation, the company quarters remained home and held a special place in their hearts. It would always be the place where Sanjana and Tejas had grown up.

Even to this day, the four of them often become nostalgic about their old house.

'Teju, how far is your college from the hostel?'

'Well, it's just about the same distance from our house to Tripathi Circle.'

For Sanjana, it was the same. Their home and the surrounding locality offered up a range of language and references comprehensible only to them.

'Oh, do you all remember Pooja, my high school buddy? She now lives near my home. It is almost like a stroll from our place to the railway station.'

'You know, one of my professors is just like Siddique Uncle,' Tejas joked. 'If he wanders too far off-topic, he can't come back!'

* * *

Moving to Bengaluru did not mean Shivaswamy's troubles dissipated; instead, a whole new set of challenges emerged. Since the rented house was situated right next to Anoop Gardenia's construction site, the clamour of building activities went on relentlessly. Until midnight, the cacophony of machinery and the glare of floodlights invaded their bedrooms. When the JCB machines were piling up the soil, clouds of dust, like angry hornets, crossed the tall compound wall and landed on their terrace, windows and doors.

When they were in Ghaziabad, they were akin to Pluto, too distant from the bustling centre. But now, they found themselves like Mercury, dangerously close to the scorching Sun, poised to smash into it at any moment.

One day, the apartment issue took an unexpected turn when a letter arrived from the builder with a new instruction: 'Please visit the registration office for the sales deed process, but, before that, please pay the pending 10 per cent and an additional eight lakh rupees due to the recent modifications.' Shivaswamy was taken aback. He promptly wrote a letter expressing his concerns and sent it via registered post: 'Please explain the extra eight lakh rupees. Allow us to move in first, and then we can complete the sales deed procedure and pay the pending 10 per cent as agreed.'

The realtor's office replied, 'Due to excessive escalation in the cost of construction materials, the agreed-upon price for the house is no longer feasible. However, despite incurring losses, we have still built the house at the price we agreed upon. We are now expecting an additional payment only to accommodate some recent modifications for the sake of convenience, and that too, merely as a cost-based adjustment. You are welcome to visit our sales office any time to learn about the changes. You can plan to move into the building whenever you wish. We are pleased to inform you that five families have already moved in. The number is increasing day by day.'

The letter prompted Shivaswamy to carry out some investigation of his own. He approached the Bihari guard at the security gate of Anoop Gardenia to get some real information on what was actually going on. Since Shivaswamy spoke fluent Hindi, the guard felt comfortable sharing inside information. While five families had, in fact, held house-warming ceremonies, only two had actually moved in, and their situation was distressing, he learnt.

BESCOM, the Bengaluru electricity supply company, had not yet provided connections. As a result, the builder supplied limited power through a diesel generator. Similarly, BWSSB, the Bengaluru water supply company, had not started supplying water to the building, so the builder filled the tanks using external suppliers. BBMP, the Bengaluru municipal corporation, had not been collecting garbage; the builder had made private arrangements to address that issue too. Just then, the guard looked around cautiously to ensure no one was eavesdropping and whispered that the corporation had not yet issued the occupancy certificate for the building either. 'It would be better for you to consider moving in once all these issues are resolved,' he advised.

* * *

To buy essential items, including groceries, Shivaswamy and Revathi often had to go to Kanakapura Road, which wasn't far for them. From their home, they had to take just one turn to get there. Kanakapura Road was a wide and busy thoroughfare. If one turned right on that road and followed the compound wall of Anoop Gardenia, one would find the main gate of the building. Twice or thrice, Shivaswamy had observed a middle-aged man on a scooter, riding in and out. He suspected that this person might be a resident—perhaps from one of the two families that already occupied the building.

There was a vegetable shop in front of the main gate. One day, as he and Revathi were buying vegetables, Shivaswamy saw the man ride in on his scooter with his wife and daughter. He jumped at the opportunity, and his suspicion was indeed correct. The family was one of the two living in Anoop Gardenia. The man's name was Kumar Gowda, and his wife's was Vanita. Kumar Gowda hailed from a village near the town of Kanakapura. He travelled to his village every Sunday to visit his parents and tend to the agricultural land they owned. He worked at the LIC office in JP Nagar. Therefore, for the sake of convenience, for both work and his visits to the village, the family had chosen to buy a flat in Anoop Gardenia.

Shivaswamy shared his story with Kumar and learnt that Kumar's apartment was on the third floor. They exchanged phone numbers, and a few days later, Shivaswamy and Revathi visited their house to witness the situation first-hand. It was as the Bihari security guard had described: the lift was non-operational since the diesel generator could only supply limited power. While it was somehow manageable for Kumar Gowda on the third floor, Shivaswamy was concerned about how he would manage without a lift on the fifth floor if he ever decided to move in.

Kumar Gowda added him to the WhatsApp group of Anoop Gardenia homeowners, which already had thirty members. He and his friend, Sandeep Kamat, administered the group. Like Shivaswamy, they had also received notices from the builder, demanding an additional eight lakh rupees. Consequently, most of the group's messages revolved around this concerning subject.

Shivaswamy then requested the administrators to add his friend Harikrishna Bhat and the others from Ghaziabad who also owned Anoop Gardenia flats.

By the time everyone was added, a heated discussion was already taking place on handling this ridiculous demand for additional payment from the builder. The owners agreed that seeking legal advice would be a good starting point. However, Sandeep Kamat, who took on the responsibility of consulting a lawyer, returned with this advice: 'Engaging in a legal battle might not favour you. It could result in years of battle, and you may be unable to enter your homes during that time. Negotiation may be the better path.'

A conference call was organized to further discuss this advice. While some owners supported the lawyer's counsel, others had doubts. Those who disagreed with the lawyer's advice wanted to at least serve a legal notice to the builder—A.P. Lakhani. In essence, no consensus was reached on the best course of action.

In addition to the pending 10 per cent payment, arranging an additional eight lakh rupees weighed heavily on Shivaswamy, causing him great uneasiness. Other expenses loomed as well. If he were to receive the apartment keys, he couldn't simply move in; work on the interiors was required. Expenses for woodwork for the kitchen, living room and bedroom fell on the buyer, not the seller. Even basic interior work in Bengaluru costs five or six lakh rupees. On top of that, there were registration expenses. He had meticulously planned for all these costs and set funds aside accordingly. But gathering an additional eight lakh rupees was never in the plan, and this caused him great anxiety.

How had Shivaswamy, a minimalist, ended up in this situation! While he was in service, he supported not only his immediate family but also his sister's family after her husband's untimely demise. He had sent enough money to his sister every month to sustain her family until his nephew finished his education and found a job as a teacher. He had also arranged his daughter's wedding reasonably well and fulfilled his son's dream of studying in the US.

Despite all these financial decisions, he had managed to purchase the apartment and paid 50 per cent of the big instalment by drawing from his provident fund and his retirement savings. After retirement, he had sought advice from an experienced financial planner and invested the remaining money in bank fixed deposits, the post office's monthly income scheme, LIC's Jeevan Shanti policy and pension schemes. Although it wouldn't offer them luxury, the amount was sufficient for him and Revathi for the remaining years of their lives. Now, this task of gathering eight lakh rupees could disrupt this hard-won financial stability. They would have to break the fixed deposits meant for their future. Who knew what circumstances lay ahead? With each passing day, the uncertainty of increasing medical expenses added to their worries, especially as they were ageing.

It was during one such day of extreme stress that Shankar, his childhood friend, gave him a call. They never held back from sharing their worries with each other. In his usual laid-back style, Shankar said, 'Hey Shivu, just because you are retired, don't sit at home and chill, my friend. If you don't keep yourself occupied, health problems will catch up, I'm telling you. You're not that old, man! You should work for a couple more years, you know?'

His words resonated with Shivaswamy. Shankar had always been street-smart. Although he had worked as an accountant in a small nut and bolt factory in the Peenya industrial town of Bengaluru for thirty years, he aspired for more. He had teamed up with his electronic engineer son and started a successful people-resource consulting company, headhunting for the thriving IT firms mushrooming in Bengaluru. No matter his success, he always stayed in touch with his friends. Even when Shivaswamy was in Ghaziabad, Shankar never let their friendship fade away. He would call at least once every three months. And, with the advent of the mobile phone, that became much more frequent.

Shivaswamy found Shankar's words practical. Two years had already passed since he retired from the public sector. He had crossed the cooling-off period, making it easy for him to take up a private job without any legal hurdles. If he worked for one or two years, he could earn the extra money the builder was asking for.

Revathi didn't like this new thought, though. Her fear was that after spending so many years in a government job, taking up a private company job now would cause him both physical and mental stress. Shivaswamy was worried about the unknown stress too, but his pride wouldn't let him admit it to Revathi.

In summary, the excruciating interview at DT Software Solutions was a direct consequence of Shivaswamy saying 'Yes' to Shankar's suggestion. In fact, it was Shankar who had suggested that he explore an HR manager's role through his consulting services. When he returned home that dreadful day, he took off his coat and shirt, turned the fan to its maximum speed and sat slumped on the sofa, feeling utterly disheartened. He realized he might be too outdated for the new job market. Even with thirty-five years of work experience, the chances of finding re-employment were slim. The idea of returning to work to earn money seemed like a joke. Should he just utilize his savings to navigate through this distressing situation?

Shivaswamy called Shankar the next day to update him on his DT Software interview. Shankar quietly listened. By then, he already knew the outcome. Whenever someone applied through his company and went for an interview, he would chase after the hiring company so restlessly that he would know the result before the applicant or sometimes even before the hiring company's HR department.

'Forget it, my friend; there are better companies out there,' he said.

Shivaswamy replied, 'No, Shankar. I don't think this will work out. Let's not try anymore. My experience is different, and what they expect here is something else.'

'Alright, I understand,' Shankar said and hung up.

Shankar was quiet because he had already received a warning from DT Software company, for sending them the wrong candidate. The message read: 'The candidate you sent us didn't fit our requirements at all; he was not even close. We had to abort the interview halfway and send him back. He argued with us over everything! As a responsible consulting company, before sending applicants to clients like us, you should screen them thoroughly. Don't waste our time by sending anyone and everyone who is retired and promises to be available.'

Even before Shivaswamy called him, Shankar had already decided not to send him for any more interviews. It was crucial for him to maintain a good reputation with companies. More importantly, he didn't want to tell his childhood friend about the warning he had received. He didn't want to hurt him.

3

The delightful news of Sanjana's pregnancy reached Shivaswamy and Revathi as they prepared to leave Ghaziabad for Bengaluru. Both of them were overjoyed. But it had also become clear to everyone that the pregnancy wasn't going to be an easy one. So, Sanjana asked them to come to the US to support her, both physically and emotionally.

They readily agreed to help and make the journey to the US. Considering the duration of the tourist visa, it would have made more sense to leave two or three months later, allowing them more time with the child right after birth. But Sanjana urgently needed their presence and was unwilling to wait. She couriered all the necessary visa documents to their Bengaluru address. She handled all the arrangements herself and ensured the documents reached them just in time for their visa interview at the US consulate office in Chennai.

They then embarked on a train journey to Chennai, where they successfully got the visa stamped on their passports. Afterwards, they visited the temples of Kanchipuram, Madurai and Mamallapuram before finally returning to Bengaluru.

Shivaswamy thought about the safety of their rented house in Bengaluru when they would be away in the US. Leaving the place unattended for such an extended period in Bengaluru could prove to be dangerous. He planned to entrust the house keys to his nephew, Prakash, who lived in Masti, and ask him to visit the house and turn on the lights at least twice a month to create the appearance of occupancy.

However, all of it proved to be unnecessary eventually. The situation surrounding the new flat took a turn for the worse, if that was even possible, in the subsequent months. Some owners again suggested hiring a lawyer and taking legal action against the builder. Other collective approaches were discussed, including approaching RERA—the Real Estate Regulatory Authority—an institution that ensured justice for homeowners, and filing a complaint against the builder. There were also suggestions for more aggressive action. Perhaps the owners could march into the building together and stage a sit-in protest until the builder addressed their concerns and came to negotiate.

When Shivaswamy told Kumar Gowda about his plan to travel to the US, Kumar discouraged him, saying, 'Sir, it's best if you stay here for now and sort out the issues with Anoop Gardenia first. The fight is gaining momentum now.' Later that evening, Sandeep Kamat too called Shivaswamy: 'Having elders like you here adds dignity to the resolution we are trying to achieve with the builder. Otherwise, those thugs think that it's just us kids making a fuss. Please reconsider your trip to America. Alternatively, let your family go now, and you can stay back here to handle the matter for a couple of months. Then you can join them. Sir, during this time in your daughter's life, your wife will be occupied, but you might feel bored being idle in the US. Besides, medical facilities in America are excellent; nobody needs to assist anyone with childbirth. My sister is there. Her deliveries happened there, and nobody from my family had to travel to help her. Do you know how healthy her children are, sir? They are like Chhota Bheems.'

Shivaswamy thought about both Kumar and Sandeep's advice, but Revathi felt uneasy about going alone. Sanjana and Teju were unsure about what to say. Ultimately, Shivaswamy decided to stay behind and address the matter at hand.

Creating a checklist, they set out on their scooter every evening, just before the rains, to purchase essential items for Revathi's journey. Two large suitcases lay open in the centre of their living room, ready to be filled. They meticulously organized and grouped items for packing. One thick-wool sweater for extreme cold, a lighter one for regular weather, four new churidars, sarees, towels, a six-month supply of medicines for various ailments, new clothes for Sanjana, Arun, their son-in-law, and Tejas, a silver anklet for the baby and eatables like chakkuli, kodubale, Mysore pak, amla pickles and groundnut chutney powder were carefully arranged and packed and sealed with love.

They double-checked all the documents—money, passport, air ticket, Aadhar card, documents sent by Sanjana for travel and stay—and arranged them in a neat leather bag purchased from DVG Road in Basavanagudi. Whenever Teju called, he took the time to explain immigration, customs, common questions, safe answers and everything else to his mum. Revathi was confident in her English-speaking skills. In her younger days, when Sanjana and Tejas were small children, she worked as an English teacher at a school in Ghaziabad for ten years.

As the day of Revathi's departure neared, both she and Shivaswamy grew increasingly tense. They repeated the same reassurances to each other. Shivaswamy had diabetes, and remembering to take his medication was a constant challenge. He lacked discipline when it came to mealtimes, which made Revathi uneasy about leaving him alone. No matter how many sambar powders, pickles, ready-to-eat breakfast items and all the condiments he loved that she prepared, she still worried that she might have forgotten something and would leave him feeling inconvenienced.

On the day before her departure, they spent quiet moments together at home. They sat on the sofa for a long time, barely speaking. It was unbearably hot outside, so they didn't venture beyond the gate all day. In the evening, around seven o'clock, they carried some chapatis, vegetable dishes, pickles, curd and rice to the terrace and enjoyed their dinner date. The terrace provided a welcome escape from the confines of the house.

When they first reached Bengaluru, they experienced a couple of weeks of cold weather. Later, as the summer set in, they developed the habit of having dinner on the terrace every evening. Summer in Bengaluru was more tolerable than in Ghaziabad. With the monsoon approaching, the weather had become a mix of heat and rain.

After dinner, they found themselves holding hands. Although the night sky was adorned with clouds, it wasn't about to rain. Stars shimmered above, and the crescent moon to the west seemed like a sketch drawn in white crayon on a blackboard. They nestled close to each other, interlocking their fingers, while their gaze rested upon the high wall of Anoop Gardenia standing before them.

As it was a Sunday, construction activities in Anoop Gardenia had ceased, granting them some respite from the usual clamour and glaring lights. To their left stood a house, not as tall as theirs, and to their right lay an empty space, enhancing their sense of solitude.

Revathi leaned on Shivaswamy's shoulder, and his heart swelled with emotion. She was the one who had kept him grounded when he was adrift. Her tender touch had soothed his body and soul. She was the reason he hadn't forsaken everything and wandered off to the Himalayas like his childhood friend Neelakanta.

That night, everything united them: the embrace of darkness, the twinkling stars above, a gentle breeze caressing their souls and their spirits close to each other. They sat together for a long time, reluctant to move. The towering wall in front of them shielded them from the harsh world beyond.

'Look how fondly that young couple has built this—our present home,' Revathi remarked, referring to their landlords. 'See how delightful it is; they should live here.'

Shivaswamy simply smiled. He suddenly remembered his childhood days at the ashram. Forty-eight years ago, under the grand tree at Siddaganga Mutt, Shankara Linga Devaru had imparted the profound philosophy of Allama Prabhu to Shivaswamy, Neelakanta and a few other students. He had spoken about the different kinds of meanings to the idea of one's abode in the material realm. He had also spoken about how the body belongs to the material world, while the spirit inhabits the invisible spheres. This had ignited in Shivaswamy and Neelakanta, both young boys back then, a quest for unconventional and philosophical interpretations of the world.

Even today, though he can recite Allama's *vachanas*—sacred maxims—from memory, he still reached for his treasured book from those days before sleeping. Revathi had affectionately named it 'The Faded Brown Book' because of its light brown cover and the faded pages that bore the marks of time. Over the years, this book had become a revered scripture, a companion, a source of wisdom and a beacon of hope for him. When darkness encroached upon his mind, the light emanating from the verses of this book guided him.

A house doesn't become one's own simply by building it. It becomes a home when it's lived in. True ownership doesn't require paperwork like sales deeds, registrations, accounts or tax receipts. If those papers are accidentally left on the windowsill, and raindrops fall on them, they all become worthless in seconds.

While sitting on the terrace, facing the building that would become their future residence, Shivaswamy found himself reminiscing about the company house in Ghaziabad. It stood as a perfect example of how a house could belong to everyone. So many families had lived there and called it *their* home before it became his, and many more must have inhabited it and claimed it as their own after he had moved on. Even in his dreams, that house brought him a sense of tranquillity. Whenever he woke up, he would close his eyes again, yearning to see it again.

* * *

By the time Shivaswamy had dropped Revathi off at the airport and returned, it was already past midnight. The house felt deserted. Sleep eluded him for hours. When he finally fell asleep, it was dawn, and the morning light streamed in through the window, flooding the room with a gentle radiance.

4

Is simplicity and detachment an innate quality, or is it learnt from the environment one grew up in, or . . . was it a combination of both?

Growing up in deprivation, Shivaswamy perhaps became more introspective and disengaged from his surroundings. His modest family comprised his parents and two sisters. Tragedy tore through their lives when his seven-year-old sister, Chandrika, affectionately known as Chandra, succumbed to typhoid at the Malur Government Hospital. That death instilled a sense of insecurity about life in Chandra's siblings, Shivaswamy and Parvathi.

Their meagre dwelling, including a small adjoining piece of land unsuitable for substantial agriculture, constituted their family's only possessions. To make ends meet, their father cultivated flowers and vegetables on that tiny plot. Each day, securing a meal was a triumph against life's relentless hardships. Fate, however, carved a different path for Shivaswamy when compassionate villagers took him and other deprived children to Siddaganga Mutt—an establishment committed to sheltering, nurturing and educating young souls battered by poverty and discrimination. The presiding seer there was the revered Sri Shivakumara Swami, known as the 'Walking God', and was celebrated for his altruism.

Without this providential intervention, Shivaswamy's life might have taken an entirely different road, possibly mirroring his father's—a life lived outside an intellectual world, working all day for a single meal. With minimal belongings—two shirts, two pairs of half-pants, two towels and a woollen muffler—he stepped into a world filled with unpredictability and promise.

Accompanying him was Neelakanta, a boy of the same age. Although they were distant relatives, they bonded better than close friends. The circumstances in Neelakanta's household mirrored those in Shivaswamy's. He was born to an older mother and had lost his father before his birth. When his mother could not care for him, the village elders included him among the children heading to Siddaganga. The items in his plastic bag were as few as those in Shivaswamy's wire basket but far more weathered. Their friendship spanned a decade, including their college days in Kolar after they left Siddaganga. After college, Neelakanta ventured forth on his own, taking an obscure passage meant for one in a million, without looking back. More on that later.

Siddaganga shaped Shivaswamy profoundly. It helped him not just with his literacy and education but also shaped his introspective journey. Shankara Linga Devaru sowed the seeds of spiritual wisdom in the boys. Following his guidance, they learnt to master self-restraint, harmonizing the mind, the intellect and the ego—an equilibrium known as 'Yogaroodha'. Early on, they delved into life's deeper layers, reciting numerous vachanas daily. It was as if Shankara Linga Devaru had channelled the spirit of Allama with his words.

When the seed of spirituality sprouts in the heart, for some, it grows in leaps and bounds while, for others, it flourishes millimetre by millimetre. If Neelakanta's faith grew quickly, Shivaswamy's grew quite slowly.

The day Shankara Linga Devaru spoke about Maya—the grand illusion—Shivaswamy noted down every word in his brown book, while Neelakanta sat and listened with unwavering attention, his eyes closed. 'Maya possesses an endless capacity to corrupt humanity. It envelops us in countless ways, crafting deceptive paths, luring us into its maze with the illusion that proclaims "This is the sole path." It creates a division between our internal and external worlds, barring us from attaining a true balance. Maya orchestrates a rhythm through the strings of language, meaning, emotion and logic, playing its tambura skilfully to entice us into its snare. Maya generates excitement to make us forget our misdeeds. It murmurs in our ears that the mist of ignorance that shrouds us is indeed knowledge. It declares with brazen assurance that every soul bears a tag, and its price is imprinted upon it. Consequently, everything becomes negotiable according to its worth and valuation. Only through relentless self-reflection and steadfast alertness can one shield oneself from Maya's beguiling veil. That's Allama's path.'

* * *

After providing them with an early education, the Mutt helped them continue their studies at a college in Kolar. They shared the same class and hostel room. Because of the path they had to take to reach there, their words and actions significantly differed, setting them apart from their contemporaries.

The Mutt that preached detachment, the childhood friend who embraced it effortlessly and the way they lived during those days forever altered how Shivaswamy perceived the world. As the stark reality of his life's journey diverged wildly from the paths he had once trodden in childhood, countless worlds collided within him ceaselessly. He remained uncertain whether his internal struggles were testaments to inner strength or reflections of a deep-seated vulnerability.

After college ended, Shivaswamy and Neelakanta, now young men, returned to Masti, but the haunting question about their future persisted, especially for Shivaswamy. It was during this tumultuous period that they met KereSwami, a sanyasi living modestly by a lake on the way to Dinneri. His actual name, Leelaradhya Dishaambara, proved too cumbersome for most people to say. So, the locals dubbed him 'KereSwami', meaning 'the sanyasi by the lake'. Some playfully twisted 'Dishaambara' in his longer name to 'Digambara Swami', meaning a naked ascetic. Though KereSwami wore a saffron robe, he never appeared to anyone as a Digambara.

KereSwami's origins remained shrouded in mystery. He was reserved, seldom indulging in conversation or offering any spiritual teachings. How he sustained himself was unknown. It was Neelakanta who told Shivaswamy about KereSwami; how Neelakanta came to know of him was also a mystery. The duo felt compelled to visit him, as if seeking something they had lost.

Unlike Shankara Linga Devaru, KereSwami offered no lengthy discourses. He often condensed his interpretation of a vachana into a single sentence, a stroke of fortune for those who listened. On occasion, he would utter a solitary word, and say, 'That's it. Understand this word; that's all you need.' A true minimalist, he remained unbothered by external presence, showing no concern whether visitors stayed long or departed abruptly.

When Shivaswamy and Neelakanta met KereSwami, they were at a critical juncture in their lives. The question before them was profound: Should they lead a conventional life, anchored in career and family, or follow figures like KereSwami or Shankara Linga Devaru? Neither of them had any idea which option to choose. Shivaswamy, however, assumed it was 'neither of the two'. It would later dawn on him that this assumption was inaccurate.

On one occasion, Shivaswamy sought KereSwami's counsel alone. 'What should I do? Embrace family life?' he asked him.

They were walking on the bund of the lake, brimming with rainwater after a full month of rain. KereSwami walked right over the muddy path, ignoring the sludge, even stepping directly onto the water's surface. Shivaswamy, on the other hand, kept his gaze fixed on the ground, making sure the muddy water wouldn't splash onto his feet. He took his steps with great caution, avoiding the muddy patches.

Without taking a moment, the Swami provided an unexpected answer. 'If you're in doubt, family life is your path,' he said and fell silent.

His words, while clear, didn't bring Shivaswamy immediate solace. Nonetheless, he trailed behind KereSwami quietly, putting his feet on the lake's bund carefully. After a few moments of silence, KereSwami suddenly stopped. He turned around and looked at Shivaswamy's face, as if assessing something. 'Only those with unwavering faith in reaching another boat should dive into the waters,' he advised. 'Let life unfold naturally. What joy is there in a fruit forced to ripen?'

That was all he said that day. It was the last time Shivaswamy saw the Swami. A sense of defeat overwhelmed him. He felt ashamed to face KereSwami again. He didn't see Neelakanta either for the next four days. It was a different matter that he would never see Neelakanta ever again. A haphazardly cut slip of paper tied to the front door latch, scribbled with the message 'I am going to the Himalayas,' was all Neelakanta left behind when he departed from his home in the stealth of the night. After this sudden departure, the true meaning of the words spoken by KereSwami became apparent to Shivaswamy. Such a question should never have arisen for someone embarking on the path of renunciation. Like Neelakanta, he should have plunged into the waters without a second thought. Those who took the plunge did not ask, 'Should I?'—they just dived in. Even if two boats sailed side by side in the same stream, crossing from one to the other demanded immense determination, a determination that solidified into an unwavering resolve. Shivaswamy lacked that level of conviction.

He followed KereSwami's advice and remained in the boat where he already was. He pursued his MA in History at Manasa Gangothri in Mysore. He passed the national exam for selection at BEL successfully and, when chosen, journeyed to Ghaziabad, undeterred by the distance. He married Revathi in a modest ceremony, steering clear of extravagant expenses. Their union was blessed with two children. The vessel of family life seemed sturdy, steering him safely through life.

* * *

How can one truly comprehend the world's intricacies without immersing oneself in it? By design, we are destined to face every conceivable experience during our earthly sojourn. The path of renunciation gains significance only after we've trodden the path of desire. Who, upon entering this world, escapes the dilemma of dual boats? Even KereSwami had his worldly vessel alongside his divine one. Didn't Allama Prabhu, who eloquently encapsulated the world in his verses, embrace asceticism only after the passing of his wife, Kamalathe?

In reality, we don't chase dichotomies like happiness–sorrow, virtue–vice, attachment–detachment or accumulation–renunciation at any time; they seek us out, touching us tenderly with their fingertips. They are the yin and yang of our lives, complementary and inseparable. They are like day and night, an unceasing cycle, repeating without our consent.

* * *

After Neelakanta's mysterious disappearance, Shivaswamy lost all contact with him. His aged, blind mother was admitted to an old people's home in Bengaluru by his relatives. Shivaswamy contemplated visiting her, wanting to inquire if Neelakanta had left any message. Yet, he hesitated and eventually decided against it. Some villagers whispered, 'He ran away to escape the burden of his old and blind mother.' Shivaswamy, who knew Neelakanta closely, dismissed it. But still, a murmur of doubt passed through his mind.

For his part, Shivaswamy vowed not to shirk any of his responsibilities. He married, gathered funds for his sister's wedding, extended support to her during her tough times, assisted her in growing flowers like their father and in managing the household, and raised and protected his children. He felt that every action of his was a deliberate effort to prevent himself from becoming another Neelakanta.

A recurring dream troubled him, though. It echoed KereSwami's words: 'Only those with unwavering faith in reaching another boat should dive into the waters.' In the vast ocean, two ships sailed parallel to each other, moving in the same direction. Shivaswamy swam between them, striving to reach one. His arms faltered, and he gasped for breath. When he glanced back, the ship he had left behind was as distant as the one he aimed to reach. A wave engulfed him, twirling him before lifting him up. He was now disoriented and couldn't distinguish between the ship he had left and the one he sought to join. The vessels were indistinguishable. He was puzzled, uncertain of the right direction. He headed towards one, but its towering masts intimidated him, and he feared he would be crushed under their weight. Exhaustion overtook him, and he halted his strokes, sinking into the dark waters.

Breathless, he woke up abruptly. This eerie dream, one that he had first dreamt on that distant night in Masti, following KereSwami's prophetic words, persisted in Ghaziabad and now haunted him in Bengaluru too.

Though Shivaswamy tried to balance all the worlds, in *vairagya*—renunciation—no such balancing exists. While he carried Allama Prabhu in his heart, the truth was that he did not secure a job because of the sage or his verses. The tree of thought that thrived in his mind held no utility for those on the outside. Yet, he managed to maintain his own form of detachment as his unique balancing act. It was remarkable how he had spent thirty-five years at BEL, or just in the world at large, really, being so different from the rest of the masses.

5

He took four days to adapt to the emptiness of his bed. Revathi was gone, and he was alone. It had been a long time since he had slept without her.

On a Monday morning, while he was chopping an onion to prepare avalakki—flattened rice—for his breakfast, he received a call from an unknown number. His eyes stung from the fumes of the onion, and tears welled up, blurring his vision. Wiping his eyes with a towel, he answered.

'Is this Shivaswamy?' asked a female voice.

'Yes.'

'I'm Anita, the executive assistant to Dhaval Thakkar, the managing director of the DT group. Our MD would like to meet with you. Would it be possible for you to visit our head office tomorrow at three in the afternoon?'

He didn't immediately understand who the caller was.

'I don't know who you are,' he replied hesitantly.

'You had an interview for the position of HR director at DT Software Solutions, a company within our group, on the twenty-fifth of last month, didn't you?' she asked.

Suddenly, it struck him. What he had forgotten was now back.

'Yes, I remember. Whom should I meet?'

'It's our MD—Dhaval Thakkar. You visited our office on Dickenson Road last time for the interview. This time, the meeting is at our head office in Sadashivanagar. Are you still interested in working for our company?' she inquired.

He wasn't sure how to respond. He hadn't expected this turn of events. The thought of the disastrous interview lingered in his mind. But now that they were reaching out again, what should he do? Should he decline or agree? He found himself in a dilemma. He debated whether he should subject himself to another round of humiliation by going for a second interview. He needed to come up with a response quickly.

She prompted him, 'Sir, if you're still interested in joining our company, our HR department will call you today. They will discuss the salary and benefits with you. The meeting with our MD will only happen after you've accepted the offer. Would you consider that?'

Two opposing voices spoke into either of his ears. One warned him that this was not it, and his past experiences said so too. The other reminded him of the outstanding balance for Anoop Gardenia. It didn't help that the construction work behind the house made its presence felt just then.

'Hello . . . Sir, are you still there?'

'Yes, I am.'

'The HR department will call you. Will you be available?'

'I will be.'

She hung up, thanking him.

After the call, he found himself in a perplexing situation. With thirty-five years of professional experience, he was well aware of the difference between successful and unsuccessful interviews. How could the interview suddenly shift from failure to success? Wasn't it clear that the interviewers had dismissed him and abandoned the interview midway? Their intent wasn't to assess him; instead, it was to overpower him. How could they now choose him? Could this be Shankar's ploy? Was he leveraging his influence within the company to make this happen?

Shivaswamy called Shankar. It seemed highly likely that he had orchestrated this situation, either to help him or to secure a commission, perhaps both. He felt angry with him for trying to do so even though he had explicitly asked him not to.

Shankar answered the phone and asked in a friendly tone, 'What's up, Shivu? Calling so early in the morning?'

Shivaswamy informed him about the call he had received. Shankar couldn't suppress his laughter. He was greatly surprised. He wondered whether his friend was telling him the truth or suffering from a delusion—likely in someone who had crossed sixty after all. He had never heard the name Anita mentioned at DT Software Solutions before. Why would the managing director, the head of all the companies under the DT Group, insist on speaking with a candidate for a mere HR manager's position? And that too for a branch and not for the corporate office? If this was the case, after the interview concluded that day, why had DT Software Solutions sent a weird message to him, implying, 'If you send any more of such candidates, our business is done!'?

'Didn't we apply for the HR manager's position?' Shankar asked.

'Yes.'

'Then why did the caller mention the HR director's position?'

'I don't know.'

Shankar found himself at a loss for words. It's rare enough when a candidate impresses the interviewers so much that they consider offering him a senior manager's position instead of just a manager's role. But what was happening here? They had initially called him for the HR manager's position, rejected him, and now, after a month, they had reached out again, this time for an HR director's position—a position three levels higher than the one he had been interviewed for. And surprisingly, they wanted him to meet with the managing director too. Something was amiss. The entire situation seemed puzzling. Nonetheless, it promised him a higher commission. Finding a director could yield double the commission compared to finding a manager. Despite the alluring prospects, he didn't want to rush into it.

Shivaswamy asked him directly, 'Are you involved in this? Please tell me straightaway.'

'I didn't do anything, Shivu. I can swear on Lord Manjunatha Swamy,' said Shankar. 'Hold on. I'll call some people in that company to check if it's true. I'll call you back. Don't answer their calls until then.'

Shivaswamy resumed the task of making breakfast. He was about to sit down to eat when Shankar's call came through.

'Shivu, what you heard is indeed true. They have chosen you. Something fishy seems to be happening. I've got some connections in their recruitment department. This way, I receive insider information unofficially. I know I shouldn't be resorting to these tricks. But, what to do, my friend? I have to feed myself too. Anyway, according to my contact, the three who interviewed you did not select you. They selected a candidate who worked for Infosys and had ten years of work experience. But their MD did not approve it and selected you after reviewing the profiles of all the candidates who came for the interview for that position! He overturned the choice made by his management. Congratulations.'

The informant had disclosed that Shivaswamy's name appeared at the bottom of the rating list submitted to the MD by the management. However, Shankar chose not to reveal this to him. After all, what purpose would it serve?

'It's strange.'

Shankar laughed. 'The company is a bit peculiar, Shivu,' he said. 'You should see the MD who wishes to meet you! He is seventy-five or eighty years old. A thick white beard! Six and a quarter feet tall! He looks like Amitabh Bachchan . . . and he speaks in the same deep voice. He is the *shahenshah* in the company. He built the company from scratch, nurtured it, elevated it and now, even though he is aged, he clings to it. When he walks in, the entire company seems to tremble. He is a Gujarati, but he was born and raised here in Bengaluru. He speaks fluent Kannada. His father had a tiny saree shop in the Chickpet area. This man is daring; he started a logistics company at a young age and eventually made it big. Even now, amidst all the various businesses under the DT Group, the transportation division forms the crux of their operations.

'Raviraj Thakkar, who interviewed you, is Dhaval Thakkar's son. However, the son is primarily in charge of the software unit. The unit is neither a full company nor as centralized as the other divisions of the DT Group; it's stuck somewhere in between. Raviraj Thakkar is not a suitable replacement to head these highly profitable companies in case anything happens to this old man. I don't think he has the ability to replace this shahenshah.'

'I don't know why he selected me. How can I face them after failing that interview so miserably?' said Shivaswamy.

'Forget about it. Those are your assumptions. They might have liked you. It depends on what you said and what the other candidates said, right? It's all relative. Don't waste your time speculating over how you were chosen. Think about the next steps. So, have they discussed your salary with you?'

'No, not yet. They will call me sometime today.'

'Listen, Shivu. Don't be a Gandhian. Don't base your demands on what you earned at BEL. This is a private company. A software company. I'm not saying BEL paid you little, but the salary structure in these companies works differently.'

'Should I ask for 10 per cent more than what I was earning at BEL when I retired?' Shivaswamy asked hesitantly.

'No, go higher.'

'Twenty-five per cent?'

'No, no. Ask for twice the amount you were earning at BEL. Bengaluru is an expensive city; the cost of living here is much higher than where you were before—in fact, it's the highest in India. Also, consider your expenses. If you start working again, there will be new costs to cover. Besides, you're staying on the outskirts of the city, and commuting surely drains your energy. Don't hesitate to ask for more. They'll expect a lot of work from you. They're even changing your position to accommodate that. It's smart to negotiate your salary properly. You should turn lemons into lemonade,' he laughed. He didn't mention that the commission he would receive from the company would be based on the salary that Shivaswamy would accept.

Throughout the day, Shivaswamy kept thinking about the strange turn of events. The thought of asking for such a substantial amount of money embarrassed him. He had already realized that Bengaluru was significantly more expensive than Ghaziabad. But still, was there any justification for asking for twice the salary?

To calm his mind, he took a leisurely stroll in the park near his home, spending an hour thinking about what he should do. He picked up the phone to tell Revathi about it, but then changed his mind. The events of that morning—the call, his conversation with Shankar, the peculiar details about the company and its MD—all appeared as elements of an April Fool's joke. He resolved to wait until he had more clarity before sharing the news with his family. At this point, he thought, it remained uncertain whether the call was authentic or just a chaotic mix-up.

When he got home, he realized there were enough household chores he could use to distract himself: to begin with, a mound of laundry that had accumulated over five days. Revathi had cultivated four flowering plants in a small patch of soil next to the front door. Realizing he hadn't watered them for two days, he set to work. Grass and weeds had sprouted between the plants, which he removed before watering the soil. By the time he completed his chores and finished reading the newspaper, lunchtime had arrived.

The phone rang, and he rushed to answer it. It was Tejas, who often called his father before going to bed, well after midnight his time. After speaking with Tejas, he checked his phone and noticed two missed calls from an unknown number. They must have come while he was busy with the laundry or tending to the plants. He suspected they were from the company and considered returning them but didn't want to appear too eager for the job.

An hour later, the same number called again. The person at the other end introduced himself as Anurag Das, an HR analyst at DT Group. He said, 'I've called to ask you a few questions and take some notes. Could you please talk to me for a few minutes?'

6

Shivaswamy navigated his scooter cautiously through Bengaluru's chaotic traffic. He hadn't quite adapted to it yet. Despite it being August, the scorching heat clung to him. He had first thought of taking the metro to the interview like he had the last time, but then he found two reasons to take the scooter out. First, he had been called to the office in Sadashivanagar, not the office near MG Road. There was no metro station near enough to this office. Second, if he kept postponing taking out the scooter every time, it would rust. He had bought this scooter in Ghaziabad twelve years ago. It became necessary when they moved from the quarters to a rented house in Surya Nagar. Every morning, he would drop Sanju off at her college, even though it meant arriving at his office forty-five minutes early.

He was quite fond of the scooter and chose not to sell it when they moved. So, he visited the RTO office and obtained a No Objection Certificate to drive it in Karnataka. Despite Tejas's repeated warnings, 'Appa, you haven't seen Bengaluru lately. It's a nightmare to drive there; it's like Delhi's Karol Bagh market.' Shivaswamy couldn't bring himself to do it. Revathi joked that owning that scooter made him feel young.

Tejas was right. For Shivaswamy, who was unfamiliar with the city, there were too many turns on the way to the Sadashivnagar office that could lead him astray. In any case, before leaving home, he wrote down the directions on a piece of paper and carried it with him. He stopped occasionally to ensure he was on the correct route, often asking the autorickshaw drivers parked on the side of the road. The drivers, in turn, asked him, 'Your scooter has UP state registration! How did you bring it from there?'

Shivaswamy had anticipated the possibility of getting lost, so he set out early. When he reached the location, he saw a grand edifice with 'DT Group of Companies' inscribed in gold on a light blue board. He found that he still had half an hour to spare. Concerned that arriving too early might not make the best impression, he parked his scooter under a tree by the roadside and began exploring the neighbourhood. Apart from the DT Group, the area was predominantly residential. However, the houses, mostly enormous mansions, were as large as any office building. He had heard that Sadashivanagar was a posh locality, but he had never seen it for himself.

As he walked, he rehearsed his answers to a potential set of questions. Waking up early that morning, he had prepared some notes, jotting down responses to questions that had tripped him up in the previous interview. He anticipated similar queries today. He recalled his previous answers and realized that they were too idealistic. Today, he intended to strike a balance.

In the morning, he reviewed the books he had relied on for thirty-five years—*HR Management*, *Organizational Behaviour* and *Strategic HR Planning*—and wrote down some key points. The night before, he had read numerous online articles about the HR demands of software companies and had acquired a better understanding of the DT Group of companies. Whether or not this attempt proved successful, he felt he should end the day with the satisfaction of having approached it with more dignity at least.

The previous day, when Anurag Das had called to inquire about his salary expectations, Shivaswamy, following Shankar's advice, requested a salary that was double his earnings at BEL. When he stated the figure he had in mind, his voice trembled. The person on the other end of the line remained silent, offering no reaction. Disgusted with himself, Shivaswamy's voice was almost apologetic as he added, 'If this poses a burden to the company, I am open to a negotiation.' The caller jotted down the figure and said that someone higher up, probably the group's HR head, a lady called Shyamala Menon, would reach out to discuss the matter further. He reassured him that he had included 'The candidate is open to negotiations' in his notes—as per his request. However, there were no subsequent calls from the HR department. By evening, Anita had called again to confirm the scheduled interview with Dhaval Thakkar.

As Shivaswamy slowly walked back to the building, he began to sweat profusely. He stood under a tall tree at the side of the road to catch his breath. The traffic on the road was sparse, with only a few luxury cars passing by. Unlike Talaghattapura, there were no street vendors here calling out loudly to sell vegetables, fruits, flowers, gas stove repairs and Jaipur carpets or offering to sharpen knives, scissors, sickles, coconut scrapers and such.

Finally, he entered the company, introduced himself to the woman at the front desk, and informed her that he was there for an interview. As soon as she realized he was there to see the managing director, she said nervously, 'I'll call him right away, sir. Please have a seat. He hasn't come to the office yet.'

In five minutes, she came to where he was sitting and said politely, 'Sir, the MD will be here in the next ten minutes. Please come inside. He has asked you to wait in the boardroom.' Then she led him to a spacious and well-organized meeting room.

The table where Shivaswamy sat was large and oval-shaped, meant to accommodate a large number of participants. In one corner of the room were displayed the accolades that the company had received. On one wall, there were various pictures of people receiving awards from prominent figures such as the central minister of transport, the chief minister of Karnataka, and the director-general of the Indian Chamber of Commerce.

Straight across from the table, on the opposite wall, and immediately visible when the door is opened, were two large portraits. One was of an elderly man wearing a traditional Gujarati turban, while the other showed a person in a suit with a stern expression. The man in the suit was younger than the man in the turban. Both portraits were adorned with garlands of flowers.

Shivaswamy put his notepad on the table and settled into a comfortable chair. 'Sir, would you like some coffee, tea or juice?' the woman asked.

'No, thank you,' he said.

'Please, sir. It's no trouble.'

'Just water.'

She leaned towards the wall and switched on the lights. Evenly spaced lamps illuminated the room beautifully. He wondered whether this luxurious room was really necessary for a conversation between two people.

She left the room. A moment later, a man in a blue uniform came in and presented two bottles of mineral water and a glass on a decorated tray.

As the clock ticked away and announced the passing of ten silent minutes, the door swung open, and an old man entered the room. Shankar's description had been on point: a tall figure with a snowy beard, peering through thick glasses, wearing a white khadi shirt and light blue trousers. His gaze fell upon Shivaswamy, assessing him without a word.

Shivaswamy stood up.

'Shivaswamy?' the old man said in his deep voice. The large conference table lay between them, and Shivaswamy was unsure whether he should walk down to the other side to shake hands. He folded his hands together in confusion and said, 'Yes, sir.'

The old man grinned, stepped closer to him, and offered a warm handshake. 'I thought you would be taller,' he said, tapping his chest and laughing heartily. 'But here you are. I am Dhaval Thakkar.'

With that introduction, they both settled into their chairs. The elderly man didn't sit facing Shivaswamy; instead, he sat beside him.

'Where is your home?'

'Talaghattapura.'

'Where is that?'

'On Kanakapura Road.'

'Well, well, well . . . you have come a long way then.'

The old man's throat was tight. He picked up Shivaswamy's glass of water and drank some from it. He was silent for a moment, as if he was recovering from speaking.

'I went through your profile. It's a blessing for our companies to have experienced people like you, who want to work even after retirement. Has the HR department discussed your salary with you? Does it meet your expectations?' he asked, taking another sip of water and locking his eyes with Shivaswamy's.

'They called me, sir. I have conveyed my expectations,' Shivaswamy said. He contemplated whether he should say, 'I'm willing to negotiate if the amount doesn't meet your company's standards,' just as he had said to the young man on the phone.

'If, for some reason, they don't agree . . . or if you have other expectations, please don't hesitate to call my secretary directly. She will take care of everything,' he said.

Shivaswamy was startled. Had this man mistaken him for somebody else? It was absurd to believe that the head of a group of companies, where twelve thousand people worked, would come forward to meet him like this. He couldn't find any words to respond and simply sat dumbfounded. Even Dhaval sat in silence. Shivaswamy only answered if Dhaval asked a question. The world's strangest interview unfolded.

A young woman in an elegant purple saree tapped on the door lightly, interrupting their conversation. Shivaswamy couldn't help but notice that she was extraordinarily beautiful. Dhaval gestured for her to come in. She said, 'Sir, I'm sorry, I wasn't aware of your arrival.'

'Mr Shivaswamy is here,' said Dhaval, as though they had known each other for a while.

She looked at Shivaswamy and smiled. 'I'm Anita. I was the one who called you yesterday.'

Shivaswamy stood up and nodded in acknowledgment.

Dhaval was displeased by her sudden presence. 'Why have you come?' he grumbled.

The young woman lowered her gaze and spoke in a hushed voice, 'Would you like something to drink, sir?'

'No,' he replied, his tone still unwelcoming.

She nodded and started to leave but paused at the doorway. 'Sir, you have a meeting with Vimal Jain and his executives at four-thirty. Should I have them come here or to your house?'

Dhaval sighed. 'Tell them to come here. Can't you see I'm already in office?'

The woman nodded once more and closed the door quietly behind her.

Dhaval was perturbed. 'I wanted to have a conversation with you. But she came in like a gust of wind,' he said.

Shivaswamy smiled politely. He didn't perceive her as a 'gust of wind'.

'Sitting in this office is always the same. I can't concentrate on anything. Let's walk down to my home. It's on the next street, right behind this building. We can talk there peacefully,' he said, rising from his seat. He was the one who had just scolded the secretary for asking if she could set up the next meeting at his home.

Shivaswamy stood up, folded his notebook, and followed him. As soon as they opened the door and stepped outside, the secretary, sitting in the cubicle, followed them.

'I'm taking him home,' Dhaval said without looking at her. Shivaswamy walked behind him. With swift strides and the gentle rustle of her saree, Anita caught up with them and asked, 'Shall I arrange for Vimal Jain and his team to meet you at your home by four-thirty then?'

'Seriously?' Dhaval retorted. 'Even at home you bother me! I can't find a moment of peace!' His words were laced with frustration.

Sensing his irritation, she remained silent.

Shivaswamy observed their interaction with curiosity, guessing that it might be routine for her to deal with his behaviour. The clock was inching towards four o'clock.

However, Dhaval wasn't thinking about her question; he was lost in his world.

'Shivaswamy?'

'Yes, sir.'

'I don't want to go home, and I don't want to stay in the office. Let's go somewhere else,' he clapped his hands together. 'To Sankey Tank! Yeah, it would be lovely to sit by the lake and chat.' Shivaswamy trailed behind him, thinking that he had, after all, come this far in this strange interview; he might as well continue. Anita followed them to the front desk in bewilderment.

Just as they were about to step out, she reached for her phone and called Dhaval's driver, Chandru. He was enjoying his coffee at Bhatta's Coffee Shop, a roadside coffee bar just two streets from Dhaval's home. Unaware that Dhaval had walked to the office, he promised to arrive in five minutes and hastily left the shop to fetch the car, leaving his half-consumed coffee behind.

As Dhaval approached the door, Anita rushed ahead and said, 'Sir, Chandru will be here in another five minutes.' Dhaval was restless. Turning towards Shivaswamy, he said, 'Let's go in your car.' Shivaswamy blushed in embarrassment.

'I haven't come in a car,' he said.

'Then?'

'I came on a scooter.'

Dhaval's eyes widened. 'A Bajaj scooter?'

'No, sir. TVS.'

'My father had a Bajaj scooter. Oh, those were the days! I used to explore the streets of Bangalore on it. I used to do all the outside work for my father's saree shop. How do you manage to kick-start yours? Like my father's—at forty-five degrees?' He mimicked the action, laughing heartily.

'No, sir. Mine has a button start,' Shivaswamy said, looking around sheepishly. Anita stood behind him. The two women at the front desk had stood up respectfully. Behind them stood three or four boys in blue uniforms. Everyone was looking at them with curiosity, but no one laughed at the MD's joke.

Dhaval turned to Shivaswamy and said, 'Come on, let's go on your scooter. It's not even two kilometres. It's even walkable . . . just the heat.'

Shivaswamy panicked. This man, the MD of the company, would have his lavish car arriving any moment now. So why the insistence on taking a ride on his scooter? How old was he? What if something untoward happened?

'You can't ride a scooter, sir,' he said anxiously.

'What?'

Anita came to Shivaswamy's aid. She said, 'Sir, your car will be here in a minute. There's no need for the scooter.'

'No, no . . . we're going on the scooter. Tell Chandru not to come. If he comes, tell him to wait here. Don't send him to Sankey Lake,' he said firmly.

Helplessly, Shivaswamy brought his scooter from the parking area and positioned it in front of the building's gate. He moved forward as much as he could, creating more space for Dhaval to sit behind him. Once Dhaval settled down, the scooter looked like a toy in comparison to his size.

As they were about to set off, Anita stepped forward, saying, 'Sir, you need a helmet.' She held out the one provided by the admin manager.

'Are you kidding me? It's just a kilometre,' Dhaval remarked.

'But you still need it,' she said.

'I don't need it,' Dhaval dismissed her and nudged Shivaswamy to start. Struggling to maintain his balance, Shivaswamy moved the scooter forward. Dhaval straightened up, and the security guards stood on either side of the open gate, waiting for them.

On the steps of the main door, Anita, the admin manager and several others stood and watched them. Anita looked worried. Through the opposite side of the gate, a white Audi drove in and stopped near her. Chandru, the driver, looked at the moving scooter carrying the two seniors, clearly puzzled by the sight.

7

As evening set in, the searing sun lingered in the sky, casting a warm golden hue. People were scattered around the serene Sankey Lake, taking walks. A few children and elders had gathered around the pigeon pond near the entrance gate. Whenever the children threw birdseed, a flock of birds would swoop down from the heavens, like a grey saree unfurling from the sky.

'We needn't walk; we can find a spot to sit and converse. I took a walk earlier in the morning. How about you?' said the MD.

'I, too, walked this morning,' Shivaswamy lied. He had not been as regular with his exercise since Revathi had gone to the US. He would stay up late reading books and delay going to bed. As a result, his mornings started later and were irregular, and his morning walk was inconsistent.

'Shivaswamy?'

'Yes, sir.'

'How old are you?' Dhaval asked, as he sat down on a stone bench.

'Sixty-two.' Shivaswamy sat down next to him.

'I am fourteen years older than you,' Dhaval said with a smile.

Although the lake was not full, it still contained a substantial amount of water, which sparkled in the sunlight.

'I wonder how long it's been since I last visited this place. It must be years,' Dhaval mused. 'I used to come here and sit with my wife. Those were the days when she was in good health.'

'How is she doing now?'

'Who?'

'Your wife.'

Dhaval smiled faintly. 'She joined *Haripada* five years ago.'

'I am sorry.' Shivaswamy expressed his condolences.

'It's all right. It's a question that needs to be asked,' Dhaval continued, 'Tell me about yourself, Shivaswamy . . . about your work experience and your family.'

Shivaswamy spoke about his education, about joining BEL and serving in Ghaziabad for thirty-five years. He also talked briefly about his background and about Revathi and their children.

Dhaval turned towards him slowly and said, 'If you don't mind, I have a question to ask. A delicate one.'

'Please, go ahead, sir.'

'Why are you trying to get a job at this age?'

Although Shivaswamy had crafted a narrative that would probably satisfy prospective employers, explaining his motivation to work after retirement, in this instance, he sensed the need to share the truth with this man. He felt that this person had more compassion than the three interviewers he had met before. He recounted the story of his struggle to secure an apartment, providing a clear picture of the challenges he had faced that led to his current financial situation. His words remained free from exaggeration or falsehood.

'*Ayyo*, Ramachandra, look at the countless hardships a man endures!' Dhaval patted Shivaswamy's shoulder with sympathy. 'After listening to your story, the businessman inside me has a question. I won't hide it. Will you leave us once you've earned your eight lakhs?' It was a straightforward question with no sarcasm.

Shivaswamy responded candidly once again. 'I'm uncertain, sir,' he said. 'I believe I possess the capacity to work for another five years. If I find it fitting, I'll continue. I'd be happy to stay if this job suits my thirty-five years of experience. But, if not, it may cause me a lot of inner conflict, which could affect my peace of mind. So, I don't know now, sir. Please forgive me if my answer disappoints you.'

Dhaval began to say something, but, at that moment, a girl of around five came running towards them, stumbled, and fell right where they were sitting.

'Oh dear!' Dhaval exclaimed as he stood up and lifted her. The girl's father reached the spot, panting heavily. 'No matter how many times I tell her not to run, she never listens!' He scolded his daughter and took her from Dhaval's arms.

'Oh, come on, my friend! If not her, who else should be running around here? Me? An old man with arthritis, sciatica and back pain?' said Dhaval, guffawed. His joke didn't go down well with the girl's father. He quickly left with his daughter.

'Raising children is so challenging. You have to let them fall, but you also have to catch them when they fall. When she falls, he catches her. In the end, when he falls, she must catch him. Father–daughter, father–son . . .' Dhaval sat down. 'Shivaswamy, I have chosen you for a special reason. I will tell you what it is. Then you can decide. Whether you want to take up this job or not is up to you. But I have chosen you.'

Shivaswamy was intrigued. The tension he had felt before the interview was gone now. Instead, he was curious.

'Shyamala presented twelve profiles to me. However, by then, they had already chosen a candidate and prepared an offer letter, awaiting my approval. The HR department requires my approval to send out offers for managerial and higher positions. This protocol applies across all divisions. My son has never liked this process. He constantly argues that I should not intervene in their selection process. This disagreement has been ongoing for some time. I'm tired of trying to persuade him about the long-term benefits of my involvement.

'Anyway, that's another story. Where was I . . .? Nowadays, I easily lose my thoughts while talking . . .'

'Shyamala put twelve profiles in front of you.'

'Yeah, that's right. No, not like that. Initially, she didn't send twelve profiles. She had already chosen a candidate and sent only that one for my approval. Later, I asked her to send me the profiles of all the candidates who had been interviewed. Along with that, I also asked for the notes they had taken during the interviews. When I asked for all this, it annoyed her. I asked for it for a different purpose, something she wouldn't understand.

'To sum it up, I carefully perused all twelve profiles and read the comments made by the interviewers. I paid particular attention to the candidate that my son Raviraj, his close friend Prabhu and Shyamala had selected. She had worked at a major corporation, perhaps Infosys or TCS—the specifics escape me. She articulated her responses cleverly, addressing technical queries on HR practices, strategies and processes. But it felt as though her practical experience fell short. I think she gave textbook answers to impress those three.

'Do you know what I thought when I read what these three had written about the candidates, Shivaswamy? The three who conducted the interviews were immature. They posed rather naive questions than practical ones. Take this question, for example; they asked everyone, including you: "If chosen, how would you acclimatize yourself here?" Absurd, isn't it? Would anyone about to welcome a daughter-in-law ask how she plans to assimilate into their family? In response, if she says in her soft voice, "I will wake up before sunrise every day, greet my mother-in-law and my father-in-law and start my day by singing *Suprabhata*," would you believe it? If you seek the right response, you must pose the right question.

'Look, your profile ended up in my hands last. Everything that the interviewers didn't appreciate about you, I did. I firmly believe that experienced people like you should be conversing with my employees as an HR executive, not a young woman who prefers reciting stuff from textbooks.

'Above all else, your response to a question struck me as classic. *When we discuss human resources, be it in software development, electronics manufacturing or constructing bridges over rivers, what distinction does it bear? Humans are humans. Every individual interacts with others, based on their intrinsic nature, upbringing and the societal culture they're part of. When an HR manager communicates with an employee, they must comprehend the subtleties of that individual's personality and adapt to their interactions accordingly. Here, the individual is paramount.* This single answer prompted me to reach out to you.'

Shivaswamy was surprised. It was true that the question had been asked, and though the words were not exactly the same as Dhaval's, he had answered with the same intent.

It was also true that Shyamala Menon was jotting everything down as quickly as a stenographer, as though doing so was easier than meeting his gaze.

What truly delighted Shivaswamy, however, and brought a smile to his face, was the fact that this person—someone holding the highest position in the company and so senior in age—had read through it all and appreciated his response.

Dhaval continued with delight after seeing Shivaswamy's smile. 'I know these folks well. The three interviewers talk as if the software business arrived from Mars. Even if I were in your position, I would provide the same answer to that question. That indicates maturity.

'Shyamala, in her comment, mentioned that your response lacked sensitivity and subtlety. Ravi stated it was too generalized, and Prabhu simply underlined it. He didn't indicate whether he liked it or not. Even if he did, these other two ensured he gave them the desired answer.

'There's much happening within the company, Shivaswamy. I will brief you on everything once you join us.'

Dhaval stood up, clutching his waist. 'I can't sit for too long. I'll stand. You can keep sitting, all right?' He positioned himself in front of him. Shivaswamy waited for what he was about to say next.

'I overruled their advice and chose you. All three were angry and left my office, showing their displeasure. According to them,

I picked you because of the salary. The TCS woman asked for more salary than you did. But that's beside the point. Don't worry now; I will increase your salary once the probationary period ends.

'I didn't really need to call you and talk to you. I asked them to send you the offer letter. But Anita insisted on my talking to you once before that. Because two of the three had written that your communication skills were not up to the mark. So, you had to come again.'

Shivaswamy's smile faded from his face. Isn't it cruel to directly tell someone with thirty-five years of work experience, 'Your communication skills are not up to the mark'? And that too, to an HR manager? What could be ruder than that? Dhaval's blunt words had toyed with Shivaswamy's emotions like a seesaw, lifting him up one moment only to throw him down the next.

Sensing Shivaswamy's displeasure, Dhaval continued in a calm and reassuring tone. 'Let me tell you my other motive in selecting you. If you hear it, you'll understand my situation better. I didn't call you for this—to assess your communication skills. Your communication skills are good enough. These guys need people who speak English like TV anchors, even if there's no substance within. I'm not running a TV station to select orators, am I?' he said with a smile.

Shivaswamy was unsure whether this man was laughing with him or at him. He remembered incidents from his childhood at school, where a boy with speech difficulties was repeatedly ridiculed by his friends who asked him to pronounce difficult words. The same is happening here. Instead of asking questions to assess him, he was talking about his company, sharing unnecessary details, as if they had known each other for many years. What did one do in this situation? Determined not to let the events of the last interview repeat themselves, Shivaswamy suppressed his irritation.

'Sir, may I ask a question?' he asked politely.

'Of course.'

'If I join your company, who will I be working for? Will I have to report to you or to those three?'

'Your question makes sense. But I don't have an answer for that right now,' Dhaval smiled again. 'Perhaps you'll be working for all of us. That's what I need.'

'Sir, I've been speaking to you candidly because you've been speaking to me in the same way. Even though we don't know each other, you've shared your company's inner workings with me. This position is not for your central office but for the software division. The daily affairs of that division are controlled by those three. They didn't choose me. If you disregard their opinion and employ me, they will reject me every day. Would it really work?'

Dhaval blinked behind his thick glasses. Then, he burst into hearty laughter and patted Shivaswamy on the shoulder. 'Experiencing that hell will be your job,' he said. 'That's precisely why I've promoted you to the role of HR director. With this new position, you'll have authority. Moreover, given that only directors and executives in top-tier positions attend my meetings, you'll engage with me directly in a more significant capacity. If they give you a hard time, we'll play a little trick and place paper pins on their chair cushions.' He winked mischievously. 'You mentioned that I'm revealing the company's secrets to you . . . I haven't disclosed the company's annual turnover or profit margin to you. What other kinds of secrets exist, Shivaswamy, that shouldn't be divulged? Besides, if you decide not to join, this might be the only encounter between us in our lifetime. So, at this stage of life, what would I achieve by bluffing with a seasoned professional like you?'

Shivaswamy smiled with a sense of bewilderment. He searched for words, uncertain about how to respond. He gathered that this man's intention was to bring him into the company to show off his power and vent his frustration, possibly directed towards his own executives. There might be an underlying message here:

'I possess the authority to override all your decisions as I see fit. I can reject the candidate chosen by you and select anyone I desire from a random pool.' Worried, he thought, *What purpose do I serve in his scheme?* It seemed wise to avoid getting entangled in such a situation. Nipping it all in the bud was wiser than facing the inevitable anguish at the end.

As Shivaswamy contemplated how to articulate his thoughts, Dhaval leaned in closer. 'I know, it seems strange to you,' he said. 'But I am subjecting you to this hardship due to a certain circumstance.' He stood up straight, holding his waist, and asked, 'Shall we walk around the lake?'

Though Dhaval looked older, his physical well-being surpassed Shivaswamy's expectations. He was surefooted and steady.

'I'll explain it briefly. The rest you will understand when you work with me in the coming days. If what I'm saying doesn't fully make sense to you now, don't worry. Please keep in mind that I do not expect anything illegal or unethical from you. You don't have to be afraid. Even though I might seem old and frail now, I am still a seasoned professional. If you know that much about me, it's enough. Gujarati Thakkars are hard-nosed businessmen, but they are honest. Have you heard of this?

'My DT Group is my empire. It began as a small logistics business and has now grown to encompass engineering consultancy, medical equipment trading and recently software solutions. Each division has a sizable workforce. In this respect, the software division is the smallest, with around four hundred or five hundred employees. However, most of my challenges stem from there. Vimal Jain manages the logistics division, while Ashok Mehta oversees the engineering consultancy and the medical equipment trading divisions. My son, Ravi, is in charge of the software division, and his right-hand man is Prabhu. The two of them were classmates and have remained steadfast friends. Prabhu is remarkably astute and executes any task with utmost precision.

'Just a few years ago, there was no software division, and we did not sell software. Only an IT department supported the other divisions. Ravi and Prabhu, however, took it upon themselves to convert that department into a division. They developed and started selling two or three products. But now, they are adamant about making this division a separate company. They want to make it public. I do not see any reason why it should become a separate company. We have reached a point where we do not see eye to eye. What was once a hairline fracture between us has now developed into a painful severance. Whether it is called a generation gap or something else, I am not sure. This division, which is growing more distant day by day, needs to be integrated back into our group. You should stay in that branch and ensure that it remains loyal to the DT Group.

'I am not creating a predisposed bias. Whether it is my left eye or my right eye, any impact on it causes me discomfort. What I am seeking is your assistance in understanding their standpoint. I would also need you to help me articulate my thoughts to them. I know it may seem simple, but what I am asking requires a great deal of experience and maturity. For most people, this maturity comes only with age. That is why I am placing my bet on you out of the twelve candidates.'

Dhaval's breath grew heavier as he walked and continued to talk. He paused to compose himself.

Shivaswamy took a moment to take it all in. 'I've never taken on an assignment like this before, sir,' he said.

'Who has, Shivaswamy?' Dhaval laughed. 'Who undertakes such work? Who should I even seek? Listen, I'll streamline your daily tasks at the office. I'll dispatch people from the main office to help you as assistants. Let's give it six months. And, if you come to me then saying that you don't like it, I won't stop you.'

Shivaswamy remained uncertain about his decision. Firstly, wasn't the job crucial for his own needs? Why should he hesitate to undertake such a task? Moreover, if he could really help this man out and his company, why shouldn't he pursue it? Yet, he hesitated. Like a swimmer caught between two ships, he found himself adrift.

They had completed a round around the lake and were nearly at the gate. The clock announced that it was six o'clock. People were making their way to the lake in small groups.

'Will you be joining tomorrow, then?' Dhaval asked.

'Could you please give me a day or two to think it over and convey my decision?'

'Sure. In any case, I'll ask Anita to send the offer letter to you,' he said with a smile.

8

Shankar called Shivaswamy and spoke non-stop, like a father trying to convince his reluctant son.

'Hey Shivu, give it some thought. Seriously, are you planning to stick it out there for the next twenty-five years? Come on! Two or three years, perhaps? This is an amazing offer, my friend! I can't work any magic to find you something like this even in any international companies.

'Look at the perks, the health insurance, and look at your position! Who's going to offer you such an amazing opportunity? Don't overthink and kill it. Don't search for excuses. Keep in mind, you have to pay for your apartment, cover your son's expenses in America and arrange for his marriage. Living expenses are mounting, and a lot of money is needed, man. Earn while you still have the energy. At our age, hardly anyone gets job offers, but you're turning down a golden chance right in your hand! Let me tell you, you don't need to stress yourself too much over the work. Just do whatever that old man asks; that's all.'

Knowing Shankar since childhood, Shivaswamy had never expected any other kind of suggestion from him. At that moment, he lacked the words to articulate the turmoil and hidden fears churning within him, and he knew that even if he did, such delicate nuances would make little impression on Shankar. All that remained for him was to sit back, take deep breaths and listen.

'I know, I know,' Shivaswamy said. 'But isn't it quite a distance to commute every day?' His voice was laced with hesitation, as if bracing himself for the fierce response Shankar was about to unleash.

'You keep saying their office is too far away, but you haven't really experienced this city yet, my friend! Here's the simple rule: MG Road is in, and ITPL tech park is out. Your office is on MG Road. What's more, there's a metro station near your house. I don't get why you're feeling unhappy about this!'

That night, Shivaswamy called Revathi and shared the news with her, without delving into all the details. Although she, too, found the salary attractive, she anxiously inquired, 'Do you really have to work again?'

He responded, 'It will be around five months until you return. I feel lonely here. Let's see, I'll give it a shot. At the very least, we'll have the money for our apartment's payment.'

She was uncertain. He tried the same story with the children and prevented them from saying anything to discourage him.

Though the company had asked him to communicate his joining date in the offer letter, he never did so. He didn't even formally confirm his acceptance. Mentally, he was planning that if he joined at all, it wouldn't be for at least another week. There were several tasks to be completed before diving into the new job. He needed to update his Bengaluru address at the Aadhaar office, close and consolidate multiple bank accounts, transfer his maturing recurring deposit from the post office, and pay his and Revathi's annual life insurance premiums. He also had to launder and iron four pairs of trousers and shirts and prepare a file with photocopies of documents the company required on his first day. Apart from all that, and most importantly, he planned to attend a meeting with a lawyer arranged by Sandeep Kamat and others that week.

* * *

The location was Adiga's Restaurant on Kanakapura Road. This lawyer was Sandeep Kamat's acquaintance. The gathering was relatively informal, more like a casual meet-up over coffee. The purpose was to discuss the next steps regarding the handover of the apartments. But the tumultuous atmosphere prevailing in the WhatsApp group appeared to have extended to the physical meeting space as well.

The gathering lacked a discernible structure. Various participants arrived at different intervals, repeatedly posing the same questions to the lawyer. Some people grew agitated, seeking strategies to gain authority over their apartments without incurring additional costs. Before the lawyer could address one query, another participant tossed a fresh question.

Most people were unacquainted with real estate intricacies, but they vehemently expressed their viewpoint anyway. The small table where the lawyer was seated was surrounded by around twenty participants, making it a challenge to accommodate everyone within hearing range. The dialogues escalated into heated debates, prompting some members to leave the restaurant and congregate outside. Eventually, the situation compelled the restaurant staff to voice their frustration too.

Sandeep had initially estimated there would be around eight to ten attendees, but things hadn't gone according to his plan. He suggested another meeting in a more serene and spacious setting, where everyone could sit comfortably and adhere to the decided agenda. Shivaswamy was among those who opted to observe silently rather than engage extensively in dialogue. Though Sandeep Kamat's initiatives were undoubtedly meant with good intentions, the lack of an organized structure to the entire thing became evident as things progressed.

Shivaswamy had chosen not to take his scooter and had walked down to the restaurant, even though it was a bit far. Kumar Gowda had been brought to the meeting by his wife, Vanita, who then took the scooter for other errands. So, he joined Shivaswamy on their walk back home.

'It's all such a headache, right?' Kumar quipped as they headed back.

'Yeah,' Shivaswamy laughed.

'You know, every time I hear them talk, I can't help but think that either we have to take the builder to court individually or simply accept the situation and pay the dues. I'm starting to lose faith that we can do anything as a group.'

'But they are asking for eight lakh rupees! Isn't that too much?' Shivaswamy exclaimed.

'Well, sir, you're still new to Bengaluru, aren't you? Right on this very road, before our project even took off, there was another one. I'll point it out to you as we walk past it. That builder is bigger than ours. Their project began three years before ours. They haven't delivered the houses yet, sir! They're facing more issues than we are. The land that the builder purchased is entangled in a legal dispute, and the case is currently in court. These builders are all sly operators, sir. They have no fear. They're ready to do whatever it takes to boost their profits.'

Shivaswamy shopped for groceries, vegetables and other daily essentials before returning home. After dinner, as he settled down to catch the news, Teju called. Shivaswamy briefed him about that day's meeting and Kumar Gowda's perspective on it.

'Appa, if there's no unity within the owners' group, this issue won't find a resolution. They'll simply bicker amongst themselves, each trying to get their way. Kumar's viewpoint seems pragmatic. If we take this to court, it could be stuck for five years; you know how those things go. On the one hand, we won't secure the house; on the other, we won't escape the lawyer's fees. If paying the builder can bring about a solution, then it's better to act sooner,' said Tejas.

Shivaswamy fell silent for a moment. 'If everyone else pays, we can follow suit. But what if they don't, and we end up being the only ones who do? The builder might just take that money without resolving anything,' he said. He had never divulged his financial struggles to his children before this.

'That's true,' Teju agreed. 'Appa, if we need to resolve the issue by paying them off, then don't worry too much. I'll complete my studies in another six months and start working here. That will certainly be helpful for us.'

By nature, Teju was more like his mother than his father: curious-minded, stating whatever he believed boldly and clearly without hesitation. He was less emotional and more practical towards the world. Sanjana, on the other hand, mostly took after their father. In her modesty, reticence and preference to keep to herself, she relied more on her heart than her head. Even academically, there was a stark difference between the two. While Teju consistently ranked first in class, she struggled every step before she finished college. She had never envied her brother though.

That night, Shivaswamy tossed and turned in bed, unable to sleep. The bright lights from the construction site of Anoop Gardenia filtered in through the white curtains of his bedroom, creating shadows. Even well past eleven, the noise of the machinery and workers was deafeningly loud. If he closed the windows, the heat and humidity would make him sweat, feel suffocated and make it impossible for him to sleep. He grabbed fresh cotton wicks from the pooja room and stuffed them in his ears. He also draped a dark bedsheet over the curtains and the window frame to block out the light. Finally, he was able to relax a little.

But his mind continued to race. If Teju completed his studies and got a job in the US, it would be easier to arrange eight lakh rupees. However, that would be unfair to him; he was still in school. If he had returned to India, established himself here, and enjoyed living in the house he had invested in, it would only be logical for him to bear the costs. Otherwise, expecting Teju to cover the expenses while he remained in the US would be unfair. It would create a life burdened by debt for both.

If Teju failed to secure a job in the US, his student visa would expire, and he would be compelled to return to India. The loan taken for his American education would need to be repaid. That could take many years on his Indian salary. In this scenario,

Shivaswamy fretted—what would Teju, and his future wife, think of him if he also had to carry the financial burden of the house? Ultimately, Shivaswamy decided that regardless of Teju's decision to come back or remain in the US, it was his own responsibility to address the matter of the house independently, avoiding any imposition on Teju.

It was the third night after the company's offer letter had arrived. He was still struggling with whether he should accept or reject the job. Whether the old managing director, who had spoken to him, was crazy or not didn't matter. For now, it seemed sensible to accept the job. If he found it frustrating later, he could quit. After all, it was a private company, and he was sixty-two years old. He decided that he would call the company the next morning and let them know that he had accepted the offer.

Just then, as if the skies were relieved that he had finally made a decision, it began to rain. Soon, his breathing grew deeper, and he finally slipped into a dreamless sleep.

9

On his first day at the company, Shivaswamy went through the formalities of filling out forms and introducing himself to various people. Anuradha, an analyst in the HR department, welcomed him and showed him around the office. Since he had come to the same office for his first interview, he was already kind of familiar with it. He was seated in a conference room and shown a video about the company. As was his habit, he took notes as he watched the video. Anuradha sat next to him throughout.

The company had been founded fifty years ago by Dinakar Ram Thakkar, the father of the current chairman and managing director, Dhaval Thakkar. Dinakar Ram was merely the titular owner; the actual operations were run by Dhaval.

In another sense, the company's history goes back even further. It had been effectively established when the Thakkar father–son duo acquired Jain Logistics, a company founded and managed by a man named Preetam Jain.

Interestingly, even though Preetam Jain sold his company to the Thakkars, he reached out to them six months later and joined the same company as an employee. He accepted the position of second-in-command. Preetam and Dhaval forged a close friendship, and Preetam eventually invested funds in the company and became a partner. His ownership, however, represented only a minor portion of the total capital.

Preetam Jain was five years older than Dhaval. He continued to serve as the head of the logistics division until he passed a decade ago. His son, Vimal Jain, assumed his role afterwards.

Shivaswamy watched the video intently, pausing it occasionally to let Anuradha explain what she knew. As he watched the images of Dinakar Ram Thakkar and Preetam Jain, he remembered the large portraits he had seen in the boardroom of the head office. These images now took on new significance in his mind.

Since its inception as a logistics company, the group's primary business had remained the same. As profits grew, the company acquired two more firms, expanding its operations. Hence, from DT Logistics, it became the DT Group of Companies. However, these new ventures were distinct from the shipping industry. One focused on medical equipment trading, while the other involved engineering consulting. 'Through this kind of diverse expansion, DT Group made its own mark in the business world,' the video's narrator said.

The medical equipment trading division imported some of the rarest medical equipment from different countries and supplied it to India's largest hospitals and research centres. It also took care of the installation and repair of such equipment. The engineering consulting division specialized in civil consulting and worked on heavy infrastructure projects such as highways, bridges, and flyovers for central and state governments. Ashok Mehta headed both divisions, with all division heads reporting to Dhaval Thakkar.

'Isn't there anything about the software division in the video?' Shivaswamy asked Anuradha.

'This is an old video, sir. It hasn't been updated yet,' she said.

'For how many years has the software division been around?' he inquired.

She stood up anxiously and said, 'I don't know, sir. Give me a moment; I'll find out and come back.'

As she headed towards the door, Shivaswamy said, 'That's okay. We'll find out together later. Come, sit down.'

* * *

A little later, Shyamala Menon, the head of HR for the entire DT Group, called Anuradha from the head office and said she would be coming to the branch office in the afternoon to speak with Shivaswamy. When Anuradha asked if she could put him on the phone instead, Shyamala declined.

Shivaswamy was directed to a small cubicle in the right-hand corner when he exited the lift on the second floor. Anuradha's face fell as she showed him to his space. After all, she, who was junior, still had a larger workspace. Shivaswamy stared at his office blankly.

He had had his own cabin at BEL for twenty years. In fact, as soon as he had stepped into the office in the morning and had met Anuradha, a 'junior', he had realized that the war had begun. Now, this was further confirmed by the workspace he had been assigned. But none of this bothered him.

'Is this space acceptable to you, sir? Ms Shyamala allocated it for you,' said Anuradha. She had already pieced together the various happenings in the office. Even before Shivaswamy set foot in the company, numerous rumours had been circulating about his appointment. In summary, she knew this much: the three senior executives had been conducting interviews for months to find an ideal HR manager for the branch. Whenever they proposed a candidate for approval, the MD would dismiss their choice in favour of an older associate. This had created tensions between the MD and the senior trio. Anuradha surmised that the current treatment of Shivaswamy was a result of these tensions.

Mallika, from the HR department at the head office, had kept her up to date about the situation. In return, she was privy to the whispers from the branch office. Their exchanges were both regular and covert. 'There's been talk about Shivaswamy,' Mallika conveyed to her. 'The man's retired and, from what I gather, he's not exactly seasoned in HR. Our MD, perhaps to showcase his dominance over his son, his daughter-in-law Dhriti and Ms Shyamala, seems to have bypassed everyone's preferences to bring him on board. Rumour has it that he's being planted as an informant for the branch. Ms Shyamala, in her ever-bold style, said to Ravi sir and Ms Dhriti, "Mark my words, I'll have him out of our company in fifteen days!" Stay clear of this mess, Anuradha. Just follow Ms Shyamala's instructions.'

'Why not? This place works for me,' said Shivaswamy, bringing Anuradha out of her reverie. 'But I'm still not clear about my responsibilities. I'll talk to Shyamala when she arrives. However, I do feel that an HR manager should have some privacy when speaking with employees. We can't always pull employees into a conference room for every discussion. Plus, with colleagues seated all around, our conversations will be audible to them. HR discussions can sometimes be sensitive and personal. If overheard, they could lead to problems,' he explained.

Anuradha jotted this down in her notebook. 'I'll let Shyamala know,' she said. She then introduced Shivaswamy to the employees on that floor. Some wondered why the HR director would be sitting there. The senior executives, HR and the administration staff usually sat on the first floor.

Lunch was being set up at the terrace garden on the fourth floor. Anuradha took him there and introduced him to several other colleagues before buying him a meal with her coupons. While they were eating at a table, several of his new colleagues came to their table to introduce themselves and exchange friendly words. Shivaswamy was well aware that employees generally wanted to be in HR's good graces.

When Debashish Sharma, a senior manager in the software delivery department, asked about his background, Anuradha observed them both closely, wondering if the question was a test, especially because of the rumours. Shivaswamy responded with a smile, 'I've been on a unique journey. I've scaled numerous peaks and navigated through many valleys. Now, here I stand before you, Mr Sharma. I bring with me over thirty-five years of experience. I possess the knack to infuse fresh perspectives into human resource management. Just wait and see. Your teams can surely trust in me.'

His voice resonated with confidence. Today, he needed to embody that very trust. Both Debashish and Anuradha seemed satisfied with his answer.

After lunch, Shivaswamy returned to his spot on the second floor. Anuradha handed him two additional forms related to health insurance to complete. As he was engrossed in filling them out, a woman's voice greeted him, 'Hello, Shivaswamy. Welcome aboard.' Looking up, it took a moment for him to recognize Shyamala Menon. Her face had somewhat faded from his memory since their interview many days ago. She had been wearing a green churidar that day; now, she was dressed in black trousers and a white top, her hair neatly pulled back, with sunglasses perched on her forehead. He stood up. She smiled and shook his hand.

'Have all the joining formalities been completed?' she asked.

Smiling, Shivaswamy asked Anuradha, 'Are these the last forms to be filled out?'

Anuradha smiled, but Shyamala did not.

'Have you had your lunch?' she asked next.

'Yes,' he replied.

She glanced at her watch. 'Oh, it's already half past two. I haven't had my lunch yet. I intended to spend an hour talking with you today, but it seems impossible. I have an important management meeting at four. I need to head back to the head office by then,' she said.

'Let's do one thing. Let's sit in the cafeteria and talk.' Without waiting for his answer, she started walking towards the lift. Shivaswamy, holding his notebook, followed her. Anuradha, too, followed them.

As Shyamala pressed the lift button, she noticed Anuradha had come along. 'I'll send Shivaswamy down in about twenty minutes,' she said to her. Anuradha understood the message and returned to her desk.

When they entered the cafeteria on the fourth floor, it was mostly empty. The catering staff were collecting trays while, in the distance, two young girls sat deeply engaged in conversation as they ate. Oblivious to the staff cleaning around them, they ate their homemade lunch.

A catering boy quickly set up a table as soon as he saw Shyamala enter the terrace and gestured to her. 'Madam, please have a seat.' Two plates were set before them. Shivaswamy returned one, indicating one would suffice. Another pair of boys served chapati and a green vegetable curry and stood nearby, waiting for further instructions.

'You've added too much oil to the sabji!' Shyamala exclaimed. One boy hurriedly fetched a senior from the kitchen. 'I'm sorry, madam. The curry appears oily because it's what's remained at the end. We were unaware that you were coming to the office today. Otherwise, we would have set aside a portion with less oil specifically for you. Please forgive us,' he explained breathlessly.

She responded with only a dismissive wave, signalling for him to leave. Once he left, her attention shifted to Shivaswamy again.

'Anuradha should have introduced you to the company today. You have been brought on board specifically for this software division.

'At first, my team from the head office managed this branch, but it proved challenging. Handling logistics and the other two divisions consumed all our energy. We believed it would be beneficial to have someone dedicated here, so we transferred Anuradha to this office. However, that alone was not enough. Raviraj and Prabhu emphasized the need for someone with managerial expertise, rather than just a junior. That's why we recruited you. Your primary focus should be on this division. I will not pull you into head office meetings. It would be a waste of your time,' she said.

Even though it was his first day, Shivaswamy smiled to himself, as if he had already understood everything about the company. It was clear that she was trying to keep him away from Dhaval.

'Alright then. I will devote my full attention to this branch,' he said.

'That's good,' Shyamala smirked as she dabbed her lips with a napkin.

'Is there anything I should focus on immediately?'

'Shivaswamy, everything in our company is "immediate",' Shyamala smiled sarcastically. Shivaswamy realized she was mocking his public sector experience, but he remained silent.

'I will be reporting to you directly, right?' asked Shivaswamy.

'Why? Do you suspect otherwise?'

'No. I'm just asking about the means to contact you and how we might schedule our meetings,' he explained.

Impatiently, she responded, 'Anuradha will provide you with all that information. Any more questions?'

'No.'

Shyamala got up and washed her hands. Shivaswamy stood at a distance, waiting for her. The catering person stood there as well.

'Tell Ganesh that the quality of food here needs to improve,' Shyamala said, walking away without glancing at him.

'What's wrong, ma'am?' the man asked, confused.

'I've already told you, haven't I? How many times do I have to say it? Who puts that much oil in the vegetables? You think anyone can come and serve whatever they like? Do you think we are gullible fools? If I get one more complaint, I'll cancel the contract. Tell Ganesh to come and see me,' she said, walking towards the lift briskly.

They stood silently in the lift. Shivaswamy pressed the button for the second floor, while she pressed the one for the ground floor. When his floor arrived, just as he stepped out, she reached out to stop the lift doors from closing and said, 'Shivaswamy?'

He turned and responded, 'Yes?'

'This isn't like your old company. There's no formality here. If you want to speak to me, just pick up the phone and call directly.' With that, she stepped back inside, and the lift doors closed.

By evening, Prabhu, the vice president of software delivery, had come to Shivaswamy's desk, spoken briefly, and left for a meeting. He still hadn't met Raviraj Thakkar, the head of the software division and Dhaval's son. Raviraj was in his first-floor office. Anuradha tried to take Shivaswamy to him twice, but he was constantly in meetings.

Shivaswamy received a laptop and took some time to familiarize himself with it. Around five o'clock, Raviraj and his wife Dhriti visited the second floor to talk to him. Extending his hand, Raviraj asked, 'Do you remember me?' Shivaswamy, smiling, replied, 'Certainly, sir,' and shook his hand.

Raviraj was dressed in a suit as usual, and stood tall like his father, but he had a more serious disposition.

'This is my wife, Dhriti.' She, too, was tall. She wore jeans and a pale-yellow top. Her face radiated health and affluence. Like her husband, she seldom smiled. She extended her long hands gently and gave him a handshake.

Raviraj said, 'I didn't want to bother you today because I knew there would be a lot of formalities that you'll have to complete. Prabhu and I will have a long discussion with you tomorrow. We will need your help in many areas.'

'Of course,' Shivaswamy responded.

'Where were you working before?' Dhriti inquired. Shivaswamy explained his background briefly. Throughout their interaction, her gaze seemed to be evaluating him, her eyes constantly on him. 'Did you meet Shyamala?' she asked.

'Yes, she was here this afternoon,' he replied.

The couple said their goodbyes, and as soon as they had stepped out of his cubicle, Dhriti asked Raviraj something in Gujarati. Shivaswamy and others nearby could hear her words but didn't fully understand them. There was no doubt that the conversation was about Shivaswamy. Raviraj didn't respond. He gently squeezed her hand and led her away.

At six in the evening, as Shivaswamy was leaving for the day, he ran into Prabhu again outside the main door. Prabhu was smoking and chatting with four other men. He smiled and approached him. 'This is our company's smokers' corner,' he said with a laugh.

'I'm sure Anuradha didn't show you this.' Then he asked, 'Do you smoke, sir?'

'No.'

Prabhu inquired about where Shivaswamy lived and how he got to the office every day.

'My house is in JP Nagar. If you like, you can come with me today. I'll drop you off halfway,' he offered.

Shivaswamy declined politely. 'The MG Road metro station is just a stone's throw away. If I take the metro from there, I'll easily get home,' he said and began walking away.

'I'll meet you tomorrow; then we can talk in detail,' Prabhu called out.

Shivaswamy responded with a smile.

He made it home, yes, but had it been comfortable? The metro was packed, and he had finally reached home by eight. He was exhausted. He wondered if this was how it was going to be every day. There were no alternatives. He knew that taking his scooter out and braving the city's traffic would be even more tiring.

He made some rice and rasam for dinner. He then called Revathi, masked his fatigue and said that the first day at work had gone smoothly. When she asked him if the commute was manageable, he responded with a muted 'somewhat'.

He called his old friend, Ram Choudhuri, who had retired from the same department at BEL and settled in Ghaziabad. After moving to Bengaluru, this was the second time that they had spoken. Shivaswamy spoke about his work in detail and shared what his new office had been like on the first day.

'Shiv, it's natural,' Choudhuri responded. 'I left Ganga Pharmaceuticals for the very reasons you're talking about. You might recall that I took a job there after I retired from BEL. You were in the city then. I couldn't adapt to the environment. Every company has its own subculture, and, if you spend your whole life working in one, you become dyed in its colours. At Ganga Pharmaceuticals, there was this young officer who used to pass orders. I just couldn't get along with him. Not that he was evil, or that such people weren't there in BEL. It's just that what was tolerable there became disgusting here. I don't really understand why that experience felt so demeaning.

'Working in a company for thirty-five years is like being married to a woman for that time. You adjust your body and mind to her completely. You both understand each other's strengths and weaknesses and learn to live with them. Joining another company at this age is like leaving your wife and marrying another woman. No matter what you do, she won't like it. You know? At this age, can you still manage to "do it" the way she prefers?'

He guffawed at his own joke. He had been senior to Shivaswamy at BEL and had retired five years before him. 'Shiv, don't exhaust yourself. When you feel it's enough, just let it go,' he said.

'Arey Bhai! I'm just wrapping up my first day's work. Let's talk about quitting in a few days,' Shivaswamy replied jovially and got off the phone. After speaking with Choudhuri, his mood lightened a bit, as if a warm breeze from Ghaziabad had caressed his cold face. He felt he just needed a good night's sleep.

10

The next day, as Shivaswamy entered the office and headed towards the lift, the receptionist hurried over to him and said, 'Sir, your seating has been changed from the cubicle on the second floor to an office room on the first floor.'

'Alright,' he replied, even though he was a bit surprised.

The new room was spacious. Adjacent to Raviraj's office was Prabhu's, and right beside that was his. His new office, with a large window, was simpler and more elegant than the offices of Raviraj and Prabhu. The situation had changed overnight and Shivaswamy wasn't sure what exactly had happened.

When Prabhu entered his room, he noticed Shivaswamy in the adjacent office through the glass doors. He smiled and went inside his office. An hour later, he knocked on Shivaswamy's door and invited him for coffee. Prabhu's white formal shirt complemented his broad shoulders and tall frame. Once they were seated in the cafeteria, Shivaswamy ordered himself a sugarless coffee.

'It's great that you've joined our company,' said Prabhu. 'This branch has struggled without an HR manager until now. We've had to rely on the head office for everything. I bore the brunt of it because I oversee software delivery here, and nearly 90 per cent of the employees in this branch are on my team. Raviraj is in charge of sales. I'd been advocating for an in-branch HR manager for quite a while, you know? But our Sadashivanagar office folks were acting deaf.' He laughed.

Shivaswamy had compiled a list of questions that he wanted to ask, particularly about the software division's products, clientele, relationship with the head office and interactions with other divisions. He felt it would be appropriate to ask Prabhu, who appeared more approachable than Shyamala and Raviraj. And he was right—Prabhu responded to all his queries in detail.

Ordering another round of coffee, Prabhu said, 'I should share a bit about my background as well . . . Ravi and I studied engineering together, right here in this city, at MS Ramaiah College. After that, I went to NITK Surathkal for my MTech, while he joined his father's business. Post my MTech, I worked for several companies and travelled extensively to countries like the UK, the USA and Germany on work assignments. Three years ago, Ravi invited me here to start a new software firm. I gladly accepted the role. We've worked tirelessly, day and night, for these three years. Now, the company is gaining a good reputation, I feel.'

'How involved is our MD in the business of this branch?' asked Shivaswamy.

Prabhu smiled. 'You're stirring up the beehive now.' He paused before continuing. 'Lately, all our problems seem to originate from there. Let me tell you something, Shivaswamy. This is a family-run company. Just calling it that doesn't convey its depth, but, if I can be more specific, it's a Gujarati family-run business . . . well, I don't need to say more, do I?

'It's only your second day here, and you're just beginning to familiarize yourself with the company. I shouldn't confuse you further. However, some things need to be said. Ravi and his father have a complex relationship. Only God knows when they're on good terms and when they're not.

'Now that Ravi's wife, Dhriti, is more involved in the company, the situation is becoming even more intricate. Dhaval Saheb wasn't keen on us venturing into software products. To him, a product is only truly a product if it's tangible! To put it another way, it wasn't so much that he disliked the software business; he just disliked Ravi diving into it. After all, by that time, Ravi had already failed in some ventures. Hence, our MD maintained a somewhat nonchalant attitude towards this division.

'It's still the case. That's why HR, finance, administration and the like are managed directly from the head office. Ravi doesn't enjoy some of the privileges that other division heads have. For instance, he couldn't even hire the manager he wanted . . .' Prabhu trailed off, regretting his final words.

Shivaswamy smiled. 'I understand. Let it go.'

They stood up to leave the cafeteria. Prabhu, in a subdued tone, said, 'Please don't assume that I rejected you when you first came here. Though your words that day were a bit idealistic, they did touch my heart.' Shivaswamy didn't say anything. They started moving towards the lift. Prabhu continued, 'But remember, Shivaswamy, we need to tread with caution here. I presume yours isn't a family with an entrepreneurial background. Neither is mine. My father was a schoolteacher. In families like ours, relationships tend to be predictable. People are usually consistent. But it's not the same in entrepreneurial families. They live and breathe business day and night. There are fights among family members—for prestige. Those who fought yesterday might unite tomorrow. Those who allied themselves with someone yesterday might fight tomorrow.

'But we need to remember that the same blood flows through all of them. They are, after all, kin. Friendships can be severed, but can kinship ever? At some point, they all might unite and exile you, the outsider, to Siberia,' he laughed.

Shivaswamy smiled again. He wondered, *Why did he say 'you' instead of 'we'? Why not, 'We might be exiled to Siberia?' Why didn't he phrase it that way?* It felt as though he was delivering this message to him with much forethought. Otherwise, there was no need to reveal all this on just their second day together.

* * *

In the afternoon, there was a long meeting between Shivaswamy, Raviraj and Prabhu. Although Shyamala was supposed to be in the meeting, she sent a message that she would not be able to make it and asked them to reschedule. Prabhu disagreed with her.

'We hired Shivaswamy precisely so our division could operate autonomously,' he argued. 'Until now, Anuradha served as a junior, and it was essential for Shyamala to attend some of the key meetings. Now with a senior HR person for this branch, how would it be any different if we still waited for Shyamala?'

Raviraj didn't agree with Prabhu's words. 'We cannot isolate Shivaswamy from the head office. Regardless of everything, he will be reporting to Shyamala,' he said. Prabhu did not accept this viewpoint.

Eventually, Shivaswamy stood up and said, 'Listen to what I have to say. There's still a lot that I need to learn about the company. However, there's one thing I wish to convey. I am capable of managing this branch autonomously from an HR perspective. I have that experience. I can communicate directly with all of you. Moreover, I will send daily updates to Shyamala. I can contact her whenever I need help. Please consider my words.'

Prabhu agreed. 'This is precisely what we expect from you.'

Raviraj's face made it clear he didn't concur. But the decisiveness of Prabhu's words sealed his lips. The meeting proceeded. The two men shared what they expected from Shivaswamy. It was clear to Shivaswamy that many of their expectations stemmed from the lack of clarity in HR policies and processes. He felt confident that he could resolve those.

It took Shivaswamy three days to turn the discussion from that day into a plan. If there were any questions, he consulted Prabhu and Anuradha. Apart from himself, Anuradha was the sole representative of the HR department in that branch. This made it crucial for him to gain her trust.

To Anuradha, Shivaswamy was the manager. Yet, she always seemed to be eluding him in some way. It wasn't challenging for him to guess why, and he decided it might be best to let it be.

When Shivaswamy wrote his plan and shared it with Anuradha, she liked it. He then forwarded it to Shyamala for her approval. Within five minutes of receiving the email, Shyamala called. As Shivaswamy tried to explain the context and content of what he had written, she cut him off, saying, 'Mr Shivaswamy, I've already mentioned that you should call me directly if you need anything.' Shivaswamy wasn't sure what she was referring to. Taking the safe route, Shivaswamy replied, 'Thank you. I will do just that.'

Her tone shifted abruptly as she said, 'In that case, what prompted you to complain to the MD that you were given a cubicle instead of an office?'

Shivaswamy was taken aback. 'Me? I complained to the MD?'

'Just because you have a past with him doesn't mean you should bring everything to his attention,' Shyamala's words dripped with resentment.

'You're under two misconceptions,' Shivaswamy replied firmly. 'First, I met Dhaval Thakkar at my interview. We were strangers before that. Let me reiterate, ours is not an old acquaintance. Second, whether I was given a cubicle or a cabin, I accepted it without complaint. I didn't discuss it with anyone. You might want to reconsider the authenticity of your source of information.'

She hung up.

In the evening, before heading home, he discussed the next day's tasks with Anuradha. During their conversation, he brought up this particular matter. She looked scared. 'Sir, Shyamala called and reprimanded me. The thing is, on the day you joined, Anita called from the MD's office in the evening, asking about how things were with you. She wanted to ensure you faced no inconvenience. It seems the MD himself had instructed her to check on you regularly. That's when I merely suggested that it might be helpful for you to have an office. That's all, sir. I didn't say anything with the intention of causing trouble. Would it not have been wrong if I had kept quiet?'

Shivaswamy laughed as if he had heard a joke. Anuradha might have tried to deflect blame to him when she spoke to Shyamala.

However, he didn't perceive it as a big mistake or betrayal on her part. He simply began thinking of ways in which he could gain her trust—as he should ideally be doing with the rest of his colleagues as well.

11

Over the next two weeks, Shivaswamy took complete control of the work in the office. The office truly needed someone with his experience. Many basic processes had been neglected for reasons stemming from the head office. They had caused this branch to falter. He began to reshape the branch in line with his own mindset. What he had said during the interview wasn't just empty talk; it proved to be true. Having worked in a big firm like BEL for so many years had given him a keen ability to understand people. A different set of people and a distinct world had thrived there. More than anything, this was a much smaller company. Here, the day-to-day issues were simple: someone behaved inappropriately with another employee; someone disregarded what a manager had said and worked as they saw fit; a certain employee was constantly late to the office; another took a month off citing their child's ill health; someone who had travelled abroad for the company found a job there and sent their resignation from there, and so on.

Were all these occurrences exclusive to DT Software Solutions? When to adhere strictly to the rule book, when to make an exception, when to be firm, and when to show compassion—none of this could be learnt from any manual. Life experience, the primary qualification needed for the HR manager's role, was the answer to such questions. Shivaswamy had it in abundance.

He understood that certain fundamental behaviours were deeply ingrained in a person. Thus, he believed that before addressing any issue, it was essential to delve into the depths of their psyche and truly understand them.

Incidentally, this belief was put to the test when he faced a peculiar case. A manager sought his help with an issue concerning his colleague. A woman in this manager's team had raised a concern, not in writing, but verbally communicated her discomfort to him. She felt uneasy about the behaviour of a male colleague in their team. His gaze often lingered on her intensely, almost piercingly. He constantly stared at her during meetings, regardless of where she was seated. On a few occasions, their hands brushed against each other's—when he handed her a whiteboard marker.

Out of a sense of responsibility, the manager approached the HR department. However, he was visibly embarrassed, perhaps more so than the young woman. Shivaswamy found himself having to coax the details out of him. The manager asserted that he hadn't observed any untoward behaviour from the young man. Other female colleagues collaborated with him without any issues. There hadn't been any prior complaints. He was known for his diligence and was crucial to the project, often working tirelessly. The young woman was equally competent and was an asset to the team.

'What is your opinion? What do you suggest we do?' Shivaswamy asked him.

'Sir, the woman might have lodged a false complaint. Or she might have misconstrued something. Replacing him in the project at this time will be very challenging. We're at a critical stage in project delivery. I really don't know what to do,' he said.

Shivaswamy corrected him, 'Please do not jump to the conclusion that it is a false complaint. We should not turn a blind eye to such incidents. First, speak to her and convey the message that you are observing his behaviour closely. Observe for yourself for a couple of weeks and take note. Then, we will sit together and contemplate the next steps. You should keep two things in mind. One, women often have a more nuanced perception when identifying inappropriate glances or behaviour than men. And two, it doesn't mean all women perceive things in the same way. Not everyone is equally sensitive. That being said, just as it's unacceptable to ignore this problem, it's also unjust to punish the young man solely on the basis of this limited evidence. You need to observe both without bias and report back to me.' Then he instructed the manager when he should meet him next.

As he was leaving, Shivaswamy said, 'One more thing. Except for the two of us, no one else should know about this. Otherwise, it could become traumatic for both the young man and the woman.'

The manager nodded in agreement.

In his work, Shivaswamy never felt the need to seek Shyamala Menon's help. The branch office operated independently. Yet, every day before leaving, he would write her a detailed report of the day's activities. She never responded to any of those emails.

* * *

Two weeks had passed since Shivaswamy had joined, and Anuradha's apprehension began to finally wane. Gradually, she started interacting more with him. Given that he was her boss, and that Shyamala's vow to have him out in two weeks had proved to be empty, she found it imperative to establish a rapport with him.

And through her, Shivaswamy began to learn the many inside stories of the company. There were two camps: the Dhaval camp and the Dhriti camp. Shyamala and Dhriti were close friends, so Shyamala clearly belonged to the Dhriti camp. She gave priority to Dhriti and Raviraj's opinions more than she did to the MD's. This was an unpalatable pill for Dhaval to swallow. The company was increasingly becoming fragmented between those who sided with the father and those who sided with the son. The rift was evident in the upper management.

While division heads Vimal Jain and Ashok Mehta were more or less aligned with the Dhaval camp, their allegiances seemed unpredictable. Vimal Jain had affection for Dhaval, a sentiment that stemmed from his father's close friendship with him. He was also a close friend of Raviraj because of their similar age. However, Ashok Mehta's loyalties were fickle. Sometimes he appeared to support the father, and sometimes the son. Since the lion's share of the company's production came from the divisions they managed, they were always careful with their words.

Shivaswamy sensed that Anuradha was not aware of what Dhaval had mentioned in his interview about the problems in making the software division a separate company. He hadn't spoken to her about it either.

Raviraj was the head of the software division, but that was only in name and title. In reality, everything operated under Prabhu's discretion. While Raviraj trusted Prabhu deeply, his wife Dhriti did not share the same sentiment. Her fear was that Dhaval might, in a show of sheer ruthlessness, make Prabhu the head of the software division and sideline his own son.

'It's like the Mahabharata unfolding here,' Shivaswamy laughed.

'True, sir. Sometimes they even drag us into it, like in your cubicle controversy. Didn't they?' said Anuradha.

12

Shivaswamy received a call from Kumar Gowda while he was in the metro. The train was leaving KR Market and was headed towards Basavanagudi. The carriage was so packed that he barely had any room to stand. Struggling to maintain his balance, he somehow managed to hold his phone in one hand and answer.

'It's been a while, sir. That's why I called.' Kumar spoke with sincere warmth. 'Aren't you alone at home? Come over for dinner tomorrow. It's Friday, so we can sit and chat at ease.' Shivaswamy was delighted and accepted the invitation immediately. After two weeks of grappling with work stress, he needed a change. He was also curious about what was going on in Anoop Gardenia.

He reached home at eight o'clock, as he had done for the past two weeks. Once inside, he called Revathi. 'What are you taking as a gift? Is there anything special about the invitation? Is it a birthday or an anniversary?' she asked him. Had he asked Kumar about that? Eventually, it was decided that he ought to take a gift. He hopped onto his scooter and headed out. It was already getting late, and the shops were closing. He went to the Royal Mart on Kanakapura Road and bought an Ajanta wall clock and had it gift-wrapped. That would suffice.

Friday morning's tasks went on without any surprises. There were two exit interviews to be conducted. The first was with a young woman who had gotten married two months ago. Her husband was based in Mumbai. She was keen on resigning from her current job to find another in Mumbai.

The second interview was with a young man who told Shivaswamy, 'The firm I'm joining plans to send me to America within the next six months. If you send me instead, I'll stay here.'

'Why is it so important for you to go abroad?' Shivaswamy inquired.

'Sir, I find it surprising hearing this from you. I've dedicated four years to this company and haven't been given an international assignment. Won't my professional profile suffer if I don't gain overseas experience?' he said.

Shivaswamy glanced at the file in front of him. The notes from his manager read, 'Accept his resignation. We cannot meet his expectations.' Prabhu had already endorsed it. Shivaswamy kept quiet, approved both resignations and shook the employees' hands before they left.

Meanwhile, Raviraj and Prabhu had gone to the head office for a crucial meeting. Even after their return, the two seemed deeply engaged in a discussion. Shivaswamy wanted to meet them, particularly to seek Raviraj's consent on certain policy modifications. But by four o'clock, since they were still engrossed in a conversation behind closed doors, Shivaswamy tapped lightly on the door. Raviraj looked up and looked a little annoyed at the interruption.

'I need your signature on some policy adjustments,' said Shivaswamy.

'I'm tied up right now. Can this wait until tomorrow?' Raviraj replied somewhat curtly.

'Alright, I'll come by on Monday.' Shivaswamy turned to leave. As he was about to close the door, Prabhu said, 'I'll drop by your office in about half an hour. We need to talk.'

'Very well,' Shivaswamy acknowledged as the door shut behind him.

Just as he had mentioned, Prabhu was in Shivaswamy's office within thirty minutes. 'Shall we head out? I can treat you to a good masala dosa at Priyadarshini,' he suggested. Shivaswamy said that he had to leave the office early that day because he had to go to a friend's house for dinner. So, they agreed to talk in the office. Prabhu came in, closed the door and sat down opposite Shivaswamy.

'There was a meeting with the MD this morning about the plans for our division for the next three months. Before the meeting even started, the MD asked where you were,' said Prabhu. He paused to observe Shivaswamy's facial expressions.

'Wasn't Shyamala there?'

'She was.'

'Then? She's the one who represents the head office. Was I needed at that meeting? Shyamala made it clear to me that I'm only supposed to be at the branch office.'

'We all assumed the same. However, today, our MD really chewed our heads off,' Prabhu sniggered.

'I've been with this company for two weeks, Prabhu. I've been watching this. It doesn't look like the disputes between the head office and the branch office are going to be resolved. It's like the central and state governments bickering when different political parties control them,' Shivaswamy said, a little frustrated.

Prabhu laughed. 'Think of it this way. If a mother-in-law and daughter-in-law are quarrelling in the living room, the household staff—the cook in the kitchen, the maid washing dishes, the gardener tending the garden—they all get free entertainment, right? It's amusing for a day. But if it's an everyday affair, it gives them a headache.'

Shivaswamy glanced at his watch. He needed to leave the office by five-thirty to make it to Kumar's place by eight o'clock. It was already five-ten. As per his daily routine, he had to send a status update email to Shyamala before leaving. But this man in front of him seemed to be repeating the same old conversations. The whole company knew Dhaval and his daughter-in-law were in a power struggle. What was the point of discussing it ad nauseam?

Noticing him checking his watch, Prabhu stood up. 'It's Friday evening, and you have dinner plans. I won't hold you up. We can talk in detail some other time. I just want to say one thing before you go. I'm telling you this now, so you'll have two days to think about it by the time we meet again on Monday.' He sat down again.

'Our MD has categorically said that you must be present at all upcoming meetings concerning our branch. That will surely make Shyamala even more upset with you. So, be ready for a boxing match,' he laughed.

'Let it be, let it be. I have to endure some inconveniences as long as I'm here,' Shivaswamy said.

Prabhu shook his head; his expression turned serious. 'That's not the point I wanted to make. I came to discuss something else, but I'll keep it brief for now. Let's talk in detail on Monday. Ravi and I have been contemplating turning the software division into a separate company.'

Prabhu paused and carefully observed Shivaswamy's face, trying to discern whether there was a hint of surprise at hearing something new or if Shivaswamy was already aware of the matter. By sensing Prabhu's intentions, Shivaswamy kept his gaze fixed on the pages of the daily organizer lying on the table and asked, 'What do you mean by turning the division into a separate company?'

Prabhu hesitated; his gaze flickered as he chose his words carefully. 'It's not as dramatic as it might sound, Shivaswamy,' he said with a faint, reassuring smile. 'The idea isn't to make the software division completely independent. It's more of a financial and legal adjustment—a way to streamline operations and improve efficiency.'

He leaned forward slightly and whispered, 'The division will still remain very much a part of the DT Group. It's just that, on paper, it will function as a separate entity for certain management purposes. Think of it as optimizing how we handle finances, reporting and compliance. Nothing more than that.'

Prabhu sat back, folding his hands together, and said, 'At the end of the day, it's all about ensuring that we stay competitive while keeping things simpler for the group as a whole. Nothing changes on the ground, really.' He chuckled, hoping to deflect further questions.

'Is our MD fine with it?' Shivaswamy asked, this time taking his turn to study Prabhu's facial expressions.

'Our MD isn't particularly fond of the idea, obviously. We tried persuading him in many ways, but his mindset is traditional. Plus, every company owner has a kind of possessiveness, you see . . . a need to hold on to their company tightly. That's causing problems. He's being a bit too much about it. He won't even listen to us, let alone entertain our ideas. This is where we need your help.'

Shivaswamy was genuinely surprised. What help could this man and his friend, who had begrudgingly accepted him into the company, possibly need from him now?

Prabhu continued. 'Even if the software division becomes a separate company, it can't sever ties with the DT group. Who's the head of the new company? Isn't it his son? We've been trying to make him realize this for the past six months. Initially, when Ravi and I approached him, he scolded us and sent us away. We attempted to negotiate through Shyamala, but that backfired. In the meantime, Dhriti has become more involved in the company's affairs. And, on some issues, even her father has spoken up, complicating matters even further.

'Now you have come. The equation can change again. It all started with the commotion that ensued when you were selected. When we tried to employ our preferred candidate, the MD selected you from our own list and sent us a coded message. Sorry, Shivaswamy, I've brought up your selection again. When the MD vehemently asserted that the company's HR management required a seasoned professional like you, we spoke for a new generation—arguing that we needed fresh blood. We were frustrated when he overruled our preferences and brought you on board.'

Why bring this up now? What's his motive for digging up the past? Shivaswami was perplexed.

Prabhu suddenly switched to an apologetic tone, almost as if he had read Shivaswamy's mind. 'However, I now see the wisdom in his decision. We certainly need someone like you in our company.

I'm sharing this with you candidly. You will always have my support. But this transition is essential. For the continued growth of this division, it needs to become independent of the DT Group. This move will be beneficial for everyone involved. Your cooperation in this matter is crucial.'

He paused. Shivaswamy didn't say anything.

'Anyway, sir, I'm aware you have plans for the evening. I won't keep you any longer,' he said, standing up.

'How can I help you, Prabhu? Shivaswamy said in a tone of despair. 'I have only been assigned the task of looking after the employees in this department.'

Roughly four weeks ago, the old man took him to Sankey Tank Lake and sought help to prevent the company from falling apart. Now, the son's representative was asking him to assist them in breaking the company up.

Shivaswamy was acutely aware of the tightrope he was walking on. Saying 'yes' would make him fall to one side, while 'no' would tip him to the other. Composure was essential in this situation. Only a serene mind could shield him from such extreme behaviour. As Allama Prabhu says: *In a shattered pot shard, can you perceive the reflection of a mirror? In the embrace of ignorance, actions contradict their essence!*

'No, no. You're not limited to this group,' Prabhu continued. 'That was evident in today's meeting. I have a feeling you'll be the referee when the two teams clash ruthlessly in the upcoming meetings,' he laughed.

'Oh, please, no, no,' Shivaswamy responded theatrically, covering his face with his hand in jest. It was already a quarter to six. He really needed to leave now.

13

When Shivaswamy entered Anoop Gardenia clutching a gift bag, he was enveloped in deep darkness. A tree-flanked pathway led to the houses of Phase I on the left and Phase II on the right. To the left stood completed houses, while the ones on the right were still under construction. Here and there, JCB machines stood bent over and silhouetted in the silence of the dark. A towering compound wall obstructed the faint streetlight, adding to the surrounding mystery. The entire area evoked the feeling of a battlefield that had quieted down after a long day of fierce combat.

The Bihari security guard at the main gate hesitated to let him venture in alone in the darkness. Having conversed with him a few times, Shivaswamy had established a friendly rapport. 'If you could wait for ten minutes, the other guard, who's gone to eat, will return. Then I could accompany you to Kumar Gowda's house. I can't leave the gate unmanned. Please sit here,' he implored.

But Shivaswamy chose not to wait. After walking a few steps, two lights twinkled from a building to the left, among the trees. He guessed these were lights from the two houses that were occupied. The light from the third floor came from Kumar's house, and he looked past two more floors to the dark fifth floor, where his house was located. Despite all the pain and uncertainty his house was causing him, Shivaswamy felt a sense of pride when he stood in the darkness and stared at that floor.

When he reached the lift, he found that it was not working. It was absurd to imagine that the lift would be working when everything around these buildings was dark and eerie, abandoned by the world. He could not see the stairs immediately either, so he called Kumar.

'Oh, did they turn off the lift? They usually do so after nine at night because they run it on a diesel generator. But it's only eight-fifteen now. Stay there, sir. I'll call the maintenance staff and have the lift turned on,' he said.

Shivaswamy stood in the darkness. The closed white doors of the six houses on the ground floor seemed to gaze unwaveringly at him. Construction materials from the neighbouring buildings were stacked on one side of this floor: mounds of sand, wooden planks, toilet commodes, iron rods and more. Cement dust tickled his nose. His breathing was the only sound. He wondered if this was the same place that haunted him with light and noise when he was outside the compound.

'Shivaswamy sir!' A voice called out, and he spun around in the darkness. Kumar's figure was vaguely visible in the corner. 'Come this way; the stairs are here. The maintenance guy has gone home, and he isn't answering the phone. The stairs are our only option. Is that alright, sir? It's the third floor, about sixty steps,' he said, switching on the flashlight on his mobile.

Now, the floor became visible. 'Of course, no problem,' Shivaswamy answered, moving towards him.

The stairs, devoid of a handrail, were unclean with scattered debris. 'Take it one step at a time, sir,' Kumar advised, leading the way up.

By the time he reached the third floor, Shivaswamy was gasping for breath. He had initially intended to climb up to the fifth floor and pause in front of his apartment for a few moments before leaving the complex. However, his exhaustion and the surrounding darkness made him realize it wouldn't be practical this time.

Kumar's was a small family. He and Vanita had a daughter who was in Grade 12. Kumar worked at LIC, and Vanita was a teacher at a private school in Konanakunte. They kept their home impeccably clean. As soon as he entered, Shivaswamy could smell the new paint. He took a moment to notice the cream-coloured square tiles, the ivory sofa, a tea table with carvings, a red carpet, the light-blue walls and a wide window draped with white curtains. The thin curtains swayed gently when the wind blew.

'Today, luckily, they finished work at seven o'clock and left. So, there is no noise, sir. Otherwise, there is no peace until midnight,' said Kumar.

Shivaswamy gave him the gift he had brought, and they sat to chat in the living room. In the meantime, Vanita arranged the meal on the dining table. The hot lentil stew, which had just been removed from the stove, was still boiling in the pot. Their daughter made a brief appearance to help her mother but soon went back to her room and closed the door. Shivaswamy and Kumar sat down to eat. Vanita said she would serve them and then sit down.

'After my wife returns from America, we will consider moving to our home in this building, just like you,' said Shivaswamy.

'How many more days will it take, Uncle?' asked Vanita.

'It may take another five or six months, I think,' he replied.

Kumar laughed and said, 'By then, we will have our eight-lakh rupee problem solved too.'

Shivaswamy laughed and then asked, 'The issues with water, power and garbage collection are all resolved, right?' He knew this question would catch them off guard because he had already assessed the situation when the lift wasn't working, but he still wanted to hear it from them.

Kumar remained silent. His silence seemed to answer the question. Before he could speak, Vanita said, 'Uncle, everything here is a problem. It's best you don't come now.'

Kumar looked at her reproachfully. 'All new apartments are like this. It will only get better after four or five families move in. Don't exaggerate and disappoint him,' he said.

'We shouldn't lie and make others suffer, especially elders. It's not good for anyone. Uncle, Phase I hasn't received the completion certificate from the BBMP. Without the certificate, no services can be set up. In the government's eyes, this is still a building unfit for habitation. We're living here almost illegally.' Her voice was filled with sorrow, despair and anger. It trembled as if she was about to cry. Shivaswamy was taken aback.

'It's not called the completion certificate; it's the occupancy certificate,' Kumar corrected her.

'Whatever. In short, it's unsuitable for living,' Vanita snapped back.

'Vanita, please. Let him eat. We can talk later,' Kumar said with an undertone of warning.

'It's all because of you!' she shot back. 'I am not scaring him, am I? I just answered his question.' She turned towards Shivaswamy. 'Uncle, I told him a million times . . . a million times! I said, "Think before you leap, for there will be consequences." But did he ever listen to me? Look at our situation now. All he cared about was how convenient it would be for him to catch a bus to his village on Saturdays and Sundays. Can you believe it? We are in this hell with our grown-up girl.'

Kumar's expression changed, and his eyes narrowed. Staring at her, he responded in a raised voice. 'It's not just about the convenient commute to my village. Was that the only reason? We had to vacate our rented house immediately once the lease ended. Weren't you happy that this place was closer to your school? Don't make baseless arguments.'

Vanita remained silent.

Shivaswamy felt a deep sorrow; he no longer had any appetite for dinner. Trying to change the subject, Kumar asked numerous questions about Shivaswamy's hometown and even inquired about his experience living in north India. The change in subject felt forced. The couple's arguments were still ringing in everyone's ears.

After the meal, the two men moved to the balcony. Vanita and her daughter served themselves some dinner and ate in front of the TV. The balcony was well-decorated. There were white-cushioned cane chairs, a rubberwood coffee table, flowerpots on one side and a carpet that resembled fresh grass, enhancing the charm of the small space. From the balcony, a star-filled sky stretched grandly over their heads. To the left, the buildings still under construction were visible. The only light in the vast darkness came from the security guard's cabin in the distance.

Kumar peeped inside the room and, after making sure that the two women were still in front of the TV, spoke softly. 'Sir, you heard what Vanita said. Our situation here is bad. We have to fight for every basic amenity. Initially, four families, including us, decided to move in together. For sure, it was some mad courage, sir. But now, only two families remain. We reside on the third floor, while Joseph Mathews and his wife occupy the one on the fourth floor. It's just the two of them. They often travel to Kerala, since their children are studying there. When they leave, they're gone for at least fifteen days. More often than not, it's just the three of us left in the building. Our daughter has grown up. At the construction site, numerous workers come and go. Such a diverse crowd! Vanita is genuinely fearful. I can understand her worries.'

Even though Kumar had been harsh with Vanita during dinner, Shivaswamy felt a sense of relief to see him showing sympathy towards her now, even though she couldn't hear them. He felt a pang of pity for the family's difficult situation. Unsure of what to say, Shivaswamy sat silently as Kumar continued speaking.

'But, contrary to her claims, we didn't move here simply because it was nearer to my village and easy to catch a bus. While that might have influenced our decision, it wasn't the sole reason, sir. Being an elder, you deserve to hear the truth from me. I yielded to temptation and brought this upon us.' He let out a heavy sigh.

'Temptation?' Shivaswamy was puzzled.

'It is *grahachara*, sir—all because of an astrological affliction. It was beyond my control. Even when one is aware of a situation, sometimes stupidity can cloud one's judgement. The folks at Anoop Gardenia had confidently convinced us that once four or five families settled in, others would follow suit, one after the other. "Come in first, and if half the building is not occupied within three months, then question me!" Sarvottama Shastri said to us,' Kumar paused.

'Who is Sarvottama Shastri?'

'He's what we call 'a 420', sir! Every time I think of him, my blood boils. I am not sure who you dealt with when buying the apartment. The one who sold apartments to nearly half the owners here was this guy, Shastri. He was a sales agent for AP Lakhani. Granted, he offered substantial discounts, but that was the only favourable thing he ever did. Everything else was a sheer scam. He has been fired from Anoop Gardenia or—more accurately—from AP Lakhani Company. He is a criminal, sir, but he has trapped us here.'

Shivaswamy couldn't fully wrap his head around this story. Such business dealings, and their associated jargon, were second nature to those immersed in them. For him, it was like stepping into an alien realm. 'How did he trap you?' he asked, a little scared.

'Sir, even as I say this, I feel embarrassed. I fear that, in your eyes, I might come across as immoral. We were already aware of the extra eight lakh rupees we're currently disputing, even before the letters were dispatched. Shastri informed us about it in advance, but it was the builder's covert plan. I admit we didn't realize it at the time, even though we had our suspicions. Shastri secretly met with the chosen six families and said, "You will receive a notice for eight lakh rupees, but I'll assist you in avoiding the payment. However, you must maintain absolute secrecy." He added, "Within fifteen days, you should relocate to your apartments. Once you've moved in, I will have the notice withdrawn for you, claiming that you are already residing there." And sir, my situation at that time was the perfect prey for his trap,' Kumar said with a sigh, looking gloomily into the dark beyond the balcony.

The story Kumar was narrating felt like a mountain road, with one twist leading to another. Hesitant that asking a question might seem like he was prying into his personal life, Shivaswamy cautiously ventured, 'What kind of situation was it, Kumar?'

'Before this, we lived in a rented house in Thyagaraja Nagar, sir. You should've seen that landlord—pale-skinned, reduced to mere bones. But deep down, he was a true demon. He occupied the ground floor and rented out four houses upstairs. He controlled the water supply, ensuring we never had a moment's peace. Friends and relatives were unwelcome. And what to say about his greed! If you dropped a rupee on cow dung, he would swoop on it like a scavenger and put it in his pocket. Every month, he would find a reason to demand more money apart from the rent. The never-ending torment there, sir, was so overwhelming that Vanita kept insisting that we leave that place.

Vanita has railed at me so much for coming here, sir. But she was the one who created a ruckus day and night to leave that house. We had to leave, and, at that very moment, Shastri came to our home and said, "Move in, and I will save you from paying eight lakh rupees." We thought everything had come together as our good fortune. We almost spat on that landlord's face when we gave him our notice. We held our heads high that we were moving to our own house.

But little did we realize that if it was a frying pan there, it would be a blazing fire here. Vanita is getting angrier every day, asking what we have achieved by coming here. What can be done, sir? Tell me, what would you have done if you were in my place?'

Shivaswamy was uncertain about what he would have done had he been in Kumar's place. Perhaps he would have acted in the same way. He shook his head. Kumar, on the other hand, did not appear to be waiting for a response.

'You got the eight lakh-rupee notice too, didn't you?' asked Shivaswamy.

'Yes, sir. After giving it to all of you, they gave it to us too, the five families who had already moved here. Those bastards even saved on postage costs. The maintenance boy slipped the notice under the door. We tried to be smart and save money, but, in the end, we were screwed in every way. In Kanakapura, there's a saying: It's about a man who was so smart that he tried to be creative and shut a door in an innovative way and ended up trapping his balls. Well, sir, that's exactly what happened to me.'

Though he laughed at his own joke, it was tinged with bitterness. Shivaswamy gave a faint nod, acknowledging Kumar's frustration. 'That's rough,' he said softly, unsure of what else to say.

A brief silence followed. Shivaswamy leaned back in his chair, his brow furrowed in thought. Kumar stood up and asked, 'Sir, shall I make some coffee?'

'No, it's late for coffee,' Shivaswamy replied. 'What did the sales guy who brought you here say?'

'Shastri! When I called him, he said, "I left AP Lakhani. I don't work for any of their properties now. Sorry, Kumar, I can't help you anymore," and hung up. Yet, just a few days later . . . you'll laugh when you hear this, sir . . . he called me and said, "Kumar, I now work for Prestige. A new project has been launched in Whitefield. It's a good one. If you know any IT engineers looking to buy a flat, please connect them with me." He was practically begging. I didn't berate him. Instead, I said, "I know five people here, Shastri. I'll give you their numbers. But what's the story with the eight lakhs, my friend?" When I dangled that carrot over his nose, he told me everything.

This entire thing was a trick by the builder—AP Lakhani. They're demanding eight lakh rupees from each of us to clear their records with the BBMP. Did you know this?'

'No,' Shivaswamy said, shocked.

'Do you know they've constructed two penthouses on the eighth floor of every building in Phase I? That's unauthorized.

Also, the basement should exclusively serve as parking, yet they've reduced ten or fifteen parking spaces to accommodate a shop. Both actions are unauthorized and aren't reflected in the official plans. Now, the BBMP is scrutinizing them and has withheld their occupancy certificate. They've built the place, and legitimizing it now will cost them crores. They're trying to pass that expense onto us, demanding eight lakh rupees each. If we all comply, they could recoup their losses and even make a profit. All their justifications are deceptive. They offset the loss from one project with another, sir. They always find a scapegoat. According to Shastri, this may not even be limited to eight lakh rupees. What to do, sir? We are cornered.'

'Oh, Kumar, I had no clue about any of this,' Shivaswamy lamented. The notion that this entire affair might exceed eight lakh rupees unsettled him deeply.

'Listen, sir . . . there's more. Those crooks knew we would oppose paying eight lakh rupees. How could they not know? They're seasoned, sir. How many times have they duped people in this way! AP Lakhani is a nationwide builder, and this is their eighth project just in Bengaluru. Think about that. That's why the folks of Anoop Gardenia made a tactical plan. They put Shastri forward, hid themselves and made five families move in here.'

'How would that help?' asked Shivaswamy.

'When a few families settled here, they would form a resident welfare association and pressure the BBMP, saying they hadn't been provided with water or electricity connections. If they also picketed in front of the BBMP office and sat on a dharna, got the news published in newspapers and even approached the court, then the BBMP, under pressure, would have to wash their hands off by giving the necessary permissions. The logic was simple. If a few families suffered due to the corporation's non-cooperation, it would stir sympathy in society, sir; that's the plan they were counting on. That is why they saw to it that the families chosen to move in included minorities, the general category and Dalits.

Look, sir, how they fool people. On the one hand, they collect money from us; on the other, they set us up to solve problems for them.' Kumar laughed sarcastically.

'Can they hand over the houses without an occupancy certificate?' asked Shivaswamy.

'They shouldn't. But here in Bengaluru, it's common, sir. Everyone tends to break the law.'

When Shivaswamy left Kumar's house that night, it was past ten o'clock. He was overwhelmed with all that he had heard from Kumar. The entire situation had gotten murkier than he had originally anticipated.

The couple came down to the security gate to see him off. Vanita had brought bisibelebath and sweets in a plastic container for the Bihari guard. She couldn't speak his language, and he couldn't speak hers. With a warm smile, he gratefully accepted the food, expressing his gratitude through his eyes.

14

Shivaswamy sat in the boardroom of the head office with his notebook. The room was rife with tension: Raviraj, Prabhu and Shyamala, all sitting in silence. Just moments earlier, when Shyamala had entered the room, he had stood up to greet her, while the other two were engrossed in their laptops. But Shyamala, as if following some protocol, first spoke to Raviraj and Prabhu, and then, seemingly noticing, said, 'Oh, Shivaswamy is here. Is everything going smoothly at the branch?' as she extended a handshake.

Before he could speak, Raviraj, without looking up from his laptop, said, 'Our MD has added him to the meeting.' Shyamala grimaced. Then, she, too, opened her laptop and hid her face behind it. Shivaswamy hadn't brought his laptop. It was a habit from his previous company. They had given him a laptop there in the last days before his retirement. Since their group head used to shout, 'If you sit doing something on your laptops while the meeting is going on, who will even hear what I am saying?', everyone had gotten used to running to meetings with notebooks instead. Shivaswamy decided that he would bring the laptop when he was here in the future, whether he used it or not. He began jotting something down in his notebook. When he raised his head, it seemed as if the two elderly people in the photo on the wall were looking at him judgementally.

Vimal Jain and Ashok Mehta entered the room. Shivaswamy knew who they were, thanks to Anuradha's descriptions. He moved to the other side of the conference table and introduced himself. Vimal Jain was the head of the group's most prominent business unit, the logistics division, while Ashok Mehta was in charge of the engineering constructions and medical equipment trading divisions. Vimal was likely in his forties, with a friendly face and a well-toned body. Extending his hand, he said, 'Our MD has spoken a lot about you.' Ashok was older, perhaps in his late fifties. He wore a light blue suit. His serious face was accentuated by a well-trimmed salt-and-pepper beard.

Then, they both exchanged a few words with Raviraj and Prabhu and sat down next to Shyamala, in the row opposite Shivaswamy. It was evident from how Vimal and Raviraj conversed that they were old friends. They were sons of the company's founders after all, so this didn't come as a surprise to Shivaswamy.

This meeting had not been planned. It came up suddenly, apparently due to some emergency. On that Monday, when Shivaswamy came to the office, he was engrossed in his work when Prabhu rushed in and said, 'There's a meeting at the head office in an hour. You're also included. Have you noticed?' Shivaswamy noticed it then. 'There's no indication of the purpose of this meeting,' he said.

'I'll tell you on the way. Come on, let's go in my car,' he said, leading him away. He drove his Honda City and told him the story all the way.

'Sir, we've discovered a bug in one of our ERP extension products—a software glitch. We had sold this product to a company in Chennai called Perumal Cements. It's been only about four to five months since the sale. While they've been longstanding customers of our logistics division, they only recently purchased our software. One of our software's modules is designed to generate financial reports. It supports the accounts department during their end-of-the-year bookkeeping. However, there was a discrepancy between our software's report and their accountant's tally. The remedy is not simple; it's projected to take a couple of months. We've already communicated with the chief financial officer of Perumal Cements. Some on their side have grasped the technical difficulty and have agreed to wait until we fix it, but not all of them. Unfortunately, the ones who haven't agreed are quite influential in the company. The company's CEO, Rajashekaran, phoned our MD directly, warning him that if we didn't address the issue within a week, they'd initiate legal proceedings against us. Our MD has convened this meeting out of sheer anxiety.'

There was heavy traffic on Sankey Road, opposite the Bangalore Golf Club. Prabhu drove the car cautiously. Shivaswamy, sitting beside him, observed him. He looked handsome in his green shirt. Shivaswamy thought he might be as old as his son-in-law Arun, or maybe a little older. He felt a sense of admiration for him—a local who had joined this Gujarati family business and adeptly managed a division. He wondered why someone so successful in his profession wasn't married yet. He wanted to know more about him.

'Sir, you know, I am terrible at explaining my work without using technical terms,' Prabhu laughed.

'I understood,' said Shivaswamy. He wasn't sure why he had been roped into this crisis. He decided not to ask; it might lead to the same drama. Prabhu drove in silence. As they parked at the head office and got out of the car, Prabhu said, 'These kinds of meetings will become routine for you. Didn't I tell you on Friday? You will be included in all matters related to our branch. I even suspect that your duties will be stretched beyond branch matters. Be prepared.'

Dhaval and Anita entered the boardroom. Dhaval, dressed in a deep navy safari suit, looked very serious. Shivaswamy wondered if this was the same man who had spoken to him so freely at Sankey Tank the other day. As Dhaval took his seat, he surveyed the room briefly through his thick glasses. To his right sat Vimal, Shyamala and Ashok. To his left were Prabhu, Raviraj and Shivaswamy.

'Aha, Shivaswamy is here! How are you, my dear man?' Breaking the moment's gravity, Dhaval stood up and walked over to Shivaswamy to shake his hand. In response, Shivaswamy also rose. Dhaval affectionately patted his left arm and said, 'I'm so glad to see you,' before returning to his seat. Dhaval's warm welcome kindled a spark of joy in Shivaswamy. In his mind, two contrasting images—one of Dhaval at Sankey Tank and the other of him in the boardroom—conjured a sense of wonder.

'Isn't the entire software branch here? What's the news?' he asked, glancing at Prabhu and then turning to Anita.

Anita replied, 'Sir, you called for this meeting. Remember, Rajashekharan from Perumal Cements called you last night?'

'Oh, Rajashekharan's issue. What's happening, Prabhu?' Dhaval asked, turning to Prabhu. 'He was quite upset, claiming something is seriously wrong with our product. He's even mentioned legal action if we fail to rectify the problem. I've taken a day's time from him to respond.'

'How can they go to court? Wasn't it their responsibility to check if all their requirements were covered when buying our product?' said Prabhu.

This angered Dhaval. 'Once created, a company's product is like a child. Those who can't nurture it shouldn't even create it,' he said.

That statement struck Raviraj and Prabhu like a sword. Raviraj tried to explain, but Dhaval cut him off, sharing an anecdote from thirty-two years ago. Back when the company was smaller, they had faced a crisis when shipping a half-tonne consignment from Mumbai to Hong Kong for their client, Neon Wesley Exports. The consignment was delayed by fifteen days due to some international unrest in the Indian Ocean. Dhaval vividly described how Preetam Jain had managed to appease the disgruntled customer. After Dhaval finished, Raviraj remarked, 'Old solutions don't always solve new problems.' His sarcasm irked Dhaval, leading to an exchange of sharp words from both sides.

Shivaswamy found the entire meeting chaotic, marked by exhortations and egos, with everyone talking at each other. He didn't dare to speak up.

Dhaval pushed his chair forward and walked towards the door. Anita stood up to follow him, indicating that the meeting was over.

Then, Shyamala said to Raviraj in a low voice, 'The question of what needs to be done with Perumal Cements is still hanging . . .'

Since the two of them were sitting opposite each other at the large table, their words were heard by everyone.

Dhaval turned around, 'Hm . . . you called me, right?'

Shyamala was taken aback by this unexpected turn of events. She had to repeat what she had said. Those seated around had heard it already. 'What should we do with Perumal Cements now?' she asked. She knew this was an explosive question.

'Someone who's listened to the Ramayana all night asks in the morning: What was the relationship between Rama and Sita?'

'No, sir. What's our immediate response?' she replied, as if defending her question.

Dhaval looked around at everyone again from behind his thick glasses. His gaze fell on Shivaswamy.

'Wait. Let's hear what Shivaswamy has to say. Let's see what he recommends,' he said, making everyone turn to him.

Shivaswamy stood up. 'It seems appropriate for one of our executives to go to Chennai and meet Rajashekaran,' he said.

Dhaval clapped his hands like a small child and grinned. 'There is the solution!'

Dismissing that, Raviraj said, 'A senior solutions architect has already been there.'

Dhaval asked, 'Was the one who went the son of the company's chairman?'

Raviraj did not answer.

Dhaval continued, 'No, not just anybody. Either you or Prabhu, or both, need to go and talk to Rajashekaran to regain his trust. If he is deeply dissatisfied, give back his money. If he wishes, he can use our product for free. And . . . Shivaswamy, you need to update me on this.' He walked out of the room.

Ashok and Vimal also rose. Vimal made a comment in Gujarati and laughed, glancing at Raviraj. Ashok joined in the laughter.

Raviraj pressed his forehead with both hands. Shyamala was busy typing on her laptop. Shivaswamy, who had stood up to respond to Dhaval's question, didn't sit down again. Vimal and Ashok exited the conference room eventually.

An unbearable silence lingered among the remaining people in the room.

'Shivaswamy, keep your advice to yourself if you haven't a clue about our business,' Shyamala snapped at him.

'You sounded like an astrologer: *Everything will be fine if we visit Chennai!* The only thing you left out was suggesting we wear a blessed talisman around our necks before setting off!' Prabhu said in a theatrical tone, and the other two on his side laughed.

Shivaswamy felt humiliated. But he responded in a calm tone, 'It's not like that, Prabhu. I had to say it because he asked me for my opinion directly. But I don't see anything wrong in what I said.'

'First get used to carrying a laptop around, then you can start giving advice,' Prabhu retorted.

Shivaswamy did not speak again. He just sat in his chair. The other three stood up and left the room.

The large boardroom was now empty, except for Shivaswamy. The only sound was the faint hum of the AC. The two elderly men in the portraits on the wall looked down at him with sympathy.

He was too distressed to even consider getting up and leaving. He sat there, unaware of how much time had passed. A short while later, Anita entered the room, pausing momentarily, surprised by the unexpected scene. She sat down next to him.

'It's been like this here for a few days,' she said softly.

Shivaswamy did not speak.

'Sir, shall I get some coffee?'

'No, thank you,' he replied, standing up and heading towards the door. She followed him, trying to say something, but the words remained unspoken. Shivaswamy left the boardroom.

He could see that Raviraj, Prabhu and Shyamala were discussing something inside Shyamala's office. The door was closed. He walked down the stairs. The office car was there; perhaps it would have taken him back to the branch office if he had asked. But Shivaswamy didn't inquire. Asking for it, if it required Shyamala's permission, seemed demeaning. He booked an Uber. Within three minutes, the taxi arrived.

More than half the day had passed at the head office. He had skipped lunch. Anuradha was waiting for him when he got to the branch to apprise him of the pending tasks before him. She left for the day by six-thirty, while Shivaswamy took another half an hour to complete his work.

As he turned off the lights in his room and prepared to leave, Prabhu emerged from his room. 'Sir, may I have a moment?' he asked.

Stepping back, Shivaswamy switched the light back on.

Prabhu followed, closing the door behind him. 'Sir, I misbehaved with you today. I spoke childishly without considering your age. Please forgive me,' he said in a low voice, without eye contact.

'It's alright, Prabhu.'

Neither of them knew what to say next. Prabhu then opened the door and returned to his room. Shivaswamy turned off the light again and headed towards the lift.

15

In a single day, Shivaswamy had witnessed both the sharp edge of anger and the quiet grace of remorse from Prabhu. The morning's ride to the head office had felt like a steady climb up a gentle slope, each moment filled with affection. By noon, Prabhu's fury struck, sending Shivaswamy's spirits plunging abruptly. Yet, by evening, it was as though he had descended into a sheltered valley—Prabhu's apology softening the sting of humiliation at least a little bit.

He finally arrived home after navigating the teeming crowds of two metro stations. When he reached the gate, he saw that the house was immersed in darkness; the power was out. His scooter stood alone in the parking area meant for a car. He entered the house, searched for a candle in the darkness, lit it, and sat quietly on the sofa. In the flickering light, his shadow loomed large on the adjacent wall, moving like a giant. Sweat clung to his skin, and his exhaustion was palpable. After ten minutes, he got up and took a cold shower in the dark.

Though not hungry, he went to the kitchen out of habit. He took the dosa batter from the fridge and placed it on the kitchen counter. Seeing the thawed contents of the fridge, he realized the power must have been out for quite some time. The glow from the gas stove illuminated the kitchen. All he had to accompany the dosas was groundnut chutney powder. The dosa tasted sour. Four pieces in, he was overcome by nausea. He rushed to the bathroom and vomited.

Revathi called just then. A sense of relief washed over him.

'Why did you eat the spoilt food? If you had prepared rice, you could've at least had it with curd,' she said. 'You can turn on the cooker and make some rice even now. It won't take long.'

'I'm tired,' he replied.

'Are you taking your pills? Have you checked your sugar levels?' she inquired. When he hesitated, she knew the answer and was upset.

Shivaswamy searched for the glucometer on the nightstand, found it, pricked his finger, took a drop of blood in the dim light of the candle, and tested his blood sugar. It was high. He concluded that this was the reason for his fatigue. He found his pills and took them.

He pulled back the curtains of the living room window and saw the street lights. As he stepped outside and stood by the gate, he noticed lights shining in the other houses down the street. He stood there for a few moments. To the left, the vacant plot was partially shrouded in darkness. He could hear faint murmurs. Once, he had seen a snake there, almost three feet long with a wheat-coloured sandy complexion. It must have been a rat snake. It had slithered gracefully along the length of the fence before disappearing into a hole. Shivaswamy wasn't frightened; instead, he was captivated by its mesmerizing shine.

In front of the gate of the house on the right stood Bhattaru, the man of that house. He appeared to be past seventy. He wore no shirt, only a sacred thread across his chest, and had a prominent belly. He leaned against the gate much like a heron. Since Revathi referred to him as 'Bhattaru'—the Kannada version of 'Pandit-ji'—Shivaswamy also addressed him by that name.

'Namaskara Bhattare, it seems you have power at home. Ours is out,' he said.

Bhattaru looked at him and asked, 'What did you say?'

Shivaswamy had to repeat himself, raising his voice.

Bhattaru's wife, seated on the step behind, said something in Sanketi. Sanketi is the dialect of a sect of Brahmins in south

Karnataka. Shivaswamy didn't understand what she said. Bhattaru then translated her words for him.

'Oh, a worker from the electricity department came this morning and disconnected your connection. It seems you haven't paid your bills for the last three months. He asked us to let you know,' Bhattaru said, and after a pause, asked, 'Why didn't you pay?'

Shivaswamy had indeed forgotten. He sighed. It was always Revathi who took care of that chore.

'In any case, the electricity office must be closed by now. Make sure you go early in the morning, before nine, and pay it,' Bhattaru advised.

Shivaswamy nodded. Just as he was about to go inside, Bhattaru's wife said something else to her husband. Bhattaru translated it for him.

'Has your daughter delivered the baby yet?'

'No, there are still three months to go.'

Another question followed: 'Are you going to America too?'

'No,' he replied. Without waiting for more questions, he retreated inside. He wasn't annoyed by the inquiries; he had yearned for the companionship of his neighbours for a long time. But tonight, he was so exhausted that he could barely stand.

He went to bed early. Sleeping without the fan was impossible. A severe headache began to set in. The candle that had faintly glowed in the corner had burnt out by midnight. The room succumbed to darkness. By three or four in the morning, sleep overcame him, and he woke up by six, as was his daily routine. His body burnt with fever. He could neither rise nor remain lying on the bed. His body curled up and shivered, as if afraid to keep pace with the world that had already begun the day.

Revathi called at seven o'clock. 'If you're so tired, don't go to the office today. Rest at home,' she said.

'Some tasks need to be completed urgently,' he replied.

Revathi was angry. 'You're speaking like a young man just starting his job. Don't they realize you're not well? If you feel so pressured, don't work at all. Just quit. I've told you before, you shouldn't be working for a private company at your age.'

She seemed to calm down only after he assured her that he wouldn't go to work that day. Before they could talk about anything else, his phone's battery died, disconnecting the call.

He could not even call the office to inform them of his absence. Holding the phone and the charger, he ran to Bhattaru's home and asked if he could charge it for ten minutes. Bhattaru graciously obliged, insisted he sit down, and offered him a cup of coffee. 'First, go to the electricity office and bring the lineman,' he suggested.

When he returned home, Shivaswamy called Anuradha. He told her he wouldn't be coming to the office and asked her to inform everyone via email.

'Yes, sir. Please take care of your health,' she replied with concern.

He visited the BESCOM office to settle the bill and submitted a request for a reconnection. After taking a tablet for his fever and sipping some hot tea, he felt a bit better and soon drifted into a deep sleep. When he woke up again, the fan was whirring above his head.

He stayed in bed until afternoon, feeling tired and dizzy. Calls began coming in one after the other. First, Prabhu inquired about his health. 'Don't worry about work, sir. If necessary, take a couple more days off,' he advised with genuine concern. Later, Teju called, sounding frantic. 'Amma told me of your condition this morning. I tried to reach you multiple times, but your phone was unreachable,' he said. He also patched in his sister, Sanju, for a conference call.

When asked what he had had for breakfast and lunch, Shivaswamy felt compelled to lie; he hadn't regained his appetite yet. After the call, as atonement for lying to his children, he prepared a meal, went outside to the Nandini milk booth, bought some yoghurt, and ate it. By evening, Anuradha had called a couple of times to seek his advice on some urgent work matters. He was able to converse with her comfortably.

By the time night fell, even though the fever had subsided, he felt drained. Revathi had called, urging him not to go to work the following day as well. He complied. That night, he slept soundly.

The next day, despite lingering fatigue, he felt healthier. By the afternoon, his appetite had returned. He cooked and ate. He completed the household chores—sweeping and mopping the floor, washing clothes and buying groceries.

In the evening, as he settled down on the terrace, a sense of tranquillity prevailed over him finally. He opened the brown book of Allama Prabhu's vachanas and began reading from the *Pranalingi Sthala*. This section of Allama's vachanas addressed a stage in one's spiritual progression where Shiva and the self are recognized as one and the same. Beside the verses, his annotations, penned in days gone by, seemed to be fading with time:

In the dense forest of existence, where paths often elude,
If one cannot find the way out or harness the ethereal breath of life,
How can he glimpse the profound—the Shiva jnana?

Written in blue ink was the interpretation: 'After delving into a dense forest, one must seek the way out. Entangled in the web of illusion and worldly desires, one must search for the path of liberation.'

While reading it, Shankara Linga Devaru's half-closed eyes came to Shivaswamy's mind. The breeze that had caressed him as he sat under the tree that day seemed to touch him now. He found himself reading the same lines repeatedly.

While relocating from Ghaziabad to Bengaluru, he had intended to visit Vijayapura. He wanted to spend a few days at the Jnana Yoga Ashram to bask in the presence of Sri Siddheshwara Swamiji—the master of vachanas—and to refresh his memories about the teachings of Vachanamruta. But from the day he had arrived, this city seemed to have wrapped itself tightly around him. Then came household pressures in their myriad forms and the resultant pain of resuming work. Each of these weighed on him and distanced him from his goal. Had he not rejoined work, the time he now spent alone would have been ideal for the solace he sought at the Jnana Yoga Ashram.

'After delving into a dense forest, one must seek the way out. Entangled in the web of illusion and worldly desires, one must search for the path of liberation.'

He recited these lines thrice like a mantra.

16

In the two days that Shivaswamy skipped work, he developed a good working relationship with Anuradha. She managed to independently seek his guidance whenever necessary. If she wanted, she could have reached out to Shyamala or the HR team at the head office, as she had done before. But she chose not to.

A meek person by nature, she had found two sources of comfort after Shivaswamy became her manager. First, she had a boss who was as old as her father, which brought a familiar warmth and made her feel safe and understood. He guided her in work matters as if he were teaching a child. Second, he displayed an unwavering emotional balance she hadn't seen in her previous managers—she had never once witnessed him lose his temper.

The office on Dickenson Road had become increasingly autonomous in human resource management. Surprisingly, Shyamala hardly intervened. After Shivaswamy joined, she seemed less concerned about this branch. Perhaps her complete immersion in the company's vast logistics division was one reason. Her initial outbursts, which seemed to have stemmed from various suspicions and rumours, had faded away.

Shivaswamy continued to send her a summary of the day's work in the evening. Since it was the third month since he had joined the company, the once-rampant rumour about her challenge—*I will drive him out in fifteen days*—gradually vanished from the minds of the employees and disappeared from cafeteria conversations. After all, such a threat from a senior management official, especially one with decades of experience and in the position of HR head, did not bode well.

Now, instead of news from the branch reaching the head office, information from the head office increasingly reached the branch. Anuradha's friend, Harini, worked in the finance department at the head office. In fact, it was Harini who had introduced Anuradha to this company. Both came from the same town. With her keen sense of hearing, Harini picked up many intricate details from the head office and its various divisions. These details would then be relayed to Anuradha and, subsequently, to Shivaswamy. Anuradha never held back information. Her job required her to spend a significant amount of time in Shivaswamy's office, and she even had her own desk set up there. The opportunities to talk were plenty.

Through this unofficial channel, many details about Dhaval Thakkar and his family reached Shivaswamy. He believed such inquisitiveness among the employees was understandable since it was a family-owned venture. This kind of curiosity wasn't there at his previous office, BEL.

Shivaswamy learnt that Dhaval and his son did not live in the same house and rarely spoke to each other. The rift between them had only deepened after the arrival of his son's wife, Dhriti. When Dhaval's wife, Sumati, was alive, she was the force that kept the family united. However, in the five years since Sumati's passing, the family had fallen apart. During this period, Dhriti had begun to assert her influence within the company. Dhaval, using various pretexts, sidelined her constantly, leading to both overt and covert power struggles.

Dhriti held no official position within the DT Group. She wasn't even an independent non-participating director. Dhaval was opposed to her holding any position. It seemed Dhaval feared her father more than his daughter-in-law. Rumours suggested that behind Dhriti's ambition to transfer the entirety of DT Group to Raviraj was her father—the puppet master. He ran a business in Jamnagar in Gujarat that was four times larger than the DT

Group. He had four daughters, all of whom had married into prosperous families. The first and the third lived in Gujarat, the second in Mumbai and Dhriti, the fourth, was based in Bengaluru.

Whether it was because she was the youngest or because he felt a sense of guilt for sending her to the far south, Dhriti's father held special affection for her. There seemed to be another reason. Among the four, she was the only daughter married into a 'small business' family. If Dhaval's enterprise was considered small, then it was beyond Shivaswamy's imagination to fathom the wealth of Dhriti's sisters.

Right from the beginning, for one reason or another, Dhaval never got along with Dhriti's father. Once, while conversing with Vimal Jain in the hallway of the head office, Dhaval burst into laughter and exclaimed, 'Did our Ravi really say that? Vimal, have you ever watched a ventriloquist act? The talking puppet show? Ravi is that puppet. It's either Dhriti or her father speaking.' Someone in a nearby cubicle overheard this, and it soon became a company-wide joke.

There was another little-known character in this family saga: Dhaval's daughter, Rashmi. She was five years older than Raviraj. The siblings never really got along. Ravi's wife, Dhriti, had a clear distaste for her. Despite the eight-year age gap, there was palpable tension between Rashmi and Dhriti. Dhriti had left Gujarat for Karnataka, while Rashmi had done the opposite. Dhriti had transitioned from a large family to a smaller one, whereas the reverse had occurred for Rashmi.

The family Rashmi had joined was no ordinary one. Dhaval had married her into a prestigious family of diamond merchants in Ahmedabad. Among the family's four sons, the youngest was Rashmi's husband, Kishan. However, there was a twist in the story. With the passing of his father, it seemed Kishan's fortune faded as well. When the assets were divided, his brothers schemed, allocating the less profitable, or, to put it bluntly, the 'useless' businesses to him. Consequently, his net worth diminished considerably. Had he managed his assets better, he could have thrived without difficulty. But Kishan lacked business acumen. He was certainly not a man of will. Being the youngest, he had grown up without bearing any significant responsibilities and was ill-prepared for the challenges that followed. He missed out on numerous business opportunities and accumulated debts. Dhaval cleared his debts on four separate occasions. Now, Kishan was merely the proprietor of two jewellery stores. In the grand context of their family's legacy, that was almost inconsequential.

When Kishan's father passed away, and there was a huge commotion in the house over dividing the property among the brothers, Rashmi wanted her father to stay with her in Ahmedabad for a few months and help Kishan. However, this idea wasn't welcomed by anyone, not even by Kishan. He didn't want his father-in-law involved in his family's affairs. As days went by, he changed his mind and yearned for his support. But, by then, it was too late. Even Dhaval hesitated. He did not know how to involve himself in a business that was not his own. There was another reason. Dhaval had little experience when it came to large business families. After inheriting his father's small saree shop, he had spent his entire life working on his own venture. Being the only child, he had never witnessed sibling disputes over inheritance.

Rashmi couldn't understand her father's apprehension. Instead, slowly, she began to see her father as the root cause of every setback Kishan encountered. These feelings grew stronger, especially after her brother, Raviraj, married a woman from a family far wealthier than their own, and particularly when Dhriti no longer looked at Rashmi with the same affection. Disheartened, Rashmi reduced her visits to Bengaluru. She had an eight-year-old son, and yet it had been years since Dhaval had last seen his grandson. There was warmth in the father–daughter relationship as long as her mother was alive. With her, it too had died.

'I forgot who said it, Anuradha. I read it somewhere long ago. Perhaps it was Shivarama Karanth, the writer. *Money is like salt.*

If there's too little, the food doesn't taste good. If it's too much, the food becomes inedible,' Shivaswamy remarked.

Anuradha smiled as she closed the lid of her lunch box and slid it into its carry bag. Her meal was minimalistic—just a chapati for the afternoon. Shivaswamy had finished his lunch too. Ever since he had fallen sick, he had been bringing lunch from home.

'It's true, sir. I neither want to earn a crore nor carry a crore's worth of problems,' she said, trying to impress her boss.

He smiled again. They both rose from the cafeteria and headed to their floor. 'It might seem that way to you and me, but the wealthy don't see it that way. They believe they have the ability to handle a crore's worth of problems while earning a crore. Maybe they do! To each their own; as much as an elephant can bear, as much as an ant can,' he said playfully. The young woman grinned in response.

Later that day, as he was getting ready to go home, Prabhu came to his cabin. He told Shivaswamy that, as was decided in the meeting the other day, he had travelled to Chennai to meet the management at Perumal Cements. Rajashekaran and his team had accepted his proposed plan to tackle the issue they were facing. 'I really should thank you for your suggestion,' he said, shaking hands with a nod. 'I'll send you the details of my meetings with them. Please update the head office,' he said.

Shivaswamy agreed. Within the next fifteen minutes, he received a summary in an email from Prabhu. He forwarded it to Anita and asked her to inform Dhaval Thakkar. Although he could have sent the email to him directly, he felt hesitant for some reason.

17

The next day, Shivaswamy was deeply engrossed in his work until noon. He was preparing for campus selections, aiming to recruit twenty-five graduates within the next sixty days. This task entailed contacting colleges in Bengaluru and creating an interview panel with Prabhu's assistance. He also needed to write to the head office, requesting two additional assistants; managing this task with Anuradha alone seemed unfeasible. Then there were the daily responsibilities that demanded his attention. Anuradha and he were fully occupied until, suddenly, Shivaswamy's mobile buzzed. An unknown number flashed on the screen. 'Sir, should I step out?' Anuradha inquired.

'No, no, stay. It seems like a wrong number,' he said, picking up the phone to answer.

'Shivaswamy. It's Dhaval.'

'Oh . . . sir. Good morning.'

'Isn't it already afternoon, Shivaswamy?'

'Oh. Good afternoon, sir,' he replied, slightly embarrassed.

Dhaval laughed. 'How are you?'

'I'm fine, sir. Work is going well. How are you, sir?'

'Thankfully, no one has ruffled my feathers yet,' Dhaval replied, his tone lighter.

'What can I assist you with, sir?'

Though Anuradha had hidden her face behind her computer, Shivaswamy knew her attention was fixed on their conversation. But he felt it wouldn't be right to ask her to leave now.

'You could have sent me the report directly,' said Dhaval.

'Oh, that . . . Sir, about Perumal Cements . . . I sent it to Anita, thinking you might be busy with something,' Shivaswamy replied.

'It's alright. Next time, send it directly to me. Moreover, I prefer the phone over emails. Just call my mobile.'

'Okay, sir.'

'If you come here, we can discuss it together. How's your day looking? Can you make it here by afternoon? I've been in the office since morning.'

'I'll be there, sir. Around two-thirty?'

'Come,' said Dhaval, and hung up.

As if she hadn't heard anything, Anuradha did not raise her head from her computer.

'Anuradha, I'll be going to the head office this afternoon. If you need anything, call me directly on my mobile. If I need to finish any tasks there, please make a list,' he instructed her. He then called the front desk to book the branch's car for the afternoon.

Shivaswamy arrived at the head office ten minutes earlier than expected, proceeded directly to the fourth floor where the MD's office was, and met Anita at her desk. She greeted him with a warmth that made him feel welcome.

He sat down on the sofa in front of her desk. As soon as she relayed the message on the intercom, the instruction to 'let him in' was given.

Dhaval stood in the corner of the room. It looked like he had just finished a call; he was still holding the phone. He was wearing a white safari suit. The colour of the clothes matched his white beard and hair.

'Shivaswamy, how have you been, my friend?' His characteristic voice boomed.

The room was expansive and opulent. The MD's chair was placed behind a heavy mahogany desk; beyond that, a glass wall offered a view of the endless sky. To the left stood a sizable bookshelf. The room was spacious enough to accommodate a hundred people comfortably. Dark brown leather sofas adorned either side. A Kashmiri carpet covered the floor. Shivaswamy had never seen an office immersed in such luxury before.

Dhaval gestured to the chair in front of his desk and then sat down.

'Shivaswamy?'

'Yes, sir.'

'You were in my dream last night,' said Dhaval. 'We were travelling together somewhere on a train. It seems you were wearing the same clothes as you are wearing now. It's like you've stepped straight out of my dream.'

Shivaswamy felt slightly at ease. With a smile, he asked, 'Where were we going, sir?'

'I don't know, Shivaswamy. All I saw was us on the move.'

'Did we reach our destination, sir? After all, it was a dream journey—no expenses.'

'Isn't that so?' Dhaval laughed. 'Look at my cheapskate mind. If it didn't cost anything, we should have just taken a plane, no?'

Shivaswamy smiled again. His mind was busy trying to guess why he might have been summoned.

'And how is our Shyamala treating you?' Dhaval asked, looking at him directly through his thick glasses. 'She's often presumptuous, you know.'

Shivaswamy became cautious. He had to choose his words carefully. He was well aware that this man wouldn't hesitate to call her in for questioning right in front of him, even over a minor issue. 'Everything is going well, sir. There are no problems. Everyone is cooperative,' he replied. Before Dhaval could say anything, the office helper entered the room.

'Would you like some coffee or tea?' the young man asked. Shivaswamy asked for a sugarless coffee. The man turned to Dhaval, 'Sir, your usual tea?'

Dhaval replied, 'No, bring me a coffee as well. And not from the vending machine. Get it from Krishna Bhavan. Oh, and if he has made hot pakodas, get those too.'

The helper nodded and left.

Dhaval, as if he had suddenly remembered something, rose from his chair and quickly moved to the window behind him. He leaned forward slightly, peering outside through the glass pane. He took off his glasses, wiped them with a handkerchief, and put them back on. Then, he looked out once more.

'Shivaswamy?'

'Yes, sir.'

'Come here.'

Shivaswamy approached him and looked out the window. The sky was filled with clouds, casting shadows over the landscape. The road below was empty, except for a few cars making their way lazily. There was a bus stop at the side of the road, a silent observer of the changing times.

'Look there—at that bus stop. I've been watching it for quite some time, perhaps for over an hour. Those two have been waiting for a bus. They seem like mother and daughter. The mother might be in her thirties, and the daughter appears to be seven or eight. What will they do if the bus doesn't come? Could there be a citywide strike today?' said Dhaval.

Shivaswamy squinted, focusing on the bus stop. The woman, presumably the mother, sat quietly in a saree, while the girl, in a churidar and kurta, seemed restless and fidgeted constantly. An autorickshaw driver driving past slowed down and stuck his head out to ask if they wanted a ride. The little girl looked at her mother's face. With a swift shake of her head, the mother declined. The autorickshaw drove away.

'Look . . .' said Dhaval with a quiver in his voice. 'When I witness the suffering of such people, I'm consumed with despair. I'm uncertain about how to act.' His voice was heavy with sorrow. 'I am overwhelmed with an urge to offer my seldom-used car to assist them. Yet, I hold back, tormented by the thought that it might embarrass them deeply.'

'What can we do, sir? The world is full of such contradictions,' Shivaswamy remarked. *In the areas surrounding Mukesh Ambani's opulent mansion in Mumbai, there are plenty of slums, as they say* . . . Even though this statement had occurred to him, he restrained himself.

The bus stop on the street and the grand fourth-floor office of a profitable company opposite it were two distinct worlds, two different poles. A fifty-foot chasm lay between them, an impassable ocean.

Dhaval, his expression altered, sat back down. He pressed the intercom and said, 'Anita, bring me yesterday's P&L report. Two copies. Just Ravi's division.'

Anita entered carrying two copies of the profit and loss report. She placed them before the two men and exited the room silently. The door closed gently behind her.

'Shivaswamy, look at the fourth line from the bottom,' said Dhaval. Shivaswamy looked. The report showed two columns: net revenue and net profit. The numbers were 144 and 52 per cent.

'Sir, I must apologize. I don't understand profit and loss statements or balance sheets. In my previous company, the accounts team never involved the HR department in these matters, so I never got accustomed to financial terms,' Shivaswamy admitted with a hint of distress in his voice.

Dhaval chuckled. 'Don't worry. You've saved your energy. Reports like these are meant for businessmen like me. To put it simply, the total revenue of the software division stands at 144 million dollars, with a profit margin of 52 per cent. This means that over half the revenue is pure profit. Now, look at the other divisions, like logistics. If their profit margin ever exceeds 18 per cent of their revenue, they consider it a huge success. Why such a difference? Could this be why so many of our young people are drawn to the software industry?' His voice held a note of wonder.

What could Shivaswamy possibly say? He had confessed his unfamiliarity with the subject at the outset. Still, gathering courage, he said, 'Perhaps one shouldn't compare businesses solely by numbers.'

Dhaval looked at him curiously. 'Everyone else seems to have the same sentiment,' he said. 'And now, you're echoing it. How can one not draw comparisons? Don't all four business divisions report directly to me? How can one be treated differently from the rest? Okay, never mind that question. It's my headache. But listen to this. My son suggests that I should be prepared to invest another fifty crore rupees. Why should I funnel such significant funds into this industry?'

'Sir, we have to expand when there is demand in new industries, don't we?'

Dhaval laughed. 'Expand for what?'

'The division's revenue would rise, sir. Moreover, DT Software Solutions would establish itself as a leading software firm here. Wouldn't that be a matter of pride, sir?'

'No,' Dhaval shook his head gravely. 'Exactly with this same logic, Ravi and Prabhu are lobbying hard to separate this division from the rest of the company. It's not just these two. There is a group behind them. It becomes unbearable to even talk about all this, Shivaswamy.

'Haven't you heard our young executives frequently use the term "organic growth"? I often wonder if they genuinely grasp its depth. A cell divides: one becomes two, two evolve into four, four multiply to eight, and so on, culminating in millions and billions of cells that shape flesh and bones, constituting the skeletal frame of a being. All this originates from a solitary cell, right? Such a process demands time, doesn't it? Don't we grant children the grace to grow, to mature at their own pace?

'But they're impatient. To them, a seed sown today should grow into a banyan tree by tomorrow. They continue with their narratives, invoking the likes of Google, HP, Amazon, Infosys and Tesla.'

By then, cups and plates brimming with coffee and pakodas had arrived. Two young helpers set them on the desk before leaving quietly. It was unclear how they had brought the pakodas from Krishna Bhavan, but here they were, elegantly presented on heavy, ornate porcelain plates.

'Shivaswamy, have some,' said Dhaval, clutching a pakoda in his left hand. With his right, he broke it, then, closing his eyes, savoured the taste with evident delight. 'If you put ten plates of pakodas in front of me and challenged me to identify which one was from Krishna Bhavan, I bet I could.'

Shivaswamy too picked up a pakoda, closed his eyes and tasted it, mirroring Dhaval's actions. The taste was truly delightful. But how and why to compare? A pakoda was a pakoda. Could there truly be a discernible difference in taste between those from Krishna Bhavan and those from Shanti Sagar if the ingredients—spices, salt and gram flour—were kept the same?

'Shivaswamy, I've heard that behind every flavour we savour, there's a tale. Only those who know the story can truly appreciate the authentic flavour. This Krishna Bhavan here is the same age as my company. Its owner is Krishna Bhat. Can you guess where he's from? Where else but Udupi! He might have known all the recipes since birth. He came to this city with just a ladle . . . Haha. He's a dear friend of mine.

'Whether he followed me or I followed him, I'm not certain. But essentially, he was nearby, running a coffee shop close to our saree store in Chickpet. Later, he moved to Sadashivanagar, near this office, and continued in the same trade, keeping the same name, Krishna Bhavan. Now, his son Govinda manages the place. Krishna, unlike me, has handed over the reins to his son. But he still drops by occasionally. Shivaswamy, it's a sight to behold! When Krishna arrives, Govinda leaves the counter immediately to head to the kitchen. So much so that Krishna often has to shout, "You've given them half the change! Finish that task, then go!" It must all be his blessings from his past lives.

'But what truly fascinates me are their pakodas. There's absolutely no difference between the pakodas Krishna used to make and the ones that Govinda makes now—not even a hint. The change in management is barely noticeable to loyal customers like me. Isn't that what succession in a company should mean? It's all about consistency, isn't it?'

Dhaval's plate was emptying quickly, while the contents on Shivaswamy's had barely reduced. Having eaten only one or two pakodas, Shivaswamy was reflecting on Dhaval's words: *Behind every flavour we savour, there's a tale.*

'That's what legacy is, isn't it?' said Shivaswamy.

'Indeed, it is. That's what I seek in my business endeavours. Is it wrong? Just as Krishna's life found meaning in the consistency of the pakodas, I hope to find purpose in my life through the company I've nurtured and grown. Krishna must have cast some spell because he succeeded. But my message here seems to fall on deaf ears. If no one feels compelled to hear my words, then what should I do, Shivaswamy? Is our legacy of no value to anyone? Does no one want our maturity?

'As we age, and our life experiences sink deeply within us like a plumb line, we see clearly what is poison and what is elixir. You've heard of Beethoven, haven't you? A towering figure in Western music. Poor soul, it's said he was completely deaf when he composed his main works. Yet, he didn't perceive it as a hindrance. In composing music, the symphonies of the inner realm are ample; "what use are ears?" he seemed to imply.

'But look at the problem. My words fail to resonate with the depth I intend, fading before they reach the ears they're meant for. Truly, it's no one's fault. Had my father spoken in this manner fifty years ago, I might not have understood him either. But still, it hurts my heart. How can I convince others that what I have built is not just a building, but my legacy?'

Dhaval rose from his chair, holding his waist as he often did. He walked to the door, then slowly returned to the window, gazing outside. 'Look, the mother and daughter are gone. They must have caught the bus,' he remarked with a smile, clapping his hands.

'Sir, would you mind if I spoke a few words?' Shivaswamy asked politely.

Dhaval came and sat down beside Shivaswamy. He remembered Dhaval doing the same during their interview. Dhaval put his hand on his shoulder and said, 'There's no need to be so formal with me.

Just speak to me as you would to a friend. The cement company's issue, and every other reason, including Prabhu's elephant-sized bug, were just excuses to meet with you and chat,' he laughed.

'Sir, I am not a businessman like you. I have never run a company like you have. I have spent my entire career in a government company and retired there. God knows to what extent I had the power and opportunities to participate in their business decisions. Given this background, my professional experience might not be of much relevance in understanding your perspective. All that is left is my broader life experience. I grew up experiencing poverty and hardships. I spent many formative years in an ashram. I have my own understanding of the world, and I can only provide insights based on that. It's up to you to determine how valuable they might be.

'Sir, isn't what you just mentioned the very thing we call the generation gap? A father dislikes what the son relishes, and the son's deeds rarely seem right to him. Doesn't a mother-in-law feel that her daughter-in-law erodes the sanctity of her kitchen—her legacy?'

Dhaval's expression darkened. As if taking a long time to absorb Shivaswamy's words, he placed both hands under his chin and fixed his gaze on him. Leaning forward, he asked in an oddly measured voice, 'So what are you telling me, Shivaswamy? That all these headaches I've been having—meetings ending in deadlock, my executives walking on eggshells, me feeling cornered in the company and in my family—are simply phantoms I've conjured? Is this entire crisis nothing more than a theatre of my own creation? Have I been throwing punches at thin air, imagining an opponent who isn't really there? Are these troubles no troubles at all, but illusions?'

He paused, studying Shivaswamy's face intently. Shivaswamy felt a chill of fear run through him.

Noticing his unease, Dhaval suddenly broke into a mischievous grin. Raising both fists, he began shadowboxing the air, muttering 'dishoom-dishoom' like a seven-year-old boy. The sombre tension cracked. With a hearty, booming laugh that filled the room, Dhaval dropped his hands and said, 'Look at me—fighting battles with my own imagination! How's that for a productive day at the office, Shivaswamy?'

Surprised by Dhaval's intensity, Shivaswamy chose his words carefully. 'Not necessarily illusions, sir. But certain perceptions can shine as brightly as truth. One must approach them with caution, sir.'

Dhaval sat in silence, and so did Shivaswamy. He felt that saying anything more might further complicate the situation. Dhaval's right elbow rested on the armrest, and his fingers brushed his chin. Shivaswamy could see the vast blue sky through the window opposite him. There were a few white clouds drifting without the promise of rain.

'Shivaswamy?'

'Yes, sir.'

'Has this never happened to you?'

'What, sir?'

'The feeling . . . that your legacy is ending after your children have grown up.'

Mixed emotions washed over Shivaswamy. Before he could say anything, Dhaval said, 'Let's do something. Let's meet again tomorrow. I have been thinking about my words for a long time. It would be unfair to ask you a question and expect you to answer immediately. Take a day to think about it. I, too, will mull over the question you have raised: Why shouldn't mine be a delusion? Can we do that?'

Shivaswamy nodded in agreement, carefully tucked away the report from Anita into his notebook and stood up. Dhaval, too, stood up.

Shivaswamy asked, 'Sir, at what time should I meet you tomorrow?'

Dhaval thought for a moment and said, 'I'll come to your office tomorrow.'

'Sir, I don't mind coming here. I'll be here at whatever time you suggest.' Shivaswamy wanted the news of this budding friendship to remain within the head office. He didn't want it spreading to the branch, where it might take on different shapes and colours.

'No, I'll come over. It's been a long time since I've been to the office on Dickenson Road. Besides, I have a friend in the neighbouring building whom I should meet,' Dhaval replied.

Shivaswamy nodded and walked towards the door. He was afraid to ask at what time he would be coming. He knew all too well how pointed questions from Anita could unsettle him. He decided he would ring Anita later to find out the time.

But before he could reach the door, Dhaval called him back.

'Shivaswamy, look at my forgetfulness. I didn't even talk about the reason why I called you.'

Shivaswamy stopped, surprised. What else could there be?

Dhaval said, 'I heard you stay in the office till eight or nine in the evening. Don't do that, please. Don't ruin your health.'

'Just occasionally, sir, not daily. Don't worry,' Shivaswamy answered, sounding surprised. 'And how did you come to know of this?'

'In this business, one needs to have spies, whether you like it or not,' Dhaval chuckled. 'If there's too much work, I'll depute a manager from here as your assistant.'

'No need, sir. The work is balanced,' Shivaswamy replied subtly.

Dhaval laughed and said, 'You'd say that if I asked you. Go now. I'll decide that.'

Shivaswamy wondered where this would lead him, but he smiled and left the room.

18

Shivaswamy stepped hesitantly into Shyamala's office. He suspected that the insult she had suffered in the previous meeting might still be lingering in her mind. However, as she was his manager, it was proper to meet with her whenever he visited the head office. Before entering her office, he had resolved not to divulge any details of his discussion with Dhaval inadvertently.

Contrary to his expectations, Shyamala welcomed him with a smile and inquired about his health with great concern. 'Is your grandchild a boy or a girl?' she asked with a smile.

'No, my daughter hasn't given birth yet,' he said.

'Don't they usually tell in advance during the scans in America?'

'I wasn't aware of that,' Shivaswamy said, surprised.

Shyamala smiled again. Her pleasant mood instilled some confidence in him. He proceeded to update her comprehensively about the activities at the branch. Since he emailed her daily before heading home, nothing about the branch was new to her. She casually asked a question or two. He, in turn, jotted down a couple of points, as if they were her suggestions, to please her. Shyamala pressed the intercom, called the office aide, and ordered coffee for both. 'I've already had mine. Drinking too much coffee keeps me awake at night,' he politely declined. She then sent the office aide to bring two glasses of apple juice instead.

Worried that it would become a problem if he hid that he had just met the MD, Shivaswamy told her that Dhaval had asked him to come to discuss the status of Perumal Cements.

She did not ask him why this issue necessitated such a long meeting.

'Oh, that's good. Sometimes, it's more convincing to talk face-to-face than to send emails. You did the right thing. Keep visiting the head office,' she said.

They then conversed on subjects other than work. The entire visit was surprisingly cordial for him. By then, the juice had also arrived, and they drank it.

'Is this also from Krishna Bhavan?' he asked, surprised. And almost immediately, regretted it. She laughed heartily. 'Did he also get you pakodas from there?' she asked with a twinkle in her eye. Shivaswamy laughed. He got ready to leave, and Shyamala extended her hand to shake his.

'Shivaswamy, Dhriti wants to meet you once,' she said.

'Who?'

'Dhriti, our MD's daughter-in-law.'

'I'll be here whenever you wish. What's the meeting about, Shyamala? Should I prepare a presentation about the branch?' he asked.

'The branch and other matters . . .' She searched for the right words. 'No presentation. Nothing needs to be prepared. She might want to discuss various things. You need to come with half a day of free time like you did today. And I'll be there as well,' she said.

Shivaswamy nodded and prepared to leave.

'How are you going?' she asked.

'I'll take the bus,' he said.

'Oh. That might be inconvenient. Let me check if the company car is available.' She reached for the intercom.

'No, no,' Shivaswamy said firmly. 'I'm not going back to the office; I'm heading home. I'll take the bus. It's more convenient.' Without hesitation, he left the room. Shyamala watched him from her seat until he crossed her room, turned right, and headed towards the lift.

He finally managed to catch a BMTC bus, but it was so crowded that he couldn't even move his feet. The bus swayed precariously from side to side, making a grating noise. After he had spent half an hour standing, and the bus had passed five or six stops, a man seated close to him, whose shoulder was practically touching his thigh, got off. Shivaswamy sat down. Someone else would have taken the seat if he had hesitated even for a second.

Taking a moment to relax, he replayed his conversation with Dhaval in his mind. It felt as though Dhaval had conveyed an indescribable anguish, a wordless agony—something he didn't know how to express, or was too embarrassed to say aloud. What was troubling him? Was it a 'maternal' concern for the company he had built and nurtured? Or a family issue, as Anuradha and others suggested? Or perhaps it was simply the challenges of ageing—a senior moment? Without him opening up, how could one ever guess what it was?

The man speaks sincerely, yet he is trapped in a windowless cell. The world's gaze eludes him. How can I help him? Apart from himself, who else can truly understand and address his dilemma?

In a corporate firm such as this, above all, even more than money, relationships determine the way forward. Beyond the clink of coins and the rustle of notes, these bonds breathe life into the company. Here, familial ties tangle themselves with business affairs: father, son and daughter-in-law at the helm, with an extended drama featuring a daughter, the son-in-law and the daughter-in-law's father, all involved in the dance. Dinakar Thakkar, Preetam Jain, Vimal Jain and Ashok Mehta—those still among us and those who have departed—are all part of the same faction. All the business heads are either blood relatives or close friends. Everyone speaks the same language. Who loves whom and who rejects whom, only God knows. In such a family business, the fiercest battles are waged not over wealth but over the delicate threads of relationships.

In the midst of this circle, what role can outsiders play? We are but water; they, blood.

What solace can I offer to this old man? I haven't scaled the mountains he has, nor descended into his valleys.

Each person's inner world was known only to them. They must illuminate their shadows. They must clear the fog of conflict within their hearts.

Only when the person seated next to him nudged him with a duffel bag, saying, 'Make way, I have to get off,' did Shivaswamy come back to reality. The bus had arrived at the last stop.

19

Shivaswamy forgot to wish Sanjana on her birthday. Surprisingly, even Revathi didn't remind him. It was Teju who finally did. 'Appa, call now. It's still eight-thirty in the evening in California. Her birthday isn't over yet.'

Shivaswamy was upset that he had forgotten, but it didn't surprise anyone. He had never been one to keep dates in mind. Revathi used to be his calendar, and now she was missing.

He called and said, 'I'm late, Putti. Don't be upset.'

'It's alright, Appa. The day isn't over yet,' she replied and giggled like a little girl. 'It may be late, but I knew you would not forget.' She knew that the depth of her father's love couldn't be measured by such a lapse of memory. Even if Shivaswamy hadn't called, she would have called and reminded him once she reached home.

She was dining at a Mexican restaurant with her husband and her mother. He could hear the piano in the background.

They chatted about her health, the weather there and a few other things, though the real joy lay more in hearing each other's voices than in any particular topic.

When Sanjana was a little girl, she made every family member's birthday special by creating hand-drawn portraits on colourful paper, decorating them with crayons and presenting them as gifts before she went to bed. Writing the card was a serious project for her. The evening before, she spread her crayons—some broken and peeling—and her treasured stack of coloured paper across the dining table. She spent a good hour sketching, carefully bordering the card with bright hues and adding flower petals around the drawing. Everyone in the family pretended not to notice her activity and then feigned surprise when she finally unveiled her masterpiece.

Once, she even made a card for her birthday, signed it with an outsized flourish, and wrote, 'To the Best Girl in the World—Happy Birthday, Sanjana!' She presented it to herself with pride and held it up for everyone to admire, and they laughed and clapped. Shivaswamy recalled her wide, toothy grin, as though she knew she was cherished beyond measure.

She stopped making these cards after leaving middle school, but their memory lingered. Each year, on her birthday, Shivaswamy would jokingly ask, 'Did you make a greeting card this time, Putti?' Without fail, she would laugh heartily. It had become their shared joke, an annual tradition that carried the echo of those childhood mornings. Every one of those cards was preserved by Revathi, carefully tucked into a plastic bag, and kept in the almirah.

'I heard they reveal the baby's gender during the scan. Is that true?' he echoed the question Shyamala had asked.

'True, Appa. But we can ask them not to tell us. Arun and I have decided not to know the gender in advance,' she replied.

Shivaswamy felt it was the right decision. After hanging up, he sank into the sofa, Sanjana's face vivid in his memory. He was reminded of a conversation he had had with her eleven years ago on her birthday at the steps of the Hanuman Mandir. That day, in the background were the sounds of aarti and bhajans.

In those days, they had left their quarters for a more expensive rented house in Surya Nagar to be closer to her school. Sanjana was quite behind in her studies. She was in the twelfth grade and attended private tuitions in two places. By late evening, she used to be so tired that she would fall asleep at her desk, her forehead resting on a book. When Shivaswamy woke up, he gently shook her awake and sent her to bed. Then she sat up, frantically searching for her book.

Putti had indeed had a learning disability, which made it difficult for her to grasp things easily, but it had remained undiagnosed. Teju's issues with his vision had been identified and easily rectified, unlike Sanju's learning struggles. When Shivaswamy remembered those days of their ignorance and the girl's hardships, his eyes grew moist.

Evenings in Surya Nagar were marked by power outages between seven and eight. Revathi used to attend a tailoring class at that time. After dropping her off at class, the two of them would go to the Hanuman temple nearby. They would sit on the steps at the top, sharing a plate of pani puri or some peanuts and biscuits. After forty-five minutes, they would pick up Revathi and go home.

Occasionally, Teju would join them; at other times, he'd study by candlelight or socialize with friends. The temple visits were a constant for father and daughter. And, thanks to those hours they spent on the steps of the temple, their bond had deepened, drawing them even closer.

Sanjana was like a tortoise, curled up inside her shell, with only a few friends by her side. After moving to Surya Nagar, the girl became even more withdrawn. Shivaswamy and Revathi thought it might be because she had left the house she had lived in since birth and entered a new environment. However, during the days they spent together, sitting on the temple steps, she opened up to her father a little at a time and told him a different story.

The cause of her desolation was the distance she had to keep from Karan, a boy in her class, who struggled as much as, or even more than, she did with her studies. What kind of relationship did they share? Did they love each other, or was she the only one in love? How could the daughter explain this to her father? Karan lived just a street away from their colony. Even when Sanjana mentioned where his house was, Shivaswamy couldn't quite picture him.

Curiously, Karan's family left town two months before they moved out of their quarters. She had never mustered the courage to speak to him, nor did he initiate any conversation. Perhaps the thought 'he is like me' mentally brought him closer to her. After he left, she felt alone in her world. She was devastated not by her family's move but by the profound loneliness she began to feel. This was all she could share with her father in bits and pieces. Shivaswamy's heart was heavy with empathy.

'Putti, it's difficult to know who desires us, but it's easy to understand whom we desire. In the end, only those we want will remain in our minds—whether they know it or not.' While saying this, the face of his childhood friend Neelakanta, blurred by the passage of time, crossed his mind.

His words resonated with her, and the image of the girl's innocent face, gazing at him with wide eyes, stayed with him—forever. It remained a secret between the two.

When Dhaval asked him, 'Weren't you ever afraid that your legacy would end with your children?' Shivaswamy's mind had wandered to Putti at the steps of that Hanuman temple. His legacy had not ended; it had only just been created that day.

20

It was Saturday, and there was to be another meeting with Ravindranath, the lawyer. This meeting was led by Sandeep Kamat from the apartment owners' group. Having learnt their lesson from the previous meeting, they organized this one at Nandana Party Hall near Konanakunte Cross.

Sandeep had messaged everyone that the hall could accommodate roughly a hundred people. Judging by the flurry of messages, the preparations appeared more thorough this time. Proper organization was imperative since the group already consisted of seventy-two owners. Besides that, there were homeowners who had invested in Phase II. The group's size had increased noticeably.

Shivaswamy had an hour to get ready before leaving. He adjusted the curtains of the living room window, fixed a small mirror to the window bars and began to shave. In the adjacent empty plot, four young boys, armed with sticks, were searching for something. One of them held a big stone. Shivaswamy watched them curiously, wondering what they were looking for.

'Over here, over here!' one of them shouted.

The others raced towards him. That's when Shivaswamy saw the snake. It slithered between the towering wall of Anoop Gardenia and the bushes in the empty plot. It wasn't the first time he had seen that snake. In fact, he had noticed it many times before, always at about the same hour when he stood by the window to shave. It would bask in the morning sun, its scales glistening, and then slowly retreat into its burrow.

The snake sensed the boys' presence and slunk away quickly. It reared its head and turned to enter its hole. Just as it was about to disappear, the boy threw the big stone at it.

Stunned, Shivaswamy let out a scream. He wasn't sure if he had cried out 'No!' or just made a sharp noise. The stone crashed into the snake's head. At that very moment, the boys with sticks struck the writhing snake violently. It became motionless. Shivaswamy's heart raced. 'What have you done?' he exclaimed in anguish.

The boys now looked up at his window. 'A big snake, Uncle. It had been evading us for days,' one said triumphantly.

'It had to be killed,' another boy justified.

'You shouldn't have killed it,' said Shivaswamy, staring at the dead snake with pity. The boys, wondering what else could have been done, looked at him in astonishment.

His heart sank. He couldn't muster the energy to shave. Instead, he simply slumped down listlessly on the sofa. He had prepared all the ingredients for breakfast before Teju's call. He was going to make upma. But now, he lacked the desire to make it. The unpleasantness of the episode left a bad taste in his mouth. After a shower, he stepped out for the meeting.

The party hall was upstairs, and the restaurant was downstairs. By the time he arrived, the small hall was packed with people. Contrary to Sandeep Kamat's claim, the hall could not comfortably seat a hundred people. At best, fifty could sit, and another fifty could stand. Considering the seventy-two homeowners present and the people accompanying them, the count easily crossed a hundred and twenty-five.

Shivaswamy managed to find a spot and leaned against a wall. There were three chairs set up on the stage. However, the only person seated was the lawyer, Ravindranath, dressed in a black coat. Shivaswamy's challenge was his height; he couldn't see much beyond the heads and backs of those in front of him. As a result, he frequently had to shuffle, stoop, stand on tiptoe and occasionally change his spot to get a clear view of the stage.

Sandeep Kamat stepped onto the stage, took the microphone and began his introductory speech. He appeared to be in his mid-thirties, and his choice of words and expressions suggested that he was city-bred. He began his speech in a formal tone, predominantly in English, sprinkling in Kannada for emphasis at certain junctures. He concisely outlined the primary purpose of the meeting.

'Many of us have paid the full amount, yet we have not received possession of our houses. What should we do? AP Lakhani Builders seems more focused on completing Phase II than on handing over the houses of Phase I. They are also working on their new project on Airport Road. I understand that some owners here have invested in Phase II. We, the owners of Phase I, genuinely do not wish for your houses to be delayed. Such misunderstandings should not occur. Whether it's Phase I or II, we all belong to the vast community of Anoop Gardenia. However, we, the residents of Phase I, have been facing these challenges after investing our money five years ago. Moreover, whatever is happening to the owners of Phase I could also happen to the owners of Phase II; hence, I seek everyone's sincere cooperation.

'One thing to note is that this is the attitude of most builders in this city. Once they have collected the money and tied us to an obligation, they feel there is no more profit to be gained from us—and they run towards the next profit-making project. What we're experiencing in Anoop Gardenia is a testament to that. It can be confidently said that the same will be the case for Phase II. By the time it's close to completion, their new project on Airport Road will likely be more lucrative and potentially steal their complete focus.

'Now, consider our issues in Phase I. What do they tell us when we approach them? They say, "Come any time, complete your registration and take possession of your homes." However, before we can do that, in addition to the final instalment, we are asked to pay an extra eight lakh rupees. Still, there is no BESCOM or BWSSB connection. The BBMP Corporation hasn't issued the occupancy certificate yet. The design they initially submitted to BBMP doesn't match the actual construction.

'They neither respond to our questions nor answer our calls. They didn't even reply to our letter, warning them of possible legal action. Given these circumstances, what should our next move be? Many of us have invested our life savings and retirement funds into buying homes here. This situation is truly disheartening.

'Today, we are joined by lawyer Ravindranath, a highly esteemed lawyer in south Bengaluru, with over forty years of experience in real estate laws. Let's hear his advice and suggestions. After listening to him, we can deliberate and decide our next steps. It would be best to conclude everything today.'

Then he handed the microphone to Ravindranath and was about to step down from the stage when the lawyer gestured for him to sit on the chair next to him. He obliged. With confidence derived from handling countless such cases, the lawyer took the microphone, tapped it once with his finger to test it, reached for the water bottle on the table in front of him, took a sip and prepared to speak.

Just then, a man from the second row stood up. 'Before the esteemed lawyer speaks, may I request a few moments?' he asked politely. The entire hall began murmuring their annoyance. The lawyer looked at Sandeep Kamat as if to ask who this was. Sandeep was a little irritated. 'I have already explained our problem in detail to Ravindranath sir,' he said, adding, 'You can ask your question during the question-and-answer session after he has given his opinion.'

'No, no. This isn't a question. I have one or two points to add to our current situation, based on what you've just said. These points must be heard before our guest shares his perspectives. His opinions might change based on them,' he said.

Sandeep looked at the lawyer. The lawyer glanced at his watch, then signalled to Sandeep to give the other man a chance. The man approached the stage. Sandeep said, 'Keep it brief. Let's not run over the lawyer's time,' and handed over the microphone.

The man who stepped on the stage appeared to be in his fifties. He was overweight, had a dark complexion and his head was mostly bald, with a few streaks of grey at the sides. 'Namaste. My name is Alluri Venkatagiri Rao. Most of my friends call me Venkat. I am a professor of Mechanical Engineering at GSIT Engineering College. And, like many here, I too am a Phase I flat owner.' His voice resonated with authority, befitting a professor, and was filled with confidence.

'First of all, I would like to thank Mr Ravindranath. My apologies for taking the floor first. I'll get straight to the point. Yesterday, we submitted our application for the registration of the Anoop Gardenia project's owners' association.

'Look, here's a copy of the application. The memorandum of association is also attached. In the list of members, we have included all the owners from Phase I and many names from Phase II who are in contact with us. This is not the final list. Before you all leave this meeting, check if your name is on it. If there are any corrections, let us know.

'To submit the application to the registrar's office, we needed at least seven members' signatures. We, the eight owners, have already done that. Everyone who's signed the application has elected me as the president of the association. No one should be alarmed by this. In our upcoming general body meeting, you can collectively elect the president and the executive committee again.'

No one could figure out where this was heading. But only the lawyer, getting the hint, interjected. 'Excuse me, mister. . .'

Venkatagiri Rao turned in that direction and responded, 'Venkat, sir.'

'Mr Venkat, you must get the deed of declaration from the builder first. Only then can the owners' association be registered,' said the lawyer.

'They have given it, sir,' Venkat put the microphone on the table, retrieved a paper from the file, handed it to the lawyer and then picked up the microphone again.

Ravindranath pulled his reading glasses from his coat pocket and read the paper silently. A hush fell over the meeting. The lawyer then raised his head and glanced at Sandeep Kamat—who, like the rest of the attendees, seemed clueless—before turning to Venkat. 'Shouldn't the other members have also been informed?' he asked.

'We wrote to everyone's address yesterday, sir. Some might have received it today,' replied Venkat.

Unyieldingly, the lawyer asked, 'Aren't you supposed to call a meeting of all the members within twenty-one days of registration to make it official?'

'That, sir, is mentioned in the letter we posted yesterday. The core committee of eight members has already decided the date for the meeting. That's what I intend to announce in this assembly,' Venkat said, turning to the audience, signalling that his conversation with the lawyer was concluded. He then spoke in a grave tone.

'We have many experienced and enthusiastic people in our group. Sandeep Kamat stands as a prime example of that enthusiasm. By now, most of you might be aware that if we take any action against the builder, and if it goes with the seal of the owners' association, it will have value. Therefore, I urge you to attend our association's general body meeting first. We've scheduled it for the twenty-first day from today, which falls on a Saturday, so it is convenient for everyone. The preceding weeks might not be as favourable due to certain festivals.

'In my opinion, it's inappropriate to delve deeper than we already have in this informal meeting today. Please, I hope no one feels disheartened by this statement. I genuinely appreciate the organizers of this meeting. As we will all be neighbours, let's maintain a cordial relationship. Also, if we decide to engage a lawyer after our general body meeting, how could we find someone more suited than Mr Ravindranath?' He then turned to the lawyer and folded his hands in gratitude.

The lawyer was confused. Venkat called seven people on the stage to stir the pot further and introduced them as the executive committee. The lawyer's expression shifted from confusion to irritation. Attempting to mask his annoyance, he stood up and said, 'Alright, it seems there is some internal discord here. Whoever invited me and those speaking now, you all need to sort it out among yourselves before you contact me.' With that, he stood up to leave.

Alluri Venkatagiri Rao, with all the drama he could muster, extended his hand to the lawyer, saying, 'We wasted your time today inadvertently. It's not Kamat's fault; he's one of our eager and young members.' He handed the lawyer an envelope and said, 'Sir, this is a small gift from our association. It contains a thousand rupees. Consider it a token of appreciation.' The lawyer took the envelope and tucked it into his pocket as he walked away.

The attendees sat as if they were watching a movie. Shivaswamy gazed in surprise at the people on stage and those around him. Soon, the hall broke into mini groups and began discussing the entire saga. The commotion in the meeting hall had returned. Sandeep Kamat, who had been the WhatsApp group's leader, sat on the stage like a statue, unable to decide whether to step down or stay put.

In the next few minutes, the ambience of the party hall changed dramatically. Owners of Phase 1 were invited to fill in their details on a form. People began to queue up, and Shivaswamy stood in one of them. Within fifteen minutes, it was his turn. His address was mentioned as that of his rented house in Ghaziabad. He crossed it out and wrote his current address in the adjacent column. They were collecting signatures from everyone on another paper. Shivaswamy held the paper in his hand and wondered about its contents. Without his reading glasses, the small letters appeared blurry. 'It's the association's bylaws, sir,' said one of the seven sages of the 'suddenly conjured' association.

As if standing in a temple queue, receiving *theertham* from one person, *akshathe* from another and *prasadam* from yet another, the people in the line checked the address, took a copy of the GB meeting, signed the bylaws and moved on. No one posed any questions. Shivaswamy, too, signed and moved on.

He stood at the door, slightly confused. He hadn't known what to expect when he arrived, and now he couldn't fully grasp what had transpired. He had hoped to meet a few people his age here. While most people in the hall appeared to be in their thirties or forties, some older people were also present. Whom should he approach? The thought made him feel awkward. Initiating conversations had never been his strength. Moreover, it seemed most people had come with someone. He had come alone.

Two men, perhaps in their forties, standing close by, were engaged in a conversation that caught his attention. 'There's no doubt that Venkat and his gang are on AP Lakhani's side. Will they ever fight for us?'

Curious, Shivaswamy turned to speak with them. However, upon realizing that he had overheard them, they, visibly unsettled, quickly moved away from him.

The only friend he had made through the home-buying process was Kumar Gowda. Strangely, he was nowhere in sight. Another acquaintance was Sandeep Kamat. He, too, was nowhere to be seen. Perhaps he had already left by then. How could he still be there after such humiliation?

The clamour in that small hall suffocated him. Before he left, he called Harikrishna Bhat from Ghaziabad to verify his address. Harikrishna mentioned that he always received mail from Anoop Gardenia, indicating that the address in their records was correct.

'But this is being handled by the association, not by Anoop Gardenia,' Shivaswamy said. In response, Harikrishna Bhat remarked, 'If they possess the addresses and phone numbers of all the buyers, then who else could have provided that?' Shivaswamy felt Harikrishna had a point.

Then, in one corner of the stage, he finally spotted Kumar Gowda, who was deeply engrossed in a discussion with Alluri Venkat. Their heads were bowed as if they were discussing a secret. Another person was with them. Shivaswamy felt happy on seeing Kumar. Intent on saying hello before leaving, he made his way onto the stage. He was also interested in getting acquainted with Venkat.

He approached them, smiled, and said, 'Hello, Kumar.' They turned towards him. None of them seemed pleased with his arrival. Kumar, forcing a smile, greeted him. 'Hello, sir, how are you?' Without waiting for a response, he quickly introduced the man beside him, 'Sir, this is my friend, Sudhindra. His flat is on the same floor as yours.' He then said to Sudhindra, 'Take Mr Shivaswamy downstairs for coffee. I'll join you there in five minutes.' Sudhindra, evidently reluctant to leave the conversation for Shivaswamy's company, showed his displeasure through his facial expressions. Venkat, on the other hand, didn't even bother to look at Shivaswamy.

Shivaswamy's face fell. 'Kumar, it's alright. I'll catch up another time,' he said, then turned to leave. The disappointment in his voice touched Kumar. He signalled Sudhindra with his eyes to go with Shivaswamy. Sudhindra reluctantly joined Shivaswamy. They descended the stairs and headed to the Darshini below. After buying coffee, they stood around a distant table. Sudhindra had no interest in talking to Shivaswamy and sipped his coffee silently. Shivaswamy asked a few friendly questions to break the awkwardness but received only curt, uninterested, one-word responses from him. He didn't even attempt to find out who Shivaswamy was.

'Sudhindra, what do you think? Did our problem get solved, or did it get more complicated?' Shivaswamy asked.

Sudhindra, suspecting they might be overheard, glanced around subtly. Then, as if about to say something, he shrugged his shoulders and fell silent. Shivaswamy didn't ask anything further. Even after they finished their coffee, Kumar hadn't joined them. Sudhindra, eager to rejoin Kumar and Venkat, headed back upstairs. Shivaswamy, however, felt no further desire to meet Kumar again. The humiliation had clouded his mind.

As Shivaswamy rode his scooter back home, he was preoccupied with the day's events. From Kumar's behaviour, he couldn't help but suspect that he might be one of the seven flat owners who had joined Venkat. He felt frustrated as he had understood nothing at the meeting. Suddenly, he thought that maybe this was how Sanjana felt in her classrooms during her school days.

When he got home, it was half past one in the afternoon, and he was very hungry. He hadn't eaten anything since morning. He had prepared everything to make upma earlier, but the incident with the snake had led to an unintentional fast. He decided to cook the upma now and eat.

When he opened the gate, he noticed the same boys from the morning again standing in the empty plot. Now, they were dressed in white dhotis with towels draped over their shoulders. Curious, he moved closer. The snake cremation rituals were underway. A young boy with matted hair and holy ash smeared on his forehead and elbows chanted mantras at the top of his lungs as the priest. He did not appear much older than the boys who had killed the snake.

On closer inspection, it became evident that they had constructed a makeshift altar using debris from the construction site at Anoop Gardenia. The altar was made up of four broken bricks with wood scraps heaped on top. On this structure lay the lifeless body of the snake, which was being anointed with turmeric, vermillion and rice and given a *kshirabhisheka*—a milk bath. Nearby, a mud pot was placed, and inside a plastic cover, were red oleander and marigold flowers. These were presumably plucked from the same fence where the snake had earlier been spotted. The snake's head was completely crushed, and its body lay in pieces.

A boy who recognized him glanced in his direction and whispered, 'The snake we killed is a cobra, uncle. If we don't cremate it properly, it will seek revenge.'

'Wasn't it a rat snake?' Shivaswamy asked. The boy didn't answer.

Shivaswamy took another look at the snake's fragmented body. The unfortunate creature, deprived of a peaceful end and lacking ears to hear the mantras, lay not in vengeance but awaiting its transformation into ashes, ready to dissolve into the *pancha bhuta*—the five essential elements of cosmic creation. The fragrant smoke from the incense stick and camphor wafted through the air, touched the snake's body, and reached Shivaswamy's breath.

The boy priest didn't like Shivaswamy's presence. He turned to the boy who had spoken to him, looked at him intently, and screamed, 'Why are you talking while the pooja is in progress?' His voice held the impatience of an elderly priest running short of time.

21

Mondays are important days in the world of corporates. After a calm and deserted weekend, coffee machines gurgle like excited dragons, spewing forth the fuel to propel another week of activity. Managers find themselves deeply immersed in weekly planning. Teams such as finance, purchasing, sales, marketing, HR and others prepare tons of reports about the past week and forecasts for the current week, which they present respectfully to their senior management. These reports burn like sacrificial offerings in management meetings, and their smoke has different effects on different people. The zeal for work peaks on Monday mornings, then gradually dwindles and settles on the valley floor by Friday evenings.

That Monday, Shivaswamy was extremely busy in his office cabin. There was a knock on the door. Since Anuradha had already come and gone ten times by then, always knocking before entering, he assumed it was her and gestured for her to come in without lifting his head from the computer.

'Good morning, Shivaswamy,' Dhaval Thakkar's voice resounded in the room.

Shivaswamy stood up in surprise. 'Oh, sir, it's you! I thought it was Anuradha.'

'Do I now have the good fortune of being Anuradha, Shivaswamy?' Dhaval laughed heartily. Whatever the joke meant, Shivaswamy joined him nervously all the same.

Earlier in the morning, he had called Anita to ask her what time Dhaval would be arriving at his office. As expected, she didn't know but promised to find out and call him back. Now, the MD was standing right in front of him.

'Come in, sir. Please have a seat.' Shivaswamy pulled a chair in front of his desk.

Dhaval looked particularly jovial, dressed in black trousers and a pale-yellow shirt. He also seemed to have had a fresh haircut and got his beard trimmed. A subtle smile played on his face. Instead of entering, he paused by the door.

'Shivaswamy?'

'Yes, sir.'

'Let's go out for lunch. You haven't brought your lunch box from home, have you? Otherwise, your wife won't let you back in with it unemptied,' he said, his eyes twinkling.

'No, sir, I haven't. My wife is in America for my daughter's pregnancy.'

'Oh, right . . . you mentioned that.' Dhaval didn't enter but stood holding the door. Shivaswamy wished he would come in and sit so he could close the door. Otherwise, his loud voice might carry across the entire floor.

Glancing at his watch, Dhaval said, 'I'll spend a few minutes with Ravi and Prabhu. After that, I need to visit a friend at Infinity Finance in the adjacent building. He's a family friend, and I promised to meet him today. We can go for lunch once I come back after meeting him. What kind of food do you prefer?'

Shivaswamy hesitated, unsure about how to respond. He rarely dined out. On the infrequent occasions he did, apart from Shanti Sagar's plate meals, which included rice, sambar, two chapatis and curry; he seldom explored any others. When his children were younger in Ghaziabad, their birthdays would be celebrated with an occasional meal out. However, they mostly relished regular north Indian fare like paratha, naan, kulcha, fried rice and pulao. Their neighbourhood lacked diverse restaurants, especially international cuisines like Mexican, Italian, Thai or Vietnamese, which were commonplace in Bengaluru. Even if such options had been available, he wasn't one to seek them out. The idea of travelling to Noida or Delhi just for a meal was also foreign to his family.

'Any kind would do, sir,' he replied.

'Alright.' Dhaval nodded. 'I will ask Anita to reserve a table somewhere nice,' he said and closed the door behind him. As Shivaswamy had suspected, their conversation echoed across the entire floor. He couldn't help but imagine that Prabhu, from his office cabin, had his eyes and ears trained his way.

He soon immersed himself in his work again. Anuradha came in and went out a few times, her eyes sparkling with curiosity.

While many in the office had heard of the MD, most had only seen him in photographs. Dhaval wasn't just anyone who would visit the office, and most of the employees here hardly had any direct dealings with the central office. Given that Dhaval was standing by the door, sharing hearty laughs and then inviting Shivaswamy to join him for lunch, it was quite intriguing news.

Thanks to the age and position gap, none of the colleagues dared ask Shivaswamy about it directly. Everyone tried to fish for details from Anuradha. But what did she know? She tried to ask Shivaswamy but could not. He did not say anything either. Now, there was a tangible witness to the claim that he was 'an old acquaintance of the MD'.

In the afternoon, Shivaswamy sat down in the back seat of the white Audi A4 with Dhaval. The luxury car moved gracefully out of the premises. Chandru, the driver, handled it with utmost caution. But the journey was short, lasting just five minutes. They turned from MG Road to Church Street and stopped in front of Coconut Grove, a Kerala-style restaurant with red terracotta walls.

They entered the restaurant and chose a table. A canopy, shaped as if it had been raised from the trunk of a coconut tree, shaded their table.

'Two Kingfisher Premiums to start with,' Dhaval ordered. He turned to Shivaswamy and asked, 'You like beer, don't you?'

'Sir, I must return to work,' Shivaswamy replied hesitantly.

'Don't worry, Shivaswamy. You'll be fine by the time you head back,' said Dhaval. 'And once you're back, don't fire anyone.' He chuckled. Shivaswamy smiled.

'If I come here and don't have a beer, my dear friend Preetam's spirit will curse me. This was his favourite place. We have been here many times. Back then, there was no office on Dickenson Road. We used to come from afar just for lunch. The last time I came with him, I was about your age. After that, it's only now that I am here.' Dhaval's voice was filled with nostalgia.

Then he rose slowly, said he'd return from the restroom, and left. From his chair, Shivaswamy surveyed the surroundings. The seated patrons and the languages they were speaking felt foreign to him. In his college days in Kolar, he'd occasionally venture to Bengaluru with friends for a day out. The travel time by bus would be around an hour and fifteen minutes. They would arrive in the morning, watch a movie, dine at a restaurant, roam around the city, and catch a bus back home in the evening. The MG Road, Brigade Road, Commercial Street and Church Street he once knew had transformed entirely. They now stood apart, resembling ambassadors representing their homeland in a foreign territory, distinct from the local essence.

Dhaval returned to the table. As if anticipating his return, a young man in a green shirt and white dhoti brought over the beer bottles, popped the caps and poured them into glasses. Following him, another server approached with a tray. On it were a gleaming white appam and several types of chutneys neatly arranged on a banana leaf. He placed them on the table and stood back with his hands folded.

Both clinked their glasses and took a big gulp of the cold beer. How many years had it been since Shivaswamy had last drunk? During his time in Ghaziabad, he would occasionally go out on Friday evenings with friends from the department, like Choudhuri and others. After crossing the age of forty-five, thanks to health issues and family responsibilities—his own and those of his friends—the frequency of those outings diminished. Eventually, they stopped. So, the cold beer felt particularly refreshing. Similarly, since he hadn't tasted Kerala-style appam in many years, that felt special too.

'Shivaswamy?'

'Yes, sir.'

'I thought a lot about what we talked about last week. That's why I've been dying to see you. I even considered coming to your home yesterday.' He grinned.

Shivaswamy thought to himself in surprise, *Oh dear! Weren't there enough strange events yesterday? The owners' meeting, the snake's death and rituals . . . Was this the only thing left to complete the circuit?*

'Why so anxious, my friend? Are you worried I might just drop by your home and make you work?'

'No, sir, certainly not. I'll invite you over once my family returns. It's a good thing you didn't come yesterday. Did I mention the flat I bought and the ongoing issues with it? There was a meeting with the owners' association for that yesterday. I was busy there for quite some time,' replied Shivaswamy.

'Ah, yes. You told me about your house-buying problem before. Where does it stand now?'

Shivaswamy narrated the story up to that point briefly.

'Oh dear. This seems like a never-ending saga for you,' he said with sympathy. He paused momentarily before continuing, 'In a way, I'm relieved. As long as that problem exists, you'll be around for me.' Then he laughed again. Shivaswamy laughed too.

'Who is your builder?'

'AP Lakhani, sir.'

Dhaval was silent for a moment. Then, chuckling, he remarked, 'Your stars appear to be severely misaligned, Shivaswamy. You always seem to stumble upon Gujarati businessmen, don't you?'

Shivaswamy laughed too and changed the subject. 'Sir, you said you gave a thought to what we talked about last week.'

Dhaval became serious. He set his glass down on the table and said, 'Hmm, about my thoughts . . . Last week, you mentioned something about this being a family feud.' He paused and looked intently at him.

Shivaswamy stammered, 'That's not what I meant, sir . . .'

'No, no . . . you were right. You guessed its source without me telling you anything about my family. Listen to me carefully . . . this "family" is a strange thing. It starts with "we" but eventually ends with "I". Look at the irony of it all, Shivaswamy. We have children to expand our family. We find partners for those children, doubling our family. Now, besides my son and daughter, I have a son-in-law and a daughter-in-law. And do they come alone? No, they bring their families too.

'As the external family grows, the internal one shrinks. In the end, only "I" will remain. Five years ago, when Sumati was alive, "we" at least referred to the two of us. Now, the "we" inside me is just "me". If even that disappears and when I shout "we", and the sound dissolves in air without a single echo, it would mean I've become a ghost. Those days are not far off,' he said with a dry laugh.

'True, sir. It's a cycle. We start alone and end alone.'

'Does it happen to you too?'

'It happens to everyone, sir. We often become possessive about our children, and this is the result. Both my children are now far away. Whether they're close or far, they need to move beyond our realm, and we must allow it.'

'I made it worse, Shivaswamy,' Dhaval stood up and clutched his waist. A waiter approached and stopped in front of him. Dhaval ordered two plates of mushroom pepper fry. On the table, the appams remained almost untouched. Shivaswamy had taken a few mouthfuls from his plate, while Dhaval hadn't tasted his at all. Shivaswamy felt that if they ordered anything else, one plate would suffice. However, he was too embarrassed to suggest sharing a plate with the company's managing director.

Dhaval held his waist and said, 'I've made another mistake, Shivaswamy. It was a grave act of selfishness, and no one will forgive me for it. I loved my company more than my children, my wife and my parents. To me, nurturing it felt more pleasurable than raising my children.

'Every time I talked about this, Preetam would recount the story of Paul Gauguin, a painter from the previous century. Alongside his passion for the company, Preetam had another obsession: reading. He shared countless tales with me.

'That painter was originally a stockbroker who supported his family, but when he was bitten by the painting bug, he left his wife and children, settled down on an island and painted incessantly. He rose to great fame but never saw his family again until his death. My story echoes his, as does Preetam's. Like that painter, we didn't run to any island yet crafted that same isolation right here. Even when my children were in the adjacent room, they felt worlds apart. I didn't know how to bridge the gap, and neither did they.

'I should have changed. I ought to have stepped back from my world for their sake. But I didn't. Now look at my story! First, the children slipped out of my gravity, and now, they demand the company. What's left for me to live for "in the name of"?'

Shivaswamy put his glass down and looked at Dhaval. He wondered if it was possible to live like this. The feeling that you couldn't break free from something you had created! Like a child who builds a sandcastle on the seashore, praying that the waves won't wash it away. In defiance, he lies on his back to the sea, as if challenging its might.

'Let go, sir,' said Shivaswamy. Dhaval, without breaking his gaze, sat back down.

'Let go, sir. You can't hold onto this any longer. There is a vachana by Allama Prabhu: "O fools are they—who cling to a lifeless body, who compare the incomparable, who adorn the body, which is but a headless corpse!" Your company has become a headless corpse to you. Don't continue adorning it. It's pointless. In the end, it will only bring you disgust. Let go.'

'Shivaswamy, recite that verse again,' Dhaval said, sitting back in his chair.

Shivaswamy did.

'Whose is it?'

'It's a vachana by Allama Prabhu.'

'I've heard of Basavanna. But I haven't heard of Allama Prabhu.'

'He was a contemporary of Basavanna, a mystic saint and a renowned poet who lived about nine hundred years ago.'

'I understood the first line: "clinging to a lifeless body". The next line was unclear to me.'

'"Who compare the incomparable," Shivaswamy recited. 'You are juxtaposing the living with the non-living. A stone remains a stone, and a cheek remains a cheek. The difference between kissing a chiselled cheek and a living cheek is as stark as the divide between day and night. This is not right, sir.'

'Oh, my God! I've spent my entire life there, Shivaswamy. And you bring this up now? How heartless you've become!' Dhaval sighed deeply, putting his elbows on the table and resting his chin on his hands. His glasses slipped off his nose, and his face was as pained as his words.

Shivaswamy realized that speaking any further would only cause more sorrow. 'I'll be back from the restroom, sir,' he announced, rising from his seat. There was no urgency, but he needed to step away.

The beer he had drunk after so many years felt pleasant and provided respite against the scorching midday sun. When he stepped out of the toilet, he looked around. At one large table, nearly fifteen to twenty people were eating, engaged in animated conversation. They might all be from the same company. At other tables, smaller groups were gathered, young families with small children, and occasionally clusters of two or three men or women. Waiters dressed in Kerala-style dhotis and green shirts swiftly moved from table to table.

As Shivaswamy returned to the table, Dhaval was still sitting in the same position, buried deep in his thoughts. He felt a surge of pity. Dhaval's face had crumpled like a flower petal crushed underfoot, reacting to the harshness of Allama's voice—a tone that felt spoken by someone other than the obedient and soft-spoken Shivaswamy. His age he had managed to conceal until now suddenly became visible. The weight of his past life seemed to resurface.

'Shivaswamy?'

'Yes, sir.'

'I have sacrificed everything for this company! Do you think it was all in vain?' he asked.

'Oh no, sir. When did I say that?' asked Shivaswamy in surprise.

'You say one thing before urinating and then backtrack right after!'

Shivaswamy laughed out loud. Only Dhaval had said those words seriously.

'Sir, I never claimed your manner of living was incorrect. Who am I, after all, to judge you? Isn't it the same as the story of the painter you told me, of the Buddha who departed from his wife and child in the dead of night? If you had questioned him whether imparting wisdom to the world held more significance than cherishing his own family, what would have been his response? I doubt he sat in the stillness, weighing such considerations before his departure.'

'You mean I shouldn't analyse the past?'

'Yes. Simply let it go,' he said.

Dhaval appeared somewhat relieved. Without heeding Shivaswamy's objections, he ordered another beer for both of them. Shivaswamy, however, only drank half of this second glass. Soon, the food arrived. The plate was laden with Malabar parotta, avial, Chettinad masala, thick Kerala rice, sambar and rich yoghurt. Having filled their stomachs with appam and beer, the two seniors left a generous portion of the scrumptious meal on the table and rose.

On the way back, silence prevailed in the car. Perhaps they were both lost in similar thoughts; they rested their heads back against the seat in contemplation. When the car turned from MG Road to Dickenson Road, Dhaval turned to him.

'Shivaswamy?'

'Yes, sir.'

'What path have you taken? What fortune have you gained? What have you lost?'

Shivaswamy smiled. 'To answer those questions, we'd need to drink another two beers, sir.'

'I'm ready.'

'I'll tell you someday when we meet again, sir. Don't expect much. I'm not a highwayman. I never dared anything. Besides raising children like all creatures do, I haven't done much worth preserving. I'm working to resolve the housing issue in my lifetime so that my children won't inherit any debt once I am gone.'

The car stopped in front of the office. Dhaval was still seated. Shivaswamy got out.

Dhaval shook his hand and said, 'Let's meet again this week. Please set aside some time.'

Shivaswamy nodded.

'Shivaswamy, it's okay to go home. It's already four o'clock. Don't go on your scooter. Take the office car.'

Shivaswamy nodded and walked in through the office gate. Dhaval's car drove away.

He walked in with a sense of unease, even though the effect of the beer had already waned. He chose the stairs to his floor, worried that someone in the lift might detect the scent of beer on him.

By the door to Raviraj's office, Raviraj and Prabhu were engaged in conversation. Shivaswamy gave them a fleeting smile as he continued to his cabin.

'Look! Shivaswamy sir is coming from a party,' Prabhu teased him with a playful wink. Shivaswamy turned and smiled back. Raviraj too was sniggering—a kind of gentle laughter that

Shivaswamy hadn't seen from him before. A sudden warmth welled up in him at that moment. Raviraj's smiling face seemed so innocent. He wanted to say something to him, but the words eluded him. For some unknown reason, thoughts of his daughter Sanjana surfaced. He slowly made his way to his room.

There were plenty of tasks to complete. By the time he was done, it was already past seven in the evening. He got on the metro and headed home.

22

When Revathi called, he was washing dishes after dinner. It was around ten at night. Revathi sounded panicked. Sanju had started bleeding that morning and was in pain. The delivery was still a month away. Arun had taken her to the hospital immediately.

Shivaswamy grew anxious. 'Did she bleed a lot? Was she tired?' he inquired.

'Not much; just spotting. She's really scared,' Revathi replied.

'Oh, God!' he exclaimed in distress. They shared a moment of silence.

'You should go to the hospital too. It would comfort her,' he said.

'Arun said it wasn't needed,' she replied. 'For some reason, she didn't want it either.'

The image of his daughter's frightened face occupied his mind. 'Stay calm. Don't panic. Everything will be alright,' he tried reassuring his wife. 'Once they return from the hospital, call me, no matter how late. I'll be waiting.'

'Did you light the lamps in the pooja room this evening?' Revathi asked.

Shivaswamy didn't respond. He had lit the lamps and offered prayers in the morning, but not in the evening.

'Put aside five hundred rupees for Dharmasthala,' she said. She had unwavering faith in the deity of Dharmasthala, Sri Manjunatheshwara Swamy. Revathi's custom was to earmark money as an offering to the god during unexpected challenges and to offer it to the temple later.

Hanging up, he sat down on the sofa for a while.

He went to the pooja room to light the lamps as Revathi had instructed. Hesitating at the door, he recalled that he had drunk alcohol that day for the first time in many years. He proceeded to the bathroom for a shower. Too impatient to wait for the water to warm up, he bathed in cold water. Afterwards, he returned to the pooja room, lit the ghee lamps, and placed a five-hundred-rupee note before the deity as an offering. Then, he sat down to meditate but found that his mind remained restless no matter how long he tried. His anxiety grew with each passing moment. Eventually, he returned to the bedroom and called his wife. It was already midnight.

'Have they returned?'

'No,' she replied.

'Call Arun,' he said. Revathi called Arun's mobile from the landline phone at home. But he didn't answer.

'Ayyō shivanē,' Shivaswamy muttered.

Revathi tried to reassure him. 'It's just a little spotting; don't panic too much. It's the eighth month. Delivery can happen. We just need to be cautious. I know this isn't labour pain. It will still take a few more days.'

'What are you doing?' he asked.

'I don't feel like doing anything. I need to cut vegetables and start cooking. Instead, I'm sitting here, reciting prayers. I thought of talking to Teju, but he's in class. I don't want to disturb him,' she said.

'No,' he said. 'Call me as soon as they come back.'

He fetched the *Shivastotra* from the pooja room and began chanting it while seated on the sofa. He then read twenty vachanas from his brown book.

Then he turned off the lights and lay down. He put his mobile phone right next to his pillow. Sleep eluded him. A headache was soon brewing. The dim light from the pooja room gently illuminated the bedroom. In that soft glow, the photos on the wall were faintly visible. In one, he and Revathi sat on chairs. Behind them stood Arun, Sanju and Teju, with Sanju in the middle. Sanju's left hand rested on Shivaswamy's left shoulder. Teju, as he usually appeared in photos, was gazing at the camera with serious eyes. The picture was taken on Sanju's wedding day.

Next to it was a photo of the siblings, their faces brimming with innocence. Sanju was a young girl attending PU College, and Teju was a high-school boy. They stood in front of the stairs at the BEL quarters, dressed in trousers and shirts. Shivaswamy rose and positioned himself in front of that photo, reflecting on the beauty of her smile.

At one in the morning, he reached for the phone to call again. However, he hesitated, thinking that calling too often would worry Revathi even more. Despite his efforts, he couldn't quell his anxiety. Restless and sleepless, he paced the house for three quarters of an hour, moving from the bedroom to the living room, then to the kitchen and back again. All the while, the mobile phone remained clutched in his hand.

When it rang, it was two in the morning. 'Has she arrived?' he asked as soon as he picked up the phone.

'She just got back,' Revathi responded. 'She's fine. There's no need to worry. They did an ultrasound scan. The baby is healthy. They said not to panic if there's occasional spotting. She needs to ensure she doesn't strain herself too much.'

'Let me speak to her,' he said. The next moment, it was Sanjana on the line.

'Appa, what's the time there? Why are you still awake? I'm alright. Sleep now, or you'll be tired tomorrow,' she chided. Her tone was comforting to him.

After the call, Shivaswamy realized his head was pounding badly. The idea of going to work in the morning felt daunting. He began to draft an email to Shyamala, indicating he wouldn't be in the office, but hesitated to send it. How would the office view it if he frequently took leaves due to health concerns? Even as the HR manager, the rules that applied to probationary employees applied to him as well. Wouldn't the company regret hiring someone over sixty and retired from the public sector?

Ultimately, he chose not to send the email. He simply shut his laptop and returned to bed. He finally fell asleep around five in the morning. But at eight o'clock, the newspaper delivery man woke him up by ringing the doorbell four times to collect his monthly payment.

23

'You know what his problem is, Shivaswamy sir . . . ?' Prabhu flicked the ash off his cigarette, took a long puff, and then carefully exhaled the smoke so that it wouldn't blow in their direction. It spiralled up into the sky and dissolved in the air.

The two of them stood on the terrace garden in the office. Around them, rows of potted plants, each with identical, evenly trimmed foliage and flowers of the same colour, looked like schoolchildren in uniform lined up for morning prayer.

Prabhu continued in an accusatory tone, 'The problem with our MD is that all his roads lead to the past. While he might have abandoned the future, he's also absent in the present. I'm not sure of the psychology behind this, sir. I wonder if I'll be the same when I reach his age. He gets stuck to one opinion and doesn't let go. He has a certain kind of attitude too—the kind that thinks, "If it's old, it must be good."

'He can't possibly adapt to the software industry because software is about the present, and he's turned his back on it. You know how elders avoid chickpeas—specifically kabuli chana—fearing they won't digest it? It's similar to that. He has a deep-rooted belief that if he can't digest something, it's not digestible for others either.'

Shivaswamy laughed. It was unclear if he was included in the category of 'elders'.

'It's true that we shouldn't only look at the road behind us. But if we only look forward without considering the road we've already travelled, that can also lead us off course; right, Prabhu?' said Shivaswamy.

Prabhu glanced at him out of the corner of his eye, wondering if he was being sarcastic. Shivaswamy, unbothered by the look, continued to sip his tea from the china cup.

'Is that what our MD sahib thinks about us?'

'No. That's just my opinion. The work you're doing for this division—building and growing—Dhaval Thakkar did that many decades ago, didn't he? He built this company from scratch. I agree with you; software and logistics are different industries. But isn't the essence of building something the same?' Over the past five months, Shivaswamy had learnt how to engage him in conversation, guiding him in the desired direction. A good lad, intelligent, but somewhat impulsive.

Prabhu lit another cigarette. 'When have we ever shown him disrespect? Even today, no one else's word holds sway in this company. But if he fosters such a possessive mindset and believes that he alone charted the right course and others should merely follow it, then what will the future of the company be? Shouldn't he pave the way if it needs to evolve with the times?

'I understand he might be close to you now. All of us have noticed your camaraderie. My words might very well reach him through you, and I'm not afraid of that. Whether you convey them or not, I needed to speak my mind.'

The words that had been unvoiced for the past five months had finally emerged. It appeared as though he believed that if the intent of his words was to scorch, then they should scorch thoroughly.

Having expressed himself so candidly, he avoided making eye contact. He left his half-smoked cigarette in the ashtray, distanced himself from Shivaswamy, walked over to the wall, and leaned against the parapet of the terrace garden.

Shivaswamy put his teacup on the table, walked over and stood beside him. From there, MG Road looked vibrant. Yet the street was choked with vehicles, lined bumper to bumper. The metro bridge hovered above the road, like an archway.

'Patience, Prabhu,' he said. 'When a leaf isn't yet detached from its tree, that means it's still fulfilling a purpose. What purpose it serves might be unknown to the surrounding leaves, to the tree, or even to that leaf itself. Everything has its time.

'All we can do is wait. We do not understand the logic of time. Patience is the only solution. I know my words won't remain just with you and will reach others. At this juncture, secrets don't hold much value. So, I guess I'm saying this to you and your friends as well: patience is the only way forward.'

Prabhu did not look at him.

24

Within a day of speaking to Prabhu, and as a sign that the matter had reached his larger network in the company, Shivaswamy received a call from Shyamala. 'How have you been, Shivaswamy? Is everything going well?' she asked casually before guiding the conversation to its real purpose. 'Dhriti wishes to see you. When can you make it here?'

He glanced at the clock. It was two-thirty. Lately, such requests from the head office had been taking up his afternoons unexpectedly, so he had started coming into the office half an hour early to complete urgent tasks in the morning. 'Shyamala, can I come tomorrow?'

'No, I'd appreciate it if you could come today. If you leave now, you might get here by three. Dhriti has specifically put aside some time in her schedule to meet with you today,' she said.

They had already made all the decisions. The meeting had been scheduled. He had no choice but to leave immediately. There was little else to say for him except, 'Okay, I'll be there.'

Shyamala told him, 'I've arranged for Ratan to pick you up. He's waiting downstairs.' Ratan was Raviraj's driver, which was also part of the plan. 'The MD isn't in the office today. Let me know if you have any work with him, and I'll handle it. Stay available here for the rest of the day,' she said.

The message to him was clear: he shouldn't disclose his arrival to Dhaval Thakkar. His daughter-in-law wanted to meet him while her father-in-law was away from the office. Acknowledging the order over the phone, he discussed outstanding tasks with Anuradha and Sudhakar before stepping out. Sudhakar, who had recently transitioned from the head office to this branch as a manager, reported to him. He was five years Anuradha's senior. Dhaval had followed through on his promise to send a manager from the headquarters to lighten Shivaswamy's workload.

If Dhriti wished to meet him without her father-in-law's knowledge, wouldn't it have been easier for her to come to this branch and sit across from him? Whenever she desired, she could have simply walked in, offering no prior intimation, and declared, 'I need to speak with you,' effectively pinning him to his chair. This branch was Raviraj's empire. Yet, she had chosen to summon him there.

Inside the lift, Shivaswamy's thoughts ran deep. Ever since joining this company, 'the owner's ego' showcased new shades of human behaviour to him. In his former government-run firm, it was about power. But here, it was about ego—*an ego that proclaimed: What you believe is yours isn't really yours; it's mine.*

Dhriti held no official role in the company. She neither participated in its proceedings nor showed any inclination to begin. Still, she competed with the MD to hold the entire organization in her grip. She played dice without showing her hand. In Shivaswamy's eyes, the elderly father-in-law and the young daughter-in-law seemed to be two sides of the same coin.

Perhaps there was another aspect to her summoning him. If she had chosen to meet at the branch office, she would've been the queen of that branch alone. But by calling him to the head office, she had positioned herself as the empress of the entire DT Group. *Even if the company changes from Dhaval to Dhriti, its name will still remain the DT Group, won't it? Such is the nature of a family business*; he mused with a smile.

When Ratan, who couldn't speak Kannada, conversed in Hindi and left Shivaswamy at the head office, it was already five minutes past three. While the father, born in Gujarat and raised in Bengaluru, had a driver from Mandya in Karnataka, the son, born and raised solely in Bengaluru, had a driver from Gujarat. Shivaswamy recalled what Anuradha had mentioned a few days ago. After Dhriti had joined the family, she seemed to prefer getting workers for chores, assistance, cooking and everything else from her hometown, Jamnagar. Perhaps even Raviraj's driver was from there.

When the car entered the office gates, Shyamala's call came through. 'We are in the conference room on the first floor. Please come here directly,' she instructed. Shyamala's office was on the first floor, while the MD's was on the fourth. Dhaval's car wasn't in its usual parking spot that day. As she had mentioned, he hadn't come to the office. From the way she emphasized 'come directly to the first floor,' it was clear that Anita should be kept out of the loop too.

As Shivaswamy entered the well-lit conference room, he saw Shyamala and Dhriti sitting opposite each other at a square table that could seat twenty people. When they heard the door open, they both turned towards him. Shyamala Menon wore a green saree and had her hair loose, in the traditional Kerala style. Dhriti wore light blue jeans and a pink kurta. She was tall and slender, mirroring Raviraj in height. He had met her only once, on the day he had joined the company five months ago, so her face had nearly faded from his memory. When Shivaswamy entered, Dhriti pointed to the chair next to Shyamala and asked him to sit down. Although Shyamala smiled and tried to make conversation, Dhriti remained serious.

Dhriti spoke swiftly and fluently, and the urban influence was evident in her words and expressions. She had developed a laser-sharp gaze that seemed to pierce through the person she spoke to.

'How is your family, Mr Swamy?' she asked. 'I heard everyone is in America, and you are here alone. It must be tough for you to be away from them all.'

Shivaswamy spoke about his family but did not delve into the real reason he had stayed back. She listened intently, her elbow resting on the table and her left hand cupping her cheek.

Then, she got straight to the point. 'Mr Swamy, my father-in-law is quite fond of you.'

Shivaswamy wondered whether her choice of 'father-in-law' over 'MD' was a deliberate attempt to steer the conversation to a more personal level. Given her lack of an official title in the company, referring to him as 'father-in-law' seemed more fitting than 'MD'.

'That's the friendship that comes with age,' he laughed.

'That might be one reason,' she said with a smile. 'But I can't say it's the only one. Aren't you younger than him?' For the first time, Shivaswamy saw a smile on her face.

'Yes,' he smiled back, 'But I'm the oldest among us who are around him, right? So, he wants to talk to me sometimes.'

'I find it comforting, Mr Swamy. My father-in-law's circle of friends is tiny. He was very fond of Vimal's father, Preetam Jain. You must have already heard much about them in this company,' she said.

That Dhaval and Preetam Jain were close friends was so well-known in the company that he had heard it many times. The amusing tales of their friendly disagreements always entertained the company. Even a decade after Preetam's passing, their stories remained in circulation. Handed down from veteran employees to newcomers, these spicy tales never lost their charm.

Just then, there was a knock on the door. It was Abhay Chand, a manager who reported to Shyamala. He needed to discuss something with her and called her out for a moment. As Shyamala stood up, Dhriti said, 'Shyamala, it's okay; you can leave. You don't need to come back. Shivaswamy will come to your desk after our conversation is over.' Shyamala exited the room. This timely departure made Shivaswamy wonder if this was also planned.

'How is the company doing, Mr Swamy?' she asked seriously, looking intently at him.

Shivaswamy felt uneasy at her gaze. What could he say about how the company was doing? Was she asking about the work in his branch specifically?

'We are working on implementing some policy-related changes, especially in retaining our talent. This is not just an issue here, but for every software company in Bengaluru,' he said. She interrupted him as he was thinking about elaborating on some HR improvements at the Dickenson Road branch.

'Not the branch; how is our DT Group doing?'

Shivaswamy felt that she had called him here with the strong intention of insulting him. He did not know what to say.

Watching him struggle to speak, she asked, 'Why, didn't my father-in-law share the details with you?'

Her sarcasm stung Shivaswamy. Yet, with restraint, he replied, 'No. He doesn't share anything he feels is unnecessary to share with me.'

His words struck her. 'That's not what I meant . . .' She was about to say something else when her phone rang. 'I'm in a meeting . . . Just five more minutes . . . I'll come over,' she said and hung up.

She stared at Shivaswamy silently for a minute. Shivaswamy felt uncomfortable and was unsure about how to interpret this silence and her piercing gaze.

'Mr Swamy, I heard the MD asked you to report on an issue with a customer in Chennai. Have you done that?'

'Yes, it's been a while.'

'It didn't reach me.'

'I didn't know I had to send it to you. I copied Shyamala and the division heads.'

'Can you send it to me today?'

'I will.'

'You should keep me in the loop on important matters.'

Shivaswamy said nothing.

'Never copy me in on emails, do you understand? Forward them to me separately.'

Shivaswamy didn't know what to say. Could he really do that? Did she even have a company email?

She dropped the subject and moved on to the next. 'I understand you advised Ravi and Prabhu to visit the troubled customer in Chennai; is that correct?'

'Yes.'

'Did they go?'

'Yes. Prabhu sent a report to me afterwards.'

'And you've forwarded it to the MD?'

'Yes.'

'Mr Swamy, let me share a little secret with you. Nobody went to Chennai.' She leaned forward with her elbows on the table and smiled.

'But Prabhu submitted a report . . .'

She laughed. 'Precisely. Are you keeping a close watch on the company?'

Shivaswamy felt cornered. She was playing a game with him that she should have been playing with her father-in-law.

'Dhriti, I don't know all that. The people who resolved the issue sent the report. I forwarded it to the MD upon his request for an update. I have neither the means nor the intention to validate it,' he replied.

'What do I care about that? I'm not interested either.' She glanced at the time on her phone. 'I have to go. So, let me be straight to the point. A ghost-like doubt has settled in my father-in-law's mind—that the company will sink if he is not there. Yet, the evidence suggests otherwise. The company is being managed efficiently by the respective business heads. The consistent growth in the company's revenue and profit year after year attests to that. Added to that, the number of employees in the company has risen by 50 per cent over the last five years. You might have noticed this in your HR records.

'While my father-in-law holds the title of MD, he seems unable to grasp the current state of the company. Most of its operations are outside his realm of experience. He struggles to comprehend them, and others refrain from pressing the matter out of respect.

'I won't beat about the bush. What certainly needs to happen now is my father-in-law's retirement. It's your job to convince him . . . And one more thing. If you help me, I will help you in return. I'm not so naive as to be unaware of why people work even after retirement. So, the help will be mutual. I must go now.' She picked up her mobile and sunglasses and, without looking at him, walked out of the room.

25

Teju laughed out loud. His laughter crossed the seas, reached Bengaluru, and made Shivaswamy laugh too. Shivaswamy had told him about his conversation with Dhriti, but he omitted the part where she said, 'If you help me, I'll help you in return.' That statement seemed a bit raw even to share with Teju.

'It's amusing, Appa, your job. You have to retire the person who hired you when you were retired,' he said.

'In a way, yes. That seems to be the expectation from both sides,' Shivaswamy replied, still laughing. Tejas was familiar with the DT Group of Companies as if he had worked there himself. Shivaswamy had told him everything. In fact, the exchange was mutual. Tejas had also shared stories of his college, hostel and friends with his father.

'Look, even though they don't say it explicitly, everyone expects me to fill Preetam Jain's shoes. I don't know who that man was, and it's been ten years since he passed away. God alone knows what void he filled in Dhaval's heart or what mountains he climbed. Can a man ever really replace another? Do you know what I feel, Teju? The more they see me in the shadow of that dead man, the deeper their disappointment seems to grow.'

'By the time you leave this job, you'll be a good actor. You could join a TV series,' Tejas said with another laugh. 'Honestly, Appa, I pity that old man. He seems to be struggling with so much uncertainty. He knows you alone can't solve all his problems. As you said, no outsiders can offer him a solution. If you're up to it, and it doesn't burden you, try to help him.'

'Now you're speaking like Dhaval's daughter-in-law. Everyone asks me to help him, but no one explains how to,' Shivaswamy said in a lighter tone.

'You know it, Appa. What he needs is for you to listen. Just continue to do that.'

That seemed like the right thing to do. 'Agreed.'

'If you had come here with Amma, none of these problems would have surfaced,' Tejas added.

Shivaswamy just laughed and hung up. After finishing the call, he imagined that Teju had probably walked into his college building. He imagined him in a T-shirt and jeans, one foot pressed against the wall of a building that resembled the age-old, British-era Central Library in Bengaluru. He could see him pushing his thick glasses up the bridge of his nose and speaking with a smile. Tejas had the habit of doing this often when he talked, ever since he started wearing glasses at seven or eight.

He was a brilliant boy, mature far beyond his years. He was fluent in multiple languages but was an introvert. When he was in the second or third grade, doubts about his vision had arisen in Revathi's mind when he came home with scribbles trying to copy what was written on the board. However, the state government doctor, who visited the school for the annual health check-up, said he was healthy and that everything, including his vision, was fine. The school also sent the report home, so they didn't take him for an eye examination. The boy didn't say anything either.

Later, Teju's PE teacher met Shivaswamy at his office. The teacher's wife worked at BEL, and he was there to pick her up. Shivaswamy recognized him and struck up a conversation. The teacher said, 'Your Tejas is smart in everything, but he seems to have a problem with his eyes. It's not at the ball, but somewhere else when he swings the bat. It seems like he struggles with hand–eye coordination. I would suggest taking him to a good eye doctor.'

When they did, they discovered he had some trouble with his vision. After that, it gradually worsened, and he had to wear thick glasses permanently.

Shivaswamy smiled, remembering the days when he had bought Teju his first pair of glasses. Still speaking in baby language, the young boy refused to wear them, no matter how many bribes were offered—strawberry ice cream, Dairy Milk chocolate, comic books. 'If you want them, put them on yourself!' he said stubbornly.

In the end, Shivaswamy, Revathi and Sanjana all had to buy a pair of cheap plastic glasses and wear them around the house to show Teju that it was no big deal. They made a game of it, and eventually, Teju gave in. The fake glasses and two of Teju's broken real glasses were still in a plastic box in the Godrej almirah.

26

The floodlights and the noise emanating from Anoop Gardenia kept Shivaswamy awake well past midnight. Just as he was preparing to head to the office in the morning, he heard a firm knock on the gate. The knocking persisted thrice, as if someone were fiddling with the latch on the gate. When he opened the door, Sanketi Bhattaru, his neighbour, stood outside. Bhattaru, who usually wore a *banian*, or vest, was dressed in a full-sleeved blue shirt and a white silk dhoti. He gave the impression that he was on his way somewhere.

'I forgot your name,' he said.

'Shivaswamy.'

'Shivaswamy avarē, I'm here because we, the residents of this street, have firmly decided to take legal action against the apartment builder across the road. This builder shows no regard for our peace and well-being; they continue their noisy construction activities late into the night. How can any of us sleep? My son and daughter-in-law have to wake up early for work, and this constant noise disrupts everyone's rest. We have tried to reason with the building manager on multiple occasions, but he is unresponsive. The owner of that building, a north Indian living in Mumbai, seems utterly indifferent to our suffering, while we have been tolerating this for six long years.

'I am not sure if you are acquainted with Gopal Rao, who lives two houses down from this vacant plot. He and his son are highly esteemed high court lawyers who have agreed to represent us. They are actively collecting signatures from all the residents on this street.

'I can see that sleepless nights are weighing on you too. Let's band together and ensure that this evil builder not only ceases his night-time activities but also halts construction during daytime hours. Come, let's go,' he said, stepping back from the gate, hoping Shivaswamy would join him.

Shivaswamy was in a dilemma. As far as he knew, all the other families on the street owned their homes, except him. Besides the ten-foot-high compound wall at the back of their houses, they had no connection to the Anoop Gardenia apartment or its builder. If the construction work stopped not only at night but also during the day, it wouldn't bother them at all; in fact, they would be happier. But it wasn't the same for him.

'I have an urgent meeting at the office. I'm already late. I'll meet you in the evening,' he sighed.

'It's just the house next door. How long will it take to sign? Just a minute.'

'No. I really don't have the time.'

Bhattaru slammed the iron gate shut and left, his frustration evident in the force with which his hands worked. Shivaswamy didn't know what else he could have said in his position. He had thought that Revathi might have shared the reason for their move from Ghaziabad with Bhattaru's wife, but that didn't appear to be the case.

He called Revathi to ask. She replied that she didn't recall mentioning it to any neighbours. She advised against signing anything, emphasizing that there was already enough chaos. Before hanging up, she added, 'Make time to go to the Dharmasthala temple. We need to fulfil the vows we made. Sanju's delivery could happen any day in the next two weeks. Go soon.'

He agreed. Later, he deliberately arrived home late, well past ten that evening, having had dinner outside. He opened the gate carefully to avoid making noise and entered the house in the dark.

The next day, Saturday morning, while he was sipping tea and reading the newspaper, the doorbell rang. His heart started pounding, suspecting it might be Bhattaru. What would he reply if he said, 'Let's go now'? He wondered for a minute if he shouldn't get the door at all. When the doorbell rang again, he left his half-drunk cup on the table and went to the door. Kumar Gowda and Vanita stood outside. They smiled at him, and, with relief, he smiled back.

He welcomed them in warmly, cleared space on the sofa, which was covered with clothes, books and old newspapers, and invited them to sit down. He then went inside and put on a shirt.

'Sorry for the trouble; we came early in the morning. We're moving out of the apartment today and just wanted to say goodbye,' said Vanita.

'Oh no. You were there in that building on our behalf. You were a bridge between us and Anoop Gardenia. Now that bridge is also gone,' Shivaswamy said sadly.

Kumar smiled regretfully. Vanita said, 'What could we do, uncle? We had hoped everything would work out, but it didn't happen. We couldn't continue staying there. We were causing our daughter a lot of distress. We'd had enough.'

'Where are you going?'

'To Banashankari,' said Kumar.

'It's not too far. We can still visit each other.'

'We tried to find a place nearby, like you, but we couldn't find the right one,' said Kumar.

Shivaswamy sighed. 'It's good that you didn't find a house here,' he said. He told them about how the neighbours on the street planned to approach the police for the night-time noise and had asked him to sign their petition.

Kumar laughed. 'What's the matter, sir? This builder troubles you in every possible way!'

Shivaswamy, too, laughed.

The couple expressed their opposing opinions.

Kumar said, 'Sir, if you sign that, it will be a conflict of interest. You will be creating trouble for yourself.'

Vanita disagreed with her husband. 'So what? Must the people living around here endure sleepless nights until the builder's work is over? And for how long? It's been going on for years! They should work during the day. At Anoop Gardenia, they begin working in the evening, using the same workers for various other projects during the day and then bringing them here exhausted in the evening.'

As the couple argued, Shivaswamy went into the kitchen to make tea. They were still arguing even as he served them tea and biscuits. To change the subject, he asked Kumar, 'There's a general body meeting called by the new association tomorrow. Are you coming?'

'No, sir. I doubt I'll have time tomorrow as we're moving into our new residence today,' Kumar replied.

By the time they left, Kumar and his wife were emotional. They bowed to touch his feet, saying, 'It is a blessing to have elders like you close.' As they crossed the gate, Vanita said, 'Uncle, you should also go to America. Don't stay here for the sake of the apartment dispute. It won't be solved anytime soon. If you go there, at least you can spend time with your grandchild.'

Kumar, as if to interrupt her, said, 'Is America as close as Mysuru that we can go there whenever we wish?'

Shivaswamy just smiled and shut the gate.

The general body meeting the next day unfolded as expected. This time, Sandeep Kamat's group had arrived armed with more strength—with eight to ten members—and was better organized. The two groups remained distinctly divided and engaged in heated arguments.

Kamat's group brought documents to the meeting and presented them, revealing that it was no longer a secret that the folks at Anoop Gardenia were helping Alluri Venkat's committee, and hence the builder.

'What's wrong with that? He is our builder. Why do you want to confront him?' Venkat asked in return. 'I can negotiate a discount with him. I can get the payment reduced by twenty-five thousand rupees for each of you,' he said.

Many people held the microphone that day. Among them, four were very vocal.

The first one said, 'Let's agree to a twenty-five-thousand-rupee discount and move on!' He was from Venkat's group.

The second one said, 'We shouldn't pay even a paisa. Let's go to court!' He was from Sandeep Kamat's group.

The third one said, 'Twenty-five thousand is too low; the reduction should be at least two lakh.'

The fourth one said, 'The shop is useful for us; let's pay for it, but the penthouses are the builder's mischief. We should not pay anything for them. Give us a breakdown of the cost of the shop and that of the penthouses.'

The meeting turned out to be even more chaotic than the previous ones. Sandeep Kamat said, 'This committee is not valid. Let's go to the registrar's office and cancel it.' However, Venkat's group managed to conduct the election on the same day and secured the majority, despite the opposition.

Someone from the crowd asked when the issues with electricity, water and waste management would be resolved, but no one had an answer. Venkat said cautiously, 'Let's explore the solutions to those issues in the upcoming meetings.' He suggested that those issues might resolve themselves after negotiations with the builder and the payment of dues.

'What if they aren't resolved even then?' the same questioner asked again.

In response, Professor Venkat said, 'Life asks for a measure of optimism from living beings.'

And that was that.

27

On Monday, the two men met at Dhaval's home. Shivaswamy had arrived at the office early that morning, completed the essential and urgent tasks and was sitting in a midday meeting when he suddenly felt he ought to meet Dhaval. Sudhakar, who had recently joined the branch office, was giving a presentation on campus hiring.

The feeling came upon him quite suddenly. Why exactly, he couldn't be sure. He stepped out of the conference room and called Anita.

'He hasn't come to the office, sir,' she said.

'Will he come today?'

'I don't know. Should I pass on a message?'

'No, that's fine,' he said, and returned to the conference room.

About twenty minutes later, Anita called. 'MD sir is at home. He's asking if you can come over there,' she said.

'I will,' he responded. She mentioned that Dhaval was free for the day, and Shivaswamy could visit whenever convenient.

That day, he had chosen to travel to the office on his scooter instead of the metro. He had also decided that he would visit Dharmasthala that week, even if it meant taking leave, and that he would personally inform the relevant office contacts of his unavailability for three days. These factors may have been at work in the background, orchestrating a meeting with Dhaval.

As he arrived at the head office, he ascended to the fourth floor to meet Anita and ask her for Dhaval's home address. Rather than providing the address directly, she phoned Chandru to bring the car. The residence was just behind the office. If one exited the office and turned either left or right onto the adjacent street, then walked a short distance keeping an eye out for the office's prominent signboard, they would stumble upon DT Paradise, a mere two-minute walk. Even so, the sleek white Audi pulled up, and a moment later, he was dropped off at Dhaval's bungalow.

The mansion was grand, spanning five levels. Shivaswamy had never been so close to such a bungalow before, let alone entering it. As soon as the car stopped under the portico, a maid approached him, as though she wanted to know who he was. The driver, Chandru, said, 'Kalpana madam, the gentleman has been called by sahib. He's from Ravi sir's office.' She welcomed him and guided him to the guest room.

A young boy presented a bottle of Bisleri and a glass. Just as Shivaswamy finished drinking and was about to put the glass down, an invitation to come inside arrived.

Dhaval sat in a spacious room on the first floor, wearing white pyjamas and a white cotton shirt, holding a book. The room evidently served as his home office, with desks and sofa sets that provided ample seating for more than twenty-five people. Seated on an easy chair, Dhaval warmly beckoned him over, saying, 'Come in, Shivaswamy,' and gestured to the sofa opposite him. 'It's delightful that you wanted to meet up. Of late, I've been hesitant to call you, wondering if I was pestering you. But not today. It's like Punyakoti seeking out Vyagra,' he said with a laugh, referring to the folk tale where Punyakoti, the cow, returns to the tiger, Vyagra, honouring her promise to be his prey.

Shivaswamy laughed as well. He surveyed the room. This single room was twice the size of his flat in Anoop Gardenia. Could this man be the sole resident of such a vast mansion? he wondered.

Dhaval Thakkar, as if sensing his thoughts, spoke up. 'Shivaswamy, I am all alone in this house. My son and my daughter-in-law left three years ago, claiming they had found happiness elsewhere. I am alone unless you count the housekeepers—Ayyappa, Chandregowda, Kalpana and Girijamma—and the security guards. If they were to forget to check whether this old man is still breathing, I could pass away in this chair, and no one would know.

'When would anyone notice, you ask? Only in the evening, when someone from the accounts department—what's his name? Anant Narayanan—came seeking my signature on high-value contracts. He would be disappointed that he had come in vain. "Oh, what would this old man have lost had he expired after signing these papers?"—that would be his sole concern,' he guffawed.

Shivaswamy did not.

A middle-aged woman brought two large glasses of lemon juice and set them on the table.

'Girijamma, Shivaswamy is diabetic. Bring him a glass with less sugar,' said Dhaval.

Shivaswamy tried to say it was okay. Ignoring him, the woman took the glass inside, returned a few minutes later with another glass, and placed it in front of him.

'Let's not sit in this room. It is the office. Only office talk will come out of it. Let's go into the garden,' Dhaval suggested, leading the way. Holding his glass, Shivaswamy quietly followed.

The space felt vast. Polished marble gleamed everywhere, and the doors were so large that an elephant could pass through. As he moved from room to room, the windows with half-drawn white curtains looked prominent. Light and space were engaged in a battle for supremacy.

How could a man's privacy remain intact when such a massive mansion had such a high ceiling, and when gigantic chandeliers hung in the middle, emitting so much light? Where could the soul find its refuge? Just as the absence of light could give rise to some maladies, Shivaswamy believed that an overabundance of light might have detrimental effects too. Some ulcers that vanished in the shadows could be aggravated in bright light.

There was an inverse relationship between one's existence and the size of one's home. The larger the home, the more one's essence seemed to diminish. Roaming within such a vast mansion might make one feel as insignificant as an ant. It was like kissing a stone cheek—the metaphor he had used while discussing the company at the Coconut Grove restaurant.

And this mansion—what a stone-carved cheek it was! Such a cheek that didn't permit the softness of the lips or the moisture of the breath to penetrate it. The salt from tears merely froze upon it, unable to elicit even the slightest sensation. Only the kisser's lips peeled and bled, while the cheek remained unaffected.

In the BEL quarters at Ghaziabad, bees had built their hives on sunlit projections from the corrugated roof. They formed thousands of chambers, filling them with sweet nectar. Once, not just one but four beehives emerged side by side. That was the year Tejas was born. Right beside the beehive grew lush moss. Having claimed the crevices, it resembled the Amazon rainforest but spread across the roof. With two bouts of monsoon rain, it became even denser.

When the children were young, their greatest adventures were wrapping themselves in shawls, wearing paper face masks, wrapping Shivaswamy's white banians around their hands as gloves and dragging a wooden stool from the house to position it under the beehive before climbing up to watch it. If a fly buzzed near their faces, they would jump off the stool and run inside, squealing, to tell their mother about their adventure.

And here, how could a worm crawl on this slippery white moonstone? To Shivaswamy, Dhaval appeared as a lone prisoner, confined within a beautiful, multistorey jail.

Dhaval walked ahead, with Shivaswamy following—a footpath wound through a lush green landscape. A fountain featured a marble woman pouring water from a colourfully decorated pot. Palm trees lined both sides of the path. Surrounding them were flowering shrubs. Shivaswamy, who came from a flower-growing family, recognized roses, jasmines, marigolds, magnolias and dahlias. However, several blossoms were unfamiliar to him; all he noticed was that they enhanced the symmetry of the footpath.

When they were seated opposite each other at the stone table in the courtyard, Shivaswamy couldn't help but ask the question that weighed on his mind: 'Sir, how do you live here all alone in such a vast mansion?'

Dhaval smiled. 'We've lived in this house for sixteen years, Shivaswamy. Preetam and Oishi's home is right next to it, and he was the reason we have these homes. By then, we'd already bought the office building here. We purchased three old bungalows behind the office at a premium, tore them down, and built two new ones for us there.

'One of the sellers, an elderly couple, pleaded with us, "Please don't demolish it. This house holds so many memories for us." Even now, when I recall their anguish that day, shivers run down my spine. Oh, what was their distress that they had to sell their home? They begged, "Please don't tear it down, not for another five years, not while we are still alive." Did Preetam agree? We cruelly laughed in their faces, telling them that they shouldn't concern themselves with the fate of the house once it was sold and the money was deposited into their account. But later, I grasped their pain when I faced a similar situation with my Nagarathpete house.

'We held a house-warming ceremony and inaugurated both houses on the same day. Look at what followed: Oishi didn't live in the new house for even two years. Preetam stayed for five years, Sumati for ten. And now, only I remain, guarding these two houses and the office day and night, like some kind of ghost.'

The woman who had served the lemon juice returned with a tray full of snacks, plates and water.

'Did your wife like this house?' Shivaswamy asked.

'When did Sumati ever like this house, Shivaswamy? She didn't want to leave our Nagarathpete house at all. We lived in that house for thirty years. It had just four rooms: one for Sumati and me, one each for our two children and one for my mother. I used to do my business work in the living room late into the night, leaving the bedroom for Sumati to sleep in. By the time we moved in there, my father had passed away. My mother lived with us for eleven years. To her, who had lived in a tiny house in a congested lane in Chickpet, our Nagarathpete house seemed as grand as a palace. She was happy, and her final years were blissful.

'My business was just taking off then, but do you know how hard it was to buy that house? It was the house Sumati herself had chosen and desired. How can I forget her tears when we had to leave it?

'When we moved from that house to this one, it wasn't just me, but our entire family that became enslaved to the office. You know how Ravi's father-in-law lives? He lives as if office and home are one and the same. But that didn't work for my family. The shift here burnt everything. The office thrived, and the home languished. My wife passed away, my son moved out and my daughter distanced herself. When family and business intertwine, it becomes unclear who would draw near and who would drift away. I still have that house in Nagarathpete. Do you know how comforting it is to go there occasionally and lie down in my bedroom?

'Do you know how much trouble a goon from that area caused me, trying to take that house from me? He was buying land and houses in the vicinity to build a shopping mall. I told him firmly I wouldn't sell it, no matter what. That set him off. "Everyone living there has sold their houses. You don't even live there. What's your problem?" he asked me. He had political connections and even became an MLA for a term—a real big shot in that area. He once sent his men to break down the front door at night to intimidate me. I responded by hiring private security and installing CCTV cameras everywhere. I even lodged a complaint against him directly with the police commissioner. After that, he backed off. But all these precautions for an empty house! No matter what, I won't sell it in this lifetime,' he said.

Shivaswamy was bewildered. Before him sat a moth, drawn to a flame, getting closer and closer until it was finally consumed.

'How many people are there in the neighbouring Vimal Jain's house?' Shivaswamy inquired.

'It's a small family. Vimal and Madhuri have just one daughter, and Vimal is Preetam's only child. Oishi often expressed her concern that the house was too big for such a small family, but no one heeded her words.

'The conversation that took place on the morning of the house-warming ceremony was amusing. The four of us—Sumati, Oishi, Preetam and I—gathered around a table, drinking tea and chatting. The topic turned to this: what was the point of building such mansions if the children moved away? The concerns seemed to weigh more on the women. You know what Preetam said? "Even after our death, Dhavoo and I will continue to live here as ghosts, ensuring a return on our investment." He laughed heartily. I did too. Both Sumati and Oishi were displeased and admonished him. "Why are you talking such nonsense on an auspicious day?" they said. Was he the kind to back down when scolded by women? He continued the dialogue, imagining how we would be as ghosts:

"Dhavoo would call out from his house, 'Preeth, where are you?'

I'd reply, 'Sitting on the air conditioner compressor, cooling my butt off. And you?'

'I've wrapped myself around the big chandelier. It feels good.'

'Are all the bulbs in the chandelier lit up?'

'No, the red ones have gone out.'

'Dhavoo, I told you, don't buy chandeliers from that fraud Manikchand. Did you listen? You bought them from him because you once had a crush on his sister when you were riding your bicycle in Chickpet. Now, suffer!'"

'Regardless of how upset the women were, he just kept talking and laughing out loud. That was his style. But ultimately, what the women said turned out to be true. Last month, Madhuri, who had come with sweets to wish me for my birthday, said, "Uncle, the house is too big for just the three of us. We are thinking of moving to a smaller one." It seems the virus of leaving has also infected

Vimal and Madhuri after Ravi and Dhriti. The days of Preeth's imagination are getting closer.'

Shivaswamy conjured up an image of two impossibly sized bungalows and two ghosts gazing at each other, talking from their windows. Since he had never seen Preetam Jain, he could ascribe any form to that spectre. However, in the other window, Dhaval did not appear as a ghost; instead, he remained a spectacled old man with a white beard, wearing white trousers and a white shirt.

'Eat this, Shivaswamy. Girijamma makes great sabudana khichdi. Here, have some.' Dhaval scooped some onto a plate and slid it in front of him. 'She's from Kundapura, the coastal town of Karnataka. Bless her heart; she learnt to cook Gujarati dishes just to please me. I actually prefer this to the authentic Gujarati. I'm much the same way, aren't I? A khichdi of Kannada and Gujarati?'

The cold evening breeze was blowing, and the garden had become chilly. Shivering, Shivaswamy stood up to depart. As he walked out of the door, he remembered that he hadn't mentioned his leave. That was, after all, the reason for his visit. When he informed Dhaval that he'd be away for three days that week, Dhaval patted him on the shoulder and said, 'No problem.'

Shivaswamy smiled. 'I'm going to Dharmasthala, sir. My wife made a vow for my daughter's safe delivery.'

Dhaval nodded and said, 'Go on, then,' but stood still, something weighing on his mind.

'Shivaswamy,' he said, 'when you brought up Dharmasthala, an old incident came to mind. There were two brothers, Gangadhar and Nani, who owned a hardware store together near Chickpet Circle. They were from Mysuru and belonged to the Vokkaliga farmers' community. Both were decent people who got along well. Their business thrived for many years. However, as is often the case among siblings, a dispute over property division arose between them. The disagreement intensified. Gangadhar, the elder brother, kept saying, "I haven't concealed anything from you. The list I've shown you represents our entire property." But Nani, the younger brother, didn't believe him. Eventually, he challenged his brother, "Would you dare swear before Lord Manjunatha Swamy in Dharmasthala?" The elder brother accepted, and both made their way to Dharmasthala. They returned, and within just three months, a tragedy struck. Gangadhar's eldest son, a young man of only twenty, took his own life by consuming poison. The police deduced it was because of a romantic entanglement. But local gossip had its own theory; many believed Gangadhar lost his son as a consequence of swearing falsely before the deity known for upholding truth.'

Shivaswamy laughed politely, not knowing how else to react. 'Even in my town, people used to go to Dharmasthala to settle property disputes,' he said and quickly left Dhaval's mansion.

He headed out onto the street, fetched his scooter from the head office and prepared to leave. He didn't enter the office; he simply didn't feel like it.

He had barely moved away from the gate when he received Dhaval's call.

'Shivaswamy?'

'Yes, sir.'

'Are you nearby?'

'Yes, sir. I'm still by the office gate.'

'Could you come over to my home for a moment?'

'I'll be there,' Shivaswamy replied. Knowing Dhaval's habit of calling back after meetings to mention forgotten details, Shivaswamy wasn't surprised by the call. He steered his scooter onto the adjacent street and pulled up at the porch at DT Paradise.

Dhaval was already outside, waiting. Kalpana, Girijamma and two other assistants stood a few steps behind him. As Shivaswamy halted his scooter, Dhaval descended the porch steps to meet him.

'Shivaswamy, will you take me to Dharmasthala with you?' Dhaval asked, his tone sincere and humble.

Shivaswamy couldn't muster a response.

28

'I don't know what to say,' Shyamala said. Then, she echoed Shivaswamy's question back to him: 'Why does he want to go to Dharmasthala with you?'

'I don't know.'

'Has he simply expressed a desire to join you?'

'Yes.'

'You should talk to Dhriti, Shivaswamy,' Shyamala advised.

'Shyamala, will you speak with her?'

'No. You talk to her. I'll text you her number,' she said. Her last sentence was a reflection of her desire to play it safe. The situation was a bit unreal to her, after all.

After his conversation with her, Shivaswamy got back to his work. No message arrived from Shyamala. Instead, forty-five minutes later, he received a call from Dhriti. 'Mr Swamy, Shyamala has informed me about the situation. It's okay from our side. For the first time in his life, he's showing a strong desire to take a leisure trip. Isn't there a direct flight from Bangalore to Dharamshala?' she asked.

'Not Dharamshala. *Dharmasthala*.'

'Where's that?'

'It's near Mangaluru, in this state. One could fly to Mangaluru and then continue by road. But I doubt our MD would agree to that.'

'Why?'

'He insists we travel as I had originally planned,' said Shivaswamy.

'And how were you planning to go?'

'I planned to take a train to Subramanya and then catch a bus from there.'

It was clear she was confused. She had never heard of those places. She didn't understand the logic of taking the train when a plane was available. For a few moments, she remained silent, searching for words. 'I'll discuss this with my father-in-law and Ravi, and then call you back,' she finally said before hanging up.

That afternoon, around three, Raviraj walked into Shivaswamy's office and closed the door behind him. Then he took a seat across the desk. He had never confronted Shivaswamy alone before, and even now, he spoke very little.

'Shivaswamy, there's no objection from our side to your trip to Dharmasthala with my father. I'm surprised he even expressed such a desire. Don't worry about applying for leave; consider this an official trip. Don't spare any expense; nothing should come out of your pocket. You can obtain an advance from the accounts section, and I'll give them the necessary instructions right away.'

Shivaswamy felt disgusted. He was angered by the thought that he seemed like a man who would fulfil his wife's vow at a temple at the company's expense. Surely, that would be an insult to anyone! When he looked at Raviraj, the man sat there impassively, as if he were there to discuss a mundane office task. His demeanour suggested he had already made all the necessary decisions regarding this trip.

'This is my personal trip, Raviraj. I am not going with your father for him. Instead, he wishes to accompany me. This is not the MD's trip; it is mine. It has nothing to do with the office,' he said.

Shivaswamy's sharp words stung Raviraj and turned his face pale. 'I am sorry; I didn't mean to offend you,' he said.

Immediately, Shivaswamy felt ashamed. He regretted that he had perhaps stooped to his level in trying to condemn the owner's ego. That man might forever wear a crown of pride on top of his head; that was his karma. But where did Shivaswamy stand?

'I'm sorry, I spoke harshly,' Shivaswamy said.

Raviraj waved his hands, indicating he wasn't upset. He then stood up to leave but hesitated. 'Shivaswamy, how old are your children?' he said finally.

The question evoked memories of the interview for Shivaswamy. 'They're adults now, Ravi. Both lead their own independent lives. Neither stays with me. Why do you ask?'

'Dhriti and I were puzzled by some of my father's remarks. He was reluctant to travel by flight or car for the trip. Even when we suggested taking Kalpana along for assistance, he refused. He said, "Shivaswamy will take me the way he took his children on trips, and he will make all the travel-related decisions."'

'Even though he didn't say it directly, his sentiments suggested as much. I'm responsible for your father during this journey. You can trust me,' Shivaswamy replied.

'I trust you completely, Shivaswamy. I'm just curious. What did he mean when he said, "He will take me the way he used to take his children?"' Raviraj asked, walking back from the door.

'Perhaps he wants to let go of all his burdens and travel with me.'

Raviraj didn't say anything further. 'You can call me anytime,' he said, standing up. 'At the very least, I'll inform our travel house to book the tickets.'

'No, I'll do it myself.'

Raviraj walked out.

Shivaswamy was surprised. If Raviraj had wanted to help, he could've said, 'I'll book the tickets.' Instead, he had said, 'I'll ask the company's travel desk to book them.' He seemed willing to assist his father, but only within the company's confines.

Two days later, the Bengaluru–Mangaluru train was set to depart from the Yeshwanthpur train station at seven in the morning. Dhaval Thakkar sat by the window, wearing a Tibetan woollen cap, white pyjamas and a shawl draped over a loose woollen sweater. He gazed in astonishment at the platform's hustle and bustle.

The light was dim, and fog restricted visibility to a few metres on the platform. Shivaswamy sat beside him, shorter in stature, dressed in a white dhoti, a light blue sweater and a brown woollen cap. He wore reading glasses and was engrossed in a newspaper.

Driver Chandregowda stood behind the coffee–tea stall on the platform, sipping hot coffee from a paper cup. He watched the two elderly men in the train window attentively. Kalpana had given him strict instructions to stay on the platform until the train departed, standing just close enough that they could call out to him if necessary.

29

Shivaswamy could not fully comprehend the meaning and significance of this Dharmasthala chapter. This chapter hardly connects any of the dots in his life in a visible way: his village life, his acquaintance with KereSwami, his friend Neelakanta, who had renounced his worldly possessions, his life in Ghaziabad, his life in Bengaluru, his involvement in the drama at the Gujarati family business, his travels on the metro, his friend Shankar, who had helped him get a job, his dream home at Anoop Gardenia that was never finished, his acquaintance with the distressed couple Kumar and Vanita, who suffered living in a house that was not yet complete, and his neighbour Sanketi Bhattaru, who was upset that he had not signed the complaint. This chapter was like a lone white swan flying among a flock of grey pigeons. It was like a man standing naked in the midst of a crowd as an embodiment of Gommateshwara.

Dhaval simply followed Shivaswamy. With the same ease with which he had spoken to his son and his daughter-in-law, he set aside his age, the pride of being the managing director of a group of companies and his responsibilities and followed Shivaswamy like a ten-year-old boy.

In keeping with the custom of Lord Manjunatha Swamy's devotees, he immersed himself in the Netravati River at the bathing ghat. From there, he squeezed himself into a Tata Sumo, so crowded with passengers that it felt like being in a tightly packed box and proceeded to the temple.

By the temple's custom, he removed his shirt, draped it over his shoulder, and waited in line for an hour for a glimpse of the deity. He followed Shivaswamy's every move, standing where he stood and sitting where he sat. When Shivaswamy offered the five hundred rupees he had brought to the offerings box, Dhaval did the same.

As Shivaswamy folded his hands in reverence and began to meditate, Dhaval said, 'Tell me your daughter's name, Shivaswamy. I will pray for her too.' Then he prayed with folded hands.

Despite his physical discomfort, Dhaval sat on the floor and dined in the temple's community hall. After their meal, the two men rested in a non-AC room at Kaveri Guesthouse, affiliated with the temple administration. Throughout the journey, Shivaswamy remained unchanged by Dhaval's presence, continuing in his typical manner, just as Dhaval had wanted. Throughout the journey, their camaraderie bore an air of benign neglect—a neglect that was strangely sought after.

In the evening, they visited Bahubali Hill to see the Bahubali statue. By the time they reached the summit, Dhaval felt exhausted, but he was also filled with joy. They sat there for over an hour, rejuvenated by the rustling green trees and cool breeze, deeply immersed in their thoughts and prayers.

While Dhaval sat with his eyes closed, Shivaswamy wandered nearby. The Bahubali Gommateshwara statue, soaring majestically to thirty-nine feet, blended seamlessly with the vast expanse of the sky, exuding an aura of tranquillity. Just as the heavens stood unadorned, so did Lord Bahubali in all his majestic glory.

From a distance, Shivaswamy's gaze fixed itself on Lord Bahubali's face. He approached slowly, his gaze unwavering, until he reached the statue's feet. At first, it was the deity's gentle countenance that captivated him, but soon it felt boundless, like gazing upon the infinite sky. The cosmic essence of Bahubali was reflected in his eyes and his soul. For Shivaswamy, the moment was unparalleled. The more he observed, the more the statue's serene and mesmerizing beauty drew him.

Bahubali's story was truly captivating. A genuine warrior didn't yield in defeat. Instead, he fought, triumphed and then magnanimously bestowed his victory upon the vanquished. He epitomized the true ascetic. Bahubali clashed with his brother Bharata, who sought the kingdom. After securing victory, he renounced it all and returned it to his brother. Yet, even after relinquishing everything and embracing asceticism, he remained tormented by the notion that he was meditating on the land that rightfully belonged to his brother. It was only when Bharata, the emperor, knelt before him, touched his feet and proclaimed, 'All this is yours. You granted it to me after winning it,' that Bahubali attained *Kevala Jnana*, the pinnacle of enlightenment.

They sat on the hill until dusk, then descended cautiously. They had journeyed to Dharmasthala on a Thursday. Although they planned to return to Bengaluru through Subramanya the next day, Dhaval said he wanted to stay another two days. This was his sole request during the entire trip.

Shivaswamy left him at the guesthouse and went out alone to call Dhriti and update her. She asked him how he was, then said she was okay with them extending their return by two days. With the help of the guesthouse manager, he found a travel agent and changed their tickets to Sunday.

On his way back to the room, Shivaswamy received a call from Revathi. He had told her before leaving Bengaluru that he was going to Dharmasthala, but he hadn't told her that Dhaval was accompanying him. To be fair, until he saw Dhaval on the railway platform, Shivaswamy wasn't entirely convinced that he would show up. So, he didn't tell anyone, including Revathi. Even though she found it strange when he mentioned it briefly, she said, 'That's good; at least you have a companion for the journey.'

The next day unfolded similarly. In the morning, they went to the temple, and in the evening, to Bahubali Hill. Since it was still early evening, they sat on the hilltop until they were content. While they spent some time together, most of it was either spent in meditation or wandering alone.

While Shivaswamy was on the hill that day, he received a call from Teju. Shivaswamy told him that he was in Dharmasthala. Teju listened, but something else was troubling him. He had seen on the news about a virus ravaging China and threatening to spread around the world. This virus, known as the coronavirus, had already been detected in Thailand, Singapore and several Middle Eastern countries. He had heard that it had the potential to disrupt lives in the same way that the SARS virus had done years ago.

'Appa, how long will it be before the virus that has reached Dubai gets to Bengaluru? You're all alone there,' he said, his voice filled with concern.

Shivaswamy was amused. 'The media tends to sensationalize things, my boy. There's no such threat here,' he reassured him.

'No, Appa,' Teju responded. 'It's not like that. If there's an outbreak like they're saying, travel systems will grind to a halt. Flights between countries will stop. We could be stuck in different places for a long time. I spoke with Sanju this morning. She's trying to extend Amma's visa. If that happens, Amma will have to stay in America for another four or five months. You know what Sanju said? "Do whatever it takes to convince Appa to come here!" Don't stay alone there, Appa. Don't be stubborn. Please come here. The apartment dispute will be resolved when it is resolved, wherever you are. You don't have to wait for it,' he pleaded. Despite Shivaswamy's attempts to reassure him, Teju's anxiety didn't wane. He spoke with the determination of a little boy intent on getting his father to say, 'Okay, I'll come!'

'Give me some time to think. I'm currently at the temple. I'll speak with you later.' Shivaswamy had to disconnect the call himself.

On Saturday, Dhaval's health deteriorated slightly. This was expected, considering the travel, the bath in the river and all the walking over the previous two days. A backache and knee pain had set in from climbing the hill for two days. Dhaval stayed in bed at the lodge that day. Shivaswamy went to the river and to the temple alone.

When he returned to the lodge, Dhaval had a fever. The lodge manager called a doctor, who concluded that it was due to exhaustion. He prescribed medicines for the next three days. Shivaswamy went to a nearby pharmacy, obtained the medicines, and gave them to Dhaval at regular intervals. He also fetched idli and chutney from a nearby restaurant and fed him. By evening, Dhaval felt somewhat better. With Shivaswamy's help, he slowly stood up, took a few steps outside, had some curd rice and then returned to bed. Shivaswamy slept lightly throughout the night, checking on Dhaval every time he stirred.

Dhaval had specifically asked him not to inform his family of his illness, so Shivaswamy refrained from calling Dhriti immediately. He decided to contact her only if Dhaval's condition worsened. Fortunately, Dhaval felt somewhat better by morning. They travelled to Subramanya and boarded the train to Bengaluru.

One adjustment that Shivaswamy made for Dhaval's sake was skipping the visit to the Subramanya temple. Traditionally, whenever he and Revathi visited Dharmasthala, they would stop at the Subramanya temple, either en route or on their way back. However, on this occasion, Shivaswamy didn't want to over-exert Dhaval.

The train rumbled through the forest and the misty hills, occasionally passing through tunnels. They slept well. When Shivaswamy woke up, the train was leaving the Sakleshpur station. Dhaval stared out of the window. The train gradually picked up speed. Noticing that Shivaswamy was awake, Dhaval turned towards him. The wind blowing through the window ruffled Dhaval's hair and white beard.

'Shivaswamy?'

'Yes, sir.'

'I wanted to speak with you yesterday, but the fever prevented me. Over these three days, I have come to a decision. Not one, but two. I'll hand over the company to Ravi as soon as I get back. One division of it should go to my daughter. They can work out the details between themselves. Second, I will move back to the house in Nagarathpete and spend the rest of my life there. My son, my daughter, my daughter-in-law and my son-in-law can decide how to divide the house in Sadashivanagar amongst themselves. If they perceive it as a haunted house and wish to sell it, they're free to do so; I won't stand in their way. Yes, when dividing the company, they should include Vimal. You know, Preetam, too, invested in the company. I have nothing to do with the company anymore,' he said. His voice was distinct and firm. The words were clear. There were no emotions.

Shivaswamy thought of KereSwami and Neelakanta. A person didn't ask for permission before diving into the water from the boat they were on; they simply leaped without hesitation. Those irresistibly drawn, as if seduced by a captivating call, found a path in the water. He was witnessing such an instance for the second time in his life—and was awestruck.

30

By the time Shivaswamy reached home, it was midnight on Sunday. He was so exhausted that he took Monday off.

At the railway station, Chandregowda was waiting for them. Despite Dhaval's insistence, Shivaswamy chose to take an autorickshaw instead of joining Dhaval in his car. As Chandregowda was about to drive away, Dhaval extended his hands from the window and grasped Shivaswamy's. 'Shivaswamy,' he said, his eyes brimming with tears, 'I will never forget the favour.'

Apart from fetching milk and curd from the dairy in the morning, Shivaswamy remained indoors the whole day. Making a strong cup of tea gave him comfort. There were many things he could let slide, but not the richness of his tea. For breakfast, he made rice roti. Using the leftover vegetables in the fridge, he prepared a flavourful sambar. After shaving and bathing, he had his lunch, settled into an afternoon nap and allowed the day to pass him by gently.

As evening approached in India, morning dawned in the US. Sanjana and Revathi called him. The outbreak of the virus from China had suddenly become a significant concern in the US. Sanjana, deeply anxious like Tejas, urged him to join them. 'Come here this week itself. I'll book the ticket for you today.'

Shivaswamy reassured her as he had reassured Tejas a couple of days ago, 'There's no virus here, nothing of that sort. Don't panic imagining things from afar.'

Revathi's feelings about the visa extension were unclear. With Sanjana also present on the call, she didn't talk much on the subject. The timing of her travel had become complicated. Had she left two months later, it would've been ideal. She could've then stayed for four months before the delivery and another two afterwards to help both the baby and the mother. But with Sanjana's escalating health concerns, and her pressing need for her mother to be there earlier, the end of Revathi's visa and Sanjana's expected delivery date were on a collision course. Extending the visa was the only option. When Revathi said, 'You should come here,' Shivaswamy didn't know how to respond.

He was surprised that no one in his family discussed his job. Did they assume he could join or leave his position upon a whim? Did they imagine him as an extra player in a cricket team, waiting on the sidelines until called? And who could blame them? When asked where he worked, 'BEL' instinctively rolled off his tongue; he had to consciously say 'DT Software Solutions'. Given this, it wasn't surprising that his family shared a similar perspective. His tenure at BEL and subsequent retirement were deeply ingrained in their memories. The new company had barely made an impression. Shivaswamy wasn't confident that Revathi was even aware of the full name of his current employer.

It was past ten o'clock at night, yet work continued at Anoop Gardenia. The impact of the neighbours' police complaint was still unclear. Shivaswamy wasn't sure if they had filed a complaint. He draped a thick bedsheet over the window and used cotton earplugs to shield himself. However, sleep evaded him.

His mind turned to Dhaval's words. He wondered what the company would be like after him. How would Raviraj and Dhriti share the power? What would it mean for the daughter to have a division? And which division? Most likely, everyone would want the logistics division. Would Raviraj and Vimal stay together? Would the company collapse, or would they all manage it collectively? Given the rumours of discord between Dhriti and

Dhaval's daughter, he had no hope of them working together harmoniously.

With Dhaval's departure, he was unsure how he would navigate his path forward. Dhaval had chosen him, despite all odds. Now, with Dhaval no longer at the company, what significance did he hold? While others occasionally praised his work and agreed with him, there was no assurance this would continue. Their reconciliation with him stemmed largely from two sources: either fear of Dhaval or as part of Dhriti's grand scheme. Without Dhaval, why would they keep him? From the first interview to this moment, over these six months, everything that happened seemed to Shivaswamy like a prank being played on him. What began as a conflict could end as a conflict.

He thought again about Dhaval's words, 'I have no more ties to the company.' The clarity and firmness of his statement made it impossible for Shivaswamy to imagine them as mere words of the moment.

Instead, a series of questions emerged: in his vulnerable state, was all this drama necessary to relinquish what he had earned? Were all those days of arguments, deliberations and decisions, capped by a four-day trip, only for this purpose? Was such theatricality necessary for an eighty-year-old man to transfer his property to his children? What compelled him to do that while on pilgrimage?

Bharata, born of the same womb and sharing the same blood, was lifted by Bahubali's powerful arms to be struck down. But moved by affection, Bahubali had gently set him back on the ground, as one might a child. Would he have done the same if Bharata were of different blood?

That stern ascetic might have walked away, but not these people. Did it matter to the world under whose control the DT Group, a private business worth several hundred crores, operated? Did it matter to the world if Dhaval Thakkar, an elderly man, lived in a lavish building with twenty rooms or in an old house with four? Did it matter if he lived in Sadashivanagar—a posh locality of the city—or on Nagarathpete Street, where the low and middle classes dwelt? Did it matter if the father referred to himself as the managing director or if the son did? Or even the daughter-in-law, for that matter?

Even after the workers at Anoop Gardenia turned off the lights and departed, Shivaswamy struggled to fall asleep for quite a while.

The next day, he left for work an hour earlier than usual. As expected, a heap of tasks was waiting for him. Anuradha and Sudhakar were also waiting for him to make many decisions. When Anuradha inquired casually about his vacation, showing no extra curiosity, he felt relieved. He realized his trip with Dhaval hadn't become office gossip. Raviraj was absent that day, and Prabhu was busy in meetings with his managers throughout.

In the middle of lunch, he received a call from a Mumbai number. He chose not to answer it. Due to the ongoing recruitment drive to fill about fifty positions, receiving calls from recruitment partner firms was common.

In fact, thanks to this recruitment drive, Shivaswamy found himself in another quandary, this time in the form of his friend Shankar. Shankar had already called him thrice. When the first two calls came, Shivaswamy was in Dharmasthala and intended to return the call after he was back in Bengaluru. When Shankar called again, he was cooking. Shankar voiced his displeasure at not being able to reach him. Shivaswamy apologized and mentioned his trip to Dharmasthala but omitted the details about Dhaval. Shankar's call was about the company's recruitment drive. He implicitly asked Shivaswamy to favour candidates from his agency. Shivaswamy stayed silent. But he was well aware that Shankar wouldn't drop the matter easily. In the past, too, Shankar had tried to pry into the company's internal affairs, but Shivaswamy had cleverly evaded him.

As he was leaving for home around six o'clock, Anita called. 'Sir, MD sir wishes to see you,' she said.

'Now?'

'If you're still at the office, you could see him. The visiting hours are until seven in the evening.'

'Visiting hours?' he asked, sounding perplexed.

'Oh, I'm sorry, sir. I assumed you were aware. MD sir has been hospitalized. It's nothing serious. He was just exhausted after his trip. Ravi sir admitted him last evening. I'm on my way out now,' she elaborated.

'Which hospital?' he asked.

'Columbia Asia Hospital in Yeshwanthpur,' she replied.

31

Kalpana was waiting for him in the hospital lobby. As he arrived, she quickly led him to the ward. To him, it felt as if he was walking through a five-star hotel. After a gentle knock and hearing 'come in' from inside, she opened the door, stepped aside to let Shivaswamy enter and then closed it behind him. The room was luxurious, befitting VIP patients. Besides Dhaval, who was on the bed, three people were seated nearby. All four turned to look at him. There was Raviraj, Dhriti and another woman—older than Dhriti.

The room, bathed in a soft, moonlight-like glow, had stark white walls and was impeccably clean, transporting visitors to an entirely different world. To Shivaswamy, it felt like an extension of Dhaval's home. An IV drip was inserted into his outstretched left arm. The state in which he lay was so starkly different from how he had been just two days before, sleeping as a pilgrim on the rough bed at Kaveri Lodge in Dharmasthala, that Shivaswamy wondered if he was the same person.

As he walked closer, Dhaval squinted to see him. He had been lying without his glasses, and Shivaswamy stood in the shadows, obscured by the IV stand. Raviraj, seated next to Dhaval, leaned over and whispered, 'It's Shivaswamy.'

'Come in, Shivaswamy,' Dhaval said warmly. Raviraj shifted and indicated a spot for him on the sofa. Dhriti smiled at him. The woman seated beside her turned with a friendly grin and introduced herself. 'I'm Madhuri Jain, Vimal Jain's wife.'

Dhaval's eyes were sunken and his hair and beard dishevelled. The white hairs on his arms stood out in the blue hospital gown. The wrinkles on his face made him look much older than he was.

'The journey must've worn you out,' Shivaswamy remarked, drawing closer.

Dhaval smiled and said, 'No, not really. Our folks here get a bit panicky. They admitted me because I coughed twice.'

Shivaswamy ran his eyes around the room. Raviraj sat with his head bowed. Dhriti and Madhuri, too, sat in silence, attentive to their conversation. Shivaswamy wondered if Dhaval had already shared the decision he had mentioned on the train with his family. Dhriti's welcoming smile hinted at it. A moment later, he felt guilt at his curiosity. After all, why should he be concerned with the private matters of another family?

Dhaval turned to Raviraj and asked something in Gujarati. Shivaswamy understood that he was asking for some time to speak with him alone. His guess was right. The three of them stood up and excused themselves.

Before leaving, Raviraj adjusted the blanket that had slipped from Dhaval's frame, retrieved a bottle of mineral water from the adjacent drawer and handed it to Shivaswamy. He then closed the door behind him. Shivaswamy put the water bottle aside.

'Shivaswamy?'

'Yes, sir.'

'I'm not sure if I expressed my gratitude adequately when I left the railway station the day before yesterday. Out of sheer goodwill, you took me to Dharmasthala,' Dhaval said, his voice filled with emotion.

'What's the big deal, sir? I was going there anyway, and you just joined me,' Shivaswamy responded.

'No, no, it's more than that. You helped me in making a decision.'

'It was not me, sir. You helped yourself,' Shivaswamy said with a gentle smile. 'In our towns, some people stand in government taluk offices to serve as witnesses. They're rent witnesses. They accept money once they've signed, often unaware of the content of the document they've endorsed. They're rarely taken seriously; for that moment, they're simply witnesses of convenience. In a way, I was that kind of witness to your decision,' Shivaswamy chuckled.

Dhaval tried to sit upright. Pointing to the lever of the hospital bed, he motioned for Shivaswamy to adjust it. Once the bed was slightly reclined, he settled down.

'Come closer,' he beckoned. Shivaswamy moved nearer. The IV tube, which was inserted into Dhaval's hand, gently brushed against his shoulder. Despite the rush-hour noise outside on the street, filled with the roar and honks of thousands of vehicles at eight in the evening, the well-insulated hospital room was very quiet.

'Shivaswamy, I called you here for a reason. I have two requests. You must not say no,' said Dhaval.

'Tell me, sir.'

'My first request is that you be there for your daughter during her delivery. Go to her home. Don't do what I did. Remember how you once told me not to live my life kissing a stone cheek? Heed your own advice. Go there, gently hold your grandchild and kiss her cherubic cheeks. Let your coarse, grey moustache tickle the baby's skin as a kind of blessing. Don't worry about work. It can wait.'

Shivaswamy sat quietly. Dhaval's words echoed the sentiments of Teju, Sanju and Revathi.

Dhaval reached out and gripped his elbow. 'Did you understand what I said?'

'Yes, sir. I've been getting the same request from my family,' Shivaswamy replied.

'Then! Don't overthink it. Go to your daughter's place. Once you return, invite me over to your home for a meal. It's been a long time since I've had a delicious bisibelebath at a Kannadiga friend's home, my dear,' he laughed.

Shivaswamy joined him. He hadn't chosen to stay here merely out of desire; there was a purpose behind it. He wondered if Dhaval had forgotten the reason and the circumstances that had led to his employment. Why would he have joined this company without a dire need? In just another month, his position would need to be confirmed. Until then, he was on probation.

Travelling to the US would mean taking several months off. Could someone on probation take that many days off, especially without medical justification? The HR rulebook certainly wouldn't allow it. Being the HR manager himself, could he bend the rules? However, he also didn't wish to counter Dhaval's kindness at that moment. It would be more appropriate to detail the reasons for his inability to leave later, he thought, and thus chose to remain silent.

Dhaval continued, 'I know why you joined my company. You told me yourself when we first met. I have done something without telling you, and I request that you accept it. I spoke to Ajay yesterday. He is a friend of mine. Do you know who he is, Shivaswamy? He is the owner of AP Lakhani Builders, from whom you bought your home. Ajay Lakhani. You told me the name of your builder once. He is an old friend of mine, from the Gujarati business community in Mumbai. One of Dhriti's sisters is settled in Mumbai. Lakhani was also there when I went to an event at their house many years ago. He is very close to Dhriti's sister's father-in-law. So, after that meeting, we collaborated on a few business ventures, which strengthened our bond. Well, those are tales from the past. These business relationships are like the sticky latex of a jackfruit. Everything clings together inside.

'I called him yesterday evening before coming here and explained your situation. He asked me to provide your name and phone number so he could retrieve all the details. An hour later, he called back and discussed it with me. Shivaswamy, your issue has been resolved. You don't owe them a single rupee.

'Don't ask me how it was settled; I won't tell you. Regardless of the answer, you'll inevitably dwell on feelings of debt, gratitude and obligation, burdening yourself with countless questions. I know you well.

'Honestly, I hesitated to share this with you initially. However, I'm telling you now solely because I want you to visit your daughter's home with a peaceful mind. Kindly accept this gesture,' he said, tenderly putting his needle-pricked hand on Shivaswamy's.

Shivaswamy took a moment to process everything Dhaval had said. He realized that Dhaval had secured a waiver for him from the owner of Anoop Gardenia. Finding it difficult to say anything immediately, he mumbled, 'Sir, why did you take so much trouble, that too in such health?'

'What trouble, Shivaswamy?' Dhaval pressed Shivaswamy's hand. The liquid flowing through the tube had chilled his hand. A cold shudder passed through him into Shivaswamy's body.

Shivaswamy was about to say something else when a nurse entered the room, followed by two more nurses and a doctor. The middle-aged doctor called out loudly from the doorway, 'How are you, Mr Thakkar?' as he moved towards him. Raviraj followed close behind.

Shivaswamy stood up and said, 'Sir, I'll be leaving.'

Dhaval didn't say anything but squeezed his hand again. As Shivaswamy reached the door, Raviraj smiled and whispered softly, 'Thanks for visiting.'

In the lobby downstairs, Dhriti, Madhuri and Kalpana were sitting on a sofa, talking. Shivaswamy didn't go over to them but pushed open the revolving door and walked out of the hospital.

32

By the time Shivaswamy arrived from the hospital at the Mysore Sandal Soap Factory metro station on Chord Road, his head was pounding again. He bought a ticket, passed through security and entered the platform mechanically. The platform was crowded, and he found himself standing when he boarded the train. It wasn't until the plump man beside him, who had leaned against him for support, said, 'Look, your phone is ringing,' that Shivaswamy realized it indeed was.

He recognized the Mumbai number from the afternoon and answered it this time.

'Is this Mr Shivaswamy?'

'Yes,' he confirmed.

'Sir, this is Ekta Deshpande from the AP Lakhani corporate office in Mumbai. I have some delightful news for you. You've been selected for our platinum gift package. This gift is unique. In APL's fifty-year history, only one other buyer has received it before you. The company will cover all remaining payment instalments you owe. Apart from that, your flat will be upgraded to include an extra bedroom beyond what you originally purchased. If an upgrade isn't available in your current project or you have another preference, you can choose from some of our other projects. There's nothing you need to do on your part. Congratulations!' she said.

Shivaswamy remained silent, leaving her puzzled. She had anticipated a different reaction, perhaps an emotional outburst or a jubilant exclamation such as, 'Oh my God! Are you serious? Don't tell me this is a practical joke!' All she could hear was the sound of the train and the murmur of people talking. She worried that she had sounded like one of those scam callers who say seductively, 'Janaab, you've won fifty lakh rupees! Please provide your bank account and other details for the money transfer, sweetheart.' Feeling daunted, she insisted, 'Sir, this is true.' Still no response. Growing suspicious, she asked in Hindi, 'Sir, you can hear me, right?'

'Yes, I'm listening,' Shivaswamy replied.

'Sir, the sales vice president of our Bangalore branch, Mr Vinay Patil, would like to meet with you tomorrow. Is that convenient? Should I schedule an appointment?' she asked.

'Why?'

'He requires your signature on the paperwork for the acceptance of the gift. He will also share more details with you in person,' she said.

Suddenly, Shivaswamy felt dizzy. It was like the weight of the surrounding crowd pressed down on him. He found it difficult to speak. The phone almost slipped from his sweaty hand.

'Sir, shall I confirm the appointment?' the woman from Mumbai asked, her tone increasingly insistent.

He ended the call and put the phone away in his pocket. When it rang again, he didn't answer but glanced at the number. The plump man leaning on him smirked and said, 'Install the Truecaller app. It's good for blocking spam calls.'

When the train arrived at Kempegowda Majestic Station, a large number of people disembarked, allowing him to find a seat. However, twice as many people boarded the train, many young men and women with laptop bags slung over their shoulders.

Shivaswamy's mind was a whirlwind of thoughts. Where would it all lead? What more would the man from A.P. Lakhani reveal the next day? What would ensue if he were to accept their gift and sign it? It might wipe out all the entangled issues in a single stroke, like all the mosquitoes with a swing of an electric flyswatter bat. The outstanding payments to Anoop Gardenia, the missed visit to witness Sanjana's childbirth, the exhausting post-retirement job, the folks at work and the torment of travelling in the metro with a laptop bag slung over his shoulder . . . every dilemma might fade away. And, if the builder took six more months to hand over the house, so what?

As the metro approached the National College stop, the phone rang again. Shivaswamy pulled it out, suspecting the same woman was calling again. But it was Teju. He had already called several times since yesterday. 'Appa, should I tell Sanju to book the tickets?' he asked.

A man standing close to him quickly moved aside to make room for another and, in doing so, inadvertently stepped on Shivaswamy's foot with his leather shoe. The pain was acute, and Shivaswamy winced. The man apologized immediately, realizing his mistake. Meanwhile, Teju, who was on the phone and had heard the commotion, asked, 'Appa, where are you?'

'On the metro,' Shivaswamy replied.

'Then go home. I'll call you back in about an hour.' Teju said and hung up.

Shivaswamy sat quietly for a while, his eyes closed. Dhaval's offer churned in his mind, like grains of sand restlessly bouncing at the bottom of a pot as jaggery melted in boiling water on a burning stove. Although the problems were resolved, a nagging regret persisted. Was it the manner in which they had been addressed? Dhaval hadn't said it outright, but he might have settled the amount with Ajay Lakhani. Even if he had, did it really matter? This wasn't a bribe; it was genuine help. And, in accepting it, he owed no one anything. He hadn't sought it; it had come unexpectedly, like a dream. Are we morally accountable for what we do in our dreams?

Questions loomed in his mind. What would he tell Kumar and Vanita if they met? What if Harikrishna called from Ghaziabad and inquired about the house dispute? Could he claim he had nothing to do with it? And if Sandeep Kamat proposed taking the builder to court and asked him to join the cause, how could he deflect?

Even if he managed to reason with everyone else, how would he explain to his wife and children how the issue was resolved?

He wondered what the future would hold if he accepted Dhaval's help and mentally went through a potential future. *If I go to America for a few months, as Teju and Sanju urge me to, I will become an outsider here. I will be erased from their immediate memory. No one understands the whole story and its nuances. Even if they do, they will not believe it. In fact, I do not even need to tell anyone. If I leave Anoop Gardenia and choose another project, as offered to me, I may distance myself from acquaintances like Kumar Gowda, Vanita, Sandeep Kamat and their circle of friends. I could permanently sever all those relationships. That means, in the end, it all comes down to figuring out how to convince my family.*

As he contemplated it, everything seemed empty to him. Empty, like when everyone left the house, and he remained alone. Empty, like the entire metro forsaken, with him as the sole passenger. Empty, like the half-constructed homes in Anoop Gardenia, their doors wide open to reveal the void within. He, the lone observer, gazed into the darkness from the balcony of his house.

Shivaswamy felt that Dhaval, in his eagerness to be unburdened, had tacitly passed something on to him. He felt invaded. His mind was tormented. Even if he were to follow Allama Prabhu for a hundred years, he would never become like him. Even after reading a thousand vachanas, none found a home in his heart.

The thought of Allama immediately brought the brown book to mind. Had he packed it at the Dharmasthala lodge, or had he inadvertently left it there? His face drained of colour. He felt as if every path had suddenly become inaccessible.

He unzipped his laptop bag, rummaging through its contents in a frenzy. The book, which had always been there, was missing. He vividly remembered putting it on a desk at Kaveri Lodge the day they had reached but couldn't recall packing it. Perhaps the colour of the table had blended with that of the book, and he had missed it. He resolved to search the kitbag he had taken on the trip as soon as he reached home.

He wasn't optimistic about finding the lost book in the kitbag, though. The sense of loss was profound, and tears threatened to spill from his eyes. The book had lightened his burdens; now, without it, he felt the overwhelming weight of the world. It had intertwined his inner and outer worlds for fifty years. Its absence meant more than the loss of a simple book. It cast him into a deep abyss. The world of illusion had somehow ensnared him.

The train glided past Banashankari, heading towards JP Nagar. Shivaswamy turned from his seat and looked out of the window. The internal light reflected on the window pane and created the illusion of another window outside. In that window too, his face gazed into the darkness. Both windows and the faces seemed to be travelling together, glimpsing each other from a distance. The shimmering image journeyed home with him.

He blocked the light with his hands and peered outside. From the elevated bridge on which they were now moving, thousands of city lights twinkled in the distance. The train sped ahead, as though determined to connect the dots.

Acknowledgements

I originally wrote this book in Kannada, titled *Ondondu Talegu Ondondu Bele*, and it was published in 2022. An incident in August 2023 spurred me to translate it into English. On the day the Kannada edition won the prestigious Book Brahma Award, the eminent Tamil novelist Charu Nivedita and the renowned Odia writer Paramita Satpathy came to present the prize. That evening, during dinner, as we—along with Satish Chapparike and other friends—were chatting about literature, reading and various other topics, Charu Nivedita asked me to speak about the novel. After I had summarized it, Paramita Satpathy remarked that it would be wonderful if the book were translated into English. When I lamented that finding the right translator was a challenge, she—herself a translator of her stories—smiled and said, 'You should do it yourself. There are advantages to that.' Her words stayed with me. Over the next three months, I sat down and completed the translation of the novel.

I find translation more difficult than writing a novel. When writing, characters gather in my mind like a bustling fair, but by the time I begin translating, they seem to disperse and leave me alone. It is like the host of a midnight party who, after all the guests have left, continues the festivities alone. Strange as it might be, there is a certain joy in that too. I might never have embarked on this translation if that conversation had never happened. My special thanks go to both Charu Nivedita and Paramita Satpathy.

I also thank Divya Dubey and my son, Shashank, for helping me revise my first translation draft.

Although I am well acquainted with Kannada publishing circles, I was new to publishing in English. A Suitable Agency stepped in to guide me, and I am grateful to both Hemali Sodhi and Ambar Sahil Chatterjee for helping bring out this book. Ambar's friendship, enthusiasm and patience have been immense. I count myself fortunate to have found a literary agent like him.

I am also indebted to Archana Nathan, my editor at Penguin Random House India, who helped refine the manuscript for an English readership. Saloni Mital handled the copy-editing, and Shadab Khan designed the cover page. My favourite writer–friends offered their feedback after reading the manuscript. I remain thankful to each of them. Finally, my thanks to my wife, Roopa, for being my first reader.